Spellbound to a Sword

Tales of Asmodora

Joseph Hearl

Dynamic Web Systems

Oviedo, Florida

Dynamic Web Systems
PO Box 621965
Oviedo, FL 32762-1965
www.DynamicWebSystems.com

Publisher's Note: This is a work of fiction. Names, characters, places, and incidents are a product of the author's imagination. Locales and public names are sometimes used for atmospheric purposes. Any resemblance to actual people, living or dead, or to businesses, companies, events, institutions, or locales is completely coincidental.

Spellbound to a Sword/Joseph Hearl. -- 1st ed.
ISBN 978-1-7331013-5-6 (Ebook)
ISBH 978-1-7331013-4-9 (Paperback)

Dedicated to the family members who pushed me to finish, the friends I served with in the Navy, and those in need of a respite from reality.

Persistence Wins.

—JOSEPH HEARL

Contents

Ordered to the Border

IT WAS ANOTHER hot day of marching. The grasses lining the road were a golden brown, reflecting the effects of the continuing drought. We were pushing both man and beast to their limit. I wondered which would break first.

Off in the distance I could see a dust cloud heading toward us. No doubt a messenger of the king. By the pace he was traversing, it must be important. Or, more likely, he thought so.

To the east were the remnants of a river. Seeing the dry bed only added to our misery. I began to think we would never get a break when word came down to halt and fall out. Like everyone else, I made my way to the water wagon.

It seemed as though we had just sat down when the command to fall in and move out came. I cussed the commander as a sadistic bastard, though I knew he was merely following orders himself.

It was around four when the messenger finally arrived. Once again, we were ordered to halt. This time we were ordered to make camp as well. For once I didn't cuss the arrival of a royal messenger, though I reserved the right to do so later. For the time being, I contentedly searched out a spot to sleep.

I had finally settled into a comfortable position, or at least what would pass for one, when a company clerk walked up. I cussed. Most times, this one included, they tell you that you have to see the commander about some urgent business. That would usually lead to being assigned some mission no one in his right mind would volunteer for.

I grumbled the entire time, as I made my way slowly toward the command tent. I noticed that the royal was gone. Smart move. Although I had no love lost for the regulars, some of our guys would sooner kill one than look at him. Most have been warned of our demeanor before being sent.

"About time you showed up," Braveer barked as I made my way to my seat. "Why is it that you're always the last to make it when I call?" I knew it was a rhetorical question, but I had to reply.

"Possibly because I'm the slowest, but more likely because I'm the last one to be notified that I'm wanted," I snapped back.

Braveer gave me a look that said watch it. I ignored it. We grew up together. That set us apart from the rest of the company. I knew just how far I could push my luck and wasn't anywhere close yet.

"Since we're all here, let's get started. As you know, I received a message from King Velouth. He received a request from Chooser to allow ten thousand of her troops to cross Asmieria. It's our job to tell her no," Braveer stated. He gave me a look that carried greater meaning than others would suspect.

"I knew I shoulda hit that royal with a lightning bolt," Cyclops whined, the fiery rings in his eyes indicating an initiate of power flaring a little.

"Or maybe you could have turned him into a toad," Shameer retorted laughing.

"Or maybe you could have sent him back in time," Hermit added, laughing louder. All of which was far beyond Cyclops' ability, though he could throw a mean fireball when the occasion called for it.

"Alright that's enough. This is no joking matter. As you all know, Chooser is one of the few ninth circle wizards alive. To me, that makes this our worst assignment yet," Braveer barked. "I've been going over our maps of the borderland and found out that they're over four hundred years old. I think the terrain has probably changed a bit since then, so I'm going to need a scouting report ASAP. Slasher, that means you and your sidekicks need to ride out immediately. It should take us two weeks or so to get there, I expect a full report to be ready by then. Well, what are you waiting for? Get lost," he commanded.

I waited outside for Cyclops & Hermit, and when they came out, I sent them to supply to requisition our usual assortment of tools & food. Cyclops and Hermit were two of the company's better wizards, though their powers were limited to around the fourth circle, peaking just below the fifth. Cyclops had lost an eye as a teenager thus gaining him his moniker. Anyone spending more than a few minutes with Hermit would soon come to understand his moniker, as the only one he can really stand to be around is Cyclops. We worked well together, and when they combined their efforts, they were able to cast spells together that were beyond either as an individual to cast, very few lower circle wizards could accomplish this without an upper circle wizards aid. I then headed over to the quartermaster to get us the best possible horses. On the bright side we wouldn't have to march in the heat. That thought was almost optimism.

We left camp as the sun was setting. I figured this would give the horses a little bit of a break before the heat of the day set in. We had a long journey ahead of us. Judging from Braveer's maps, at least a three-day journey if we rode nonstop. Of course, the horses would drop dead, but hey we'd get there in three days. Not going to happen. I figured we'd ride hard the first day, stopping an hour after noon or so before the heat reached its peak. After a couple of hours of sleep, and giving the horses a rest, we'd ride on, stopping just after daybreak. This way we wouldn't have to exhaust the horses from the heat of the day.

The first leg of the trip went by uneventfully. We managed to find a small stand of trees to nap under. We hung a tarp to give us sufficient shade. We continued on as planned, leaving many miles behind us. I hoped the remainder of the journey would go as smoothly but doubted it. Having been with the company for twenty-five years, I learned that optimism doesn't pay. Expect the worst and you're seldom disappointed.

We spotted some old burned out buildings shortly after midmorning of the second day. They looked like a good place to make camp, so we did. Cyclops managed to kill a good-sized rabbit, so we were spared from having to eat the hardtack we had brought. My optimism was beginning to return. I assigned Cyclops the first watch then it would be Hermits turn then mine.

I slept fairly peacefully, although a beautiful female voice kept faintly calling to me, 'Phoenix. Phoenix.' I awoke with a start. Hermit was standing over me.

"How do you do that," he asked.

"Do what," I asked in reply.

"Wake up before I wake you," he stated.

I stretched and shook the cobwebs out of my head. "Couldn't tell ya," I replied. I didn't mention the woman's voice. I relieved myself on a nearby tree, before assuming the watch. I grabbed a cup of coffee from the pot Hermit had made to keep himself awake and began scanning the area for any possible threats not expecting to find any.

With about an hour to go before we would get under way, that feeling of something amiss began to swell in the back of my mind. I looked around and around, saw nothing wrong, yet couldn't shake the trepidation. My hand went down to the sword I kept on my side. It did nothing to allay the feeling of something amiss. The feeling grew stronger, until I realized that the ground had started to tremble. It was a faint tremble, but a definite tremble. I woke Hermit and Cyclops.

They felt the tremble right away and grabbed for their weapons. We set out to find the source of the tremble, realizing that it could well be an earthquake, for which the region was known. Hermit managed to find the trouble by falling through the ground into a tunnel. Cyclops jumped in after him. I grabbed some rope from the supply horse. Fortunately, rope is part of our usual supply for our recon missions.

I tied the rope off on a tree that though dead, seemed sound enough to handle the task. I lowered the rope into the hole for them to climb, but I got a little careless and fell in with them when the ground gave way. My feeling of trepidation was in full swing now. A noise to my left caused me to draw my sword. It glowed with an ambience I had never witnessed in the over thirty-five years that I've wielded it.

A loud shriek emanated from the area where I had heard the first noise. Cyclops and Hermit both unleashed the spells they had prepared in the direction of the sound. I thought it quaint at times that they seemed to know which spell the other would use and complimented each other's power by casting a similar spell. They were only fourth circle initiates, but working together as they did, they could have been sixth.

Their spells went off quickly and simultaneously, one flashing fire, the other I couldn't tell, but they were followed by a thump. I made my way towards the charred remains lying on the tunnel floor. I kicked it over with my boot. The charred almost unrecognizable face of a hobgoblin stared back up at me. We quickly returned to our guard. Hobgoblins never traveled alone. Nor could they have created the trembling we had felt earlier. Hermit leaned back against the tunnel wall, then quickly lunged away yelping. "That things hot," he exclaimed.

"No shit, I just hit it with a fireball," Cyclops chided.

"Your spell didn't make it that hot," Hermit retorted. I cautiously put a hand toward the wall. Any hotter and it would be lava. Something didn't add up, and we really didn't have time to investigate. I motioned to them to get out via the rope I had lowered earlier.

"If we're still alive after this mission, maybe we can come back and investigate," I suggested. My comment didn't escape my comrade's notice. Our current mission was dangerous. Chooser was a powerful woman, even without her magic. Her kingdom was one of the richest in the known world. Her elite guard were reported to be changelings, the most viscous and feared relative of lycanthropy ever to walk the earth. No two changelings were alike. All were a mishmash of ursine, feline, and canine parts that changed every full moon. They were once human, but once infected and changed they could never resume human form again.

Sword in hand, I covered their retreat up the rope. Hermit and Cyclops kept a spell on their lips as I climbed out. "We'd better leave a marker to warn the company. I'll do that while you two see what you can do about blocking that hole," I commanded. They both muttered obscenities under their breath as I walked away, to which I couldn't help grinning.

We accomplished our tasks as quickly as possible then continued with our journey. We had only lost about an hour, which shouldn't be too critical. Of course, Braveer would think otherwise. But what he doesn't know won't hurt him, or us. As we traveled on, I couldn't help pondering the events of the recent past. First there was the woman's voice calling me, then the tremors, then the red-hot wall. Then there was my sword glowing like it did. I've known that it was a sword of major power from the first time I grabbed its hilt. Yet it never ceased to amaze me. What did it mean?

We stopped to eat our hardtack around midnight. One thing about these recon missions, we didn't get a chance to eat very often, or well. I could still taste the rabbit we had eaten the day before. I almost got indigestion before I finished the hardtack. It's said that an army travels on its stomach. If they're eating hardtack, it's to dull the pain.

After eating, we remounted and continued on. By daybreak, we could see the Dragore Mountains looming large in front of us. Had it not been so dark, we would have seen them five hours earlier. A vague notion tugged at the back of my mind. I couldn't quite figure out what it was that I was trying to remember. I put it off as fatigue and ordered a halt. We would set up camp here.

Cyclops managed to get us two swiyote, an herbivore that looked like a cross between a coyote and a swine. We wouldn't have to eat hardtack on this mission again, providing we could have fire. For all his faults, Cyclops was an excellent hunter.

After eating, I settled into sleep to prepare for my turn at watch. Once more I heard the woman's voice calling me. Louder this time, as if nearer. I was drawn toward it like a moth to a flame. "Phoenix, Phoenix," she called. "Where are you," I asked. I heard no reply. The voice slowly faded. I woke to find myself clutching my sword's hilt tightly. I scanned the terrain. Hermit was sitting drinking a cup of coffee. I got up and relieved myself, then him. There was no way I'd be able to fall back asleep and it was close to my time to stand watch anyway.

I let them both sleep about an extra hour or so to make up for the day before; then, we went on our way. The path was treacherous and winding as it made its way up and over the mountain. About halfway up the mountainside, a large cavern was torn into the rock. A legend of ages ago flooded my mind. The thought I couldn't quite pinpoint made itself clear. Hell, even the name of the range screamed it, Dragore, the largest dragon ever to inhabit the region of man. Dragore was the dragon whose wrath had decimated civilizations five thousand or so years ago, until the full council of wizards joined forces to defeat her.

I let myself run through the gambit of possibilities until I neared panic. I steeled myself all the while continuing on. Cyclops saw me lost in thoughts and asked, "Do you know where we're going?" I glowered back in my reply. "You don't have to bite my head off," he retorted. "You'd think he was King Slasher," he snorted to Hermit. Hermit ignored him, lost in his own thoughts.

The further we made it up the mountain, the stronger the feeling of panic grew. Cyclops continued to rant on as we traveled, while Hermit rode in silence. It occurred to me that when the council of wizards defeated Dragore, they had placed spells to prevent anyone from entering the cavern and risk reanimating her. From our reactions, the spells induced fear and were still quite active. Finally, as we crested the mountain, the spells began to abate. Cyclops stopped his ranting, and Hermit broke his silence. "What happened back there," he asked.

"Ever hear of Dragore, the dragon," I asked in reply.

"Yeah, I remember hearing some myth when I was a kid, who hasn't," he asked. "Why?"

"We just passed her lair. The council of wizards that defeated her placed a lot of spells on it to keep people out. And when I say council, I mean every wizard of the sixth circle and higher at the time, and a few lower to boot," I replied.

"You're telling me that stuff about a giant dragon that terrorized civilization is true," Hermit asked incredulously. I nodded in reply. We rode on in silence. Most humans have never seen a dragon before, myself included. Nor did I want to.

It had taken a full day to reach the mountains peak. About two hours before daylight we could see campfires in the distance, near the base of the mountains. We stopped and set up a camp, envious of those in the distance for their fires. We wouldn't have such a luxury.

We had managed to find some large boulders to hide our camp behind. In the morning sun I could see that the enemy was encamped at the base of the mountain near a stream that flowed down from a spring near the middle of the mountain. I looked around to see what assets we had. None. No fire, no water, no nothing that would be considered a comfort. I must be getting too old for this shit.

We rested in shifts as before. Once we were all awake and alert Hermit and Cyclops set out to spy on the encampment below, while I surveyed the terrain. We had the advantage of the high ground, which most military minds would agree was a major plus. There were a sufficient number of large rocks around to use as ammunition for siege engines such as catapults. The only real navigable path up the mountainside was narrow, not fit for more than three abreast in combat. Optimistically we would have several advantages, except for a wizard capable of matching Chooser's power, which hopefully wouldn't really be necessary.

I was just about finished with my map when Hermit and Cyclops came rushing back. They were out of breath and paler than I remembered ever seeing them before.

"She's here," Cyclops gasped.

"Who," I asked though not wanting an answer.

"Chooser, who do you think," Hermit, snapped annoyed. The look I flashed him told him I knew who but didn't want to be bothered with it.

I composed myself then asked, "How many troops are down there?"

"Maybe you didn't hear me," Hermit said annoyed. "Chooser here. Down there," he reiterated pointing toward the encampment for emphasis.

"I heard you. That doesn't tell me how many troops we're facing," I remarked impatiently.

"About ten thousand," Cyclops answered.

"That's the number that Braveer used. I want to know how many exactly. Am I to believe that she has ten thousand infantries with her? No cavalry? No archers," I berated them. "What about her apprentices and generals?"

I leaned against a boulder and stared down the mountain. I tried to imagine what she looked like. From all reports she was a remarkable beauty. Young and beautiful is the normal description. I wondered if it were natural or magically enhanced. She was after all a ninth circle initiate. Wizards of that power could easily alter their appearance. My curiosity got the better of me, so I asked, "Is she as pretty as rumor has it."

"That's what you want to know? There is something wrong with you," Hermit chided.

"I'll go down on the next survey," I stated flatly.

"Be my guest," Hermit laughed.

Cyclops looked quizzically at my statement. "Since when do you do the spying," he asked.

"Since I need accurate information that you and your sidekick don't seem able to gather," I replied. "Get some rest. We'll leave after sunset."

As we made our way down the mountain, I felt as giddy as a choirboy with a crush. I tried everything I could to calm my nerves, with limited success. I finally convinced myself that it was just doing a strange task and tried to put it out of my mind.

When we reached the outer perimeter of the encampment, I used hand signals to instruct Cyclops to head east. I headed west, doing my best to avoid detection. I found the horse corral and quickly counted the head. Four thousand head, as best as I could figure. These were cavalry horses, and a rather large number of them. I continued to skirt around the camp westward. I came upon another corral of horses. These appeared to be draft horses like the kind used to haul heavy wagons. I passed by heading toward an area of tents. In front of the larger one I could see Chooser's banner. This was obviously what had sent Hermit and Cyclops into their panic.

I was about to move on when I noticed the flap to the tent begin to move. I did my best to stay out of sight while straining to see who or what came out. She emerged like she was floating on air. She was tall, about five-ten, slender, graceful, and agile. Her face was angelic and tan. She glanced in my direction and my heart skipped a beat, in part from a fear of being seen, and another part from the sheer elation of seeing such beauty. If it was magically enhanced, it didn't matter. She was near perfection. She had a perfect little nose, full cheeks, and a delicate curve to her face that could captivate a man's every thought. Her best feature, by far were her captivating green eyes. In them I could see the powerful glow of an initiate of the ninth circle. My heart stopped for a second fearing I had been spotted. I remained motionless for what seemed like an eternity before she walked away towards a larger, less decorative tent. When I was sure she was gone, I quietly made my way back towards the mountains.

Cyclops was waiting for me when I reached the base of the mountain. "Where the hell have you been," he whispered harshly.

"Watching a goddess," I whispered back. "Let's get back to camp before someone sees us." With that we made our way back toward camp. Once we were safe at camp, Cyclops began grilling me.

"What do you mean 'you were watching a goddess'," Cyclops demanded.

"Just what I said. I was watching a goddess, Chooser," I replied.

"You saw her," Hermit asked incredulously.

"Oh, she is beautiful," I lamented. "Tall. About up to here," I said holding my hand to her approximate height. "And slender. Like that girl you had two months ago," I suggested to Hermit. "Only her looks!! Wow! Beautiful Green eyes, with a tan complexion, a face that could take a man's breath away. A goddess," I finished.

"Terrific! We're out numbered, and Slasher has a crush on the enemy leader," Hermit exclaimed.

"So, when's the wedding," Cyclops chided. I ignored them but began to suspect it had been too long since we had been to a town with a decent brothel. I had never let them get to me before, and I wasn't going to start anything new.

"Listen, I think we have as much information as we're going to get for now, Let's get some sleep and see what we can see tomorrow," I said. "Hermit, you take first watch."

I had a hard time falling asleep. When I did, I had the same dream I had had the last few nights. Somewhere in the distance a woman was calling to me. I could hear her voice as plain as day, yet I couldn't see her. I called out for her and received no reply. Then there was the name she called me, Phoenix. A name I hadn't heard in thirty some odd years. To everyone that knew me I was Slasher, wielder of a magic sword. Only Braveer knew me as otherwise and he dared not call me by it.

The next day we managed to put together a more comprehensive account of the encampment below. Hermit had pulled himself together enough to do his job, which is how we found out that all of Chooser's top generals were with her below us. Some were mere military men, though most were wizards. They didn't seem to be aware of our presence, which was what we wanted and hoped it would stay that way. It made gathering intelligence easier. Sometime during the night another large force of troops had arrived to bolster their numbers, which was now close to a hundred thousand.

As we finished collecting our information, my mind kept going back to the night before and Chooser. I had seen beautiful women before, even made love to a few, but something about her wouldn't let me be. It wasn't anything I could put my finger on. It made doing my work difficult.

It was near dusk when we heard a noise that made our hearts stop. We stopped in our tracks and stared at each other. Changelings! Changelings are creatures that like lycanthropy were once human, but unlike lycanthropes, changelings can never resume human form. The biggest difference between the two, lycanthropes become werewolves, whereas changelings are a mesh of ursine, canine, and feline components that changed with each new full moon, and these were Chooser's reported personal guard! My hand went quickly to the hilt of my sword. Without hesitation I drew the weapon from its scabbard. We gathered close, each scanning a different direction hoping not to see any movement. No such luck.

Cyclops was the first to spot them. He alerted us by unleashing the fireball spell he had prepared the moment we heard the first blood-curdling screech. There were two of them, one of which was still smoking from Cyclops' spell. Without waiting for them to attack us, I launched myself at the two beasts. My sword cut a wide swath, slicing through one of the beast's midsection. In a fluid motion I swung my sword over my head and down onto its head, the blade cleaving it in two.

As I began to turn my attention to the other creature, I felt a sharp pain in my left side. With the blade in my right hand, I swung in the direction of my antagonist. The head of the second creature rolled over the rocky terrain. I looked around to see if there were any other threats. Not seeing any, I raced back to my two companions grabbing my side. "We better get out of here," I suggested. They nodded dumbfounded.

They quickly gathered our supplies and necessary belongings, mounted our steeds, and raced up the mountain. I had grabbed a piece of cloth and held it over my wound. Behind and below us, Chooser's encampment began to show signs of life. My side was burning where the creature had sliced me with what I assumed were its claws. I kept my hand and cloth over it to help stem the flow of blood and fought to keep myself in the saddle. As we crested the mountain, I lost the fight. I don't know whether it was the loss of blood or the rock that my head hit that caused me to lose consciousness, but either way I did.

Phoenix Rising

TWO WOMEN were beckoning me. One knew my name, the other I could see. The latter was the young lady whose looks had captivated my mind. She seemed genuinely concerned for my wellbeing, to a point. I gave into the former. That is, I followed her voice. She led me back to myself. Once there I woke up, regrettably.

"Doctor. He's coming to," a woman's voice said.

"Welcome back to the living," the doctor remarked as I opened my eyes. I couldn't decide which hurt more, the knot on my head, or my side, which felt as though it were on fire.

"What hit me," I asked. "A rock and a changeling, but not in that order," Hermit replied.

"I don't remember any of it. I mean, I remember hearing the changelings and drawing my sword, but nothing after that," I said.

"Wouldn't you know he'd play humble to the hilt," Cyclops exclaimed.

"He's probably suffering from a mild case of amnesia," the doctor explained. "He did hit his head rather hard."

"Good, so somebody please fill me in," I pleaded.

As Hermit explained my actions to me, I listened intently. Then laughed. "You really don't expect me to believe I'd attack two changlings with a sword," I chuckled, all the while thinking about my sword.

"Believe it," Cyclops confirmed. I stared at them in half disbelief. My thoughts went to my sword, and so did my hand.

Braveer witnessed my action. "No one could get it off you," he said. I glanced up at him then at my hand. I hadn't been aware of my actions.

"Where are we," I asked to change the subject.

"The scene of the crime," Hermit joked. He went on to explain, "The Company was coming up the mountain as you fell off your horse."

It seemed my sword had taken control of me and had made me attack two changelings. I found it disturbing that I would attack not just one, but two changlings. I had never heard of anyone going against the creatures with weapons and winning before. It normally took a wizard of the seventh circle or better to win such a battle. That made twice in a week's span that my sword had shown some of its powers. I still hadn't figured out what the glowing was all about. Taking over my body and making me forget about it bothered me but had happened at least once before. Braveer had told me about a past instance from our youth, which I preferred to not think about.

The doctor checked my wounds then gave me a vile tasting potion he said would ease the pain. It must have also been designed to knock you out, because the next thing I knew, I was dreaming again.

Chooser inhabited my dream. "You're absolutely beautiful," I told her, knowing I'd never get the chance to tell her for real.

"Thank you," she replied blushing, which made her look even more remarkable than before. "You must come to me," she said. Something about the way she said it struck me as odd. It wasn't how you would expect a dream figure to make such a statement. Her voice was tinged with concern, not the typical flirtatious 'come hither' you get from dream girls.

"Why," I asked not knowing what kind of answer I would get.

"Because I can help you," she said flooring me.

"What do you mean you can help me," I asked laughingly.

"From the changeling disease," she explained.

I awoke with a start and sat upright. I reached down and ripped off the bandage from my side. I felt faint from what I saw. The wound was almost healed. I now knew two things for certain. I was infected with a virus that would change me into a mindless wild beast and Chooser had visited me in my dream through the use of a spell. I half blushed realizing that I had actually told her how beautiful she was.

It was now sometime after sunset. I got up and left the medical tent. The nurse that had announced my return to consciousness tried to stop me from leaving. I gave a look that suggested it would be in her own best interest not to, so she acquiesced. Outside of the medical tent, I scanned the camp until I found Braveer's tent then made a beeline to it.

"I'll be needing my box," I told him solemnly as I entered.

"You haven't looked at it in all these years, why now? Changeling piss you off that much," he asked adding "not that I'm complaining."

"Funny you should mention changelings, because I'm doomed to become one unless I can find a cure," I replied just as solemnly. He visibly paled and fumbled for my box, a small chest really. The chest was imbued with powerful magic that enabled it to hold far more than one might expect it to hold. I had given it to him when I joined the company.

I looked down at the ebony chest with its intricate golden ruins drawn by my hand in my long-ago youth. I traced my finger along a path through the ruins unlocking the chest. Inside, on top, lie two necklaces. One held a medallion of a flaming bird, a phoenix, the other a locket. The medallion was a symbol of power once wielded by a wizard of the ninth circle, me. The other necklace held a locket with a lock of hair from my one true love. A woman I later found in the arms of my best friend the night I slew them both. That day smashed into the front of my mind, forcing me to relive those horrific events.

It was the summer of my seventeenth year. I was always exploring the countryside with my two favorite companions, Firewind and Christine. Firewind and I had been friends since we could walk, having lived next door to each other. Christine was the love of my life. She lived down the road apiece, on her daddy's farm. My father was a farmer too and they would help each other out during harvest time. She was the most beautiful thing

I had ever laid my eyes upon and I loved her from the start.

Firewind and I had taken up the arcane art at an early age both of us excelling at it. By the time we were twelve, we were already at the seventh circle. Most wizards took thirty years to reach that level of proficiency. We had the good fortune to have an excellent teacher. Cyclone was a member of the ninth circle content to spend his final days in a small village teaching eager young minds. He assured us that our power was our own doing, and we ate it up.

By seventeen, we had learned all that he could teach us, and more. I had learned to transform myself into a flaming bird, becoming Phoenix. Firewind could enshroud himself in flames, floating across the terrain at tremendous speed. Christine never seemed interested in learning about magic. She was content to just hang around her two personal magicians, watching with fascination as we gained power from each experience.

We had traveled further than we had ever traveled before. We weren't afraid of running into any of the creatures that were known to inhabit this region. Few creatures known to man could face one-ninth-circle wizard, let alone two.

As we broke through the woods, we saw a cavern leading down into the ground, from which we could sense immense energy of a magical nature. Being the adventurous types that we were, we made a couple of torches and headed down. The cavern seemed unnatural, more likely manmade than naturally occurring. After about two hundred feet, it forked. We decided to split up to cover the ground more quickly. Christine and I took the left fork, Firewind the one on the right. We would keep our senses alert for active magic in case one of us should run into trouble.

Christine and I had gone fifty feet or so around a bend when we found a small room carved into the left wall. I magically checked for traps then we entered. It seemed to be a shrine of sorts complete with an altar in the center of the room. Upon the altar was a ring. It seemed innocent enough, but I was cautious to check for unseen power. As I did so, Christine snatched the ring from the altar. "Christine! Don't you realize how dangerous that is," I scolded.

"Why? Nothing happened," she retorted.

"That ring is emanating magic. You don't know what spells are on it," I continued berating her.

"You wouldn't let anything happen to me," she reasoned as she slipped it on her finger. I watched intently, yet nothing seemed to happen. She kissed me on my cheek and grabbed my arm.

We went further into the cavern which dead ended in another room. Like the last room, this one seemed to be a shrine. Instead of a ring on the altar though, there was a sword. Only it wasn't exactly on the altar, it was hovering over it. The power emanating from the altar was staggering. Even without trying to I could tell that the sword was the source of the power. I cautiously reached out and grabbed the hilt of the sword. Holding it in my hand I marveled at the intricate ruins that decorated its length. I found a scabbard next to the altar and sheathed this magnificent work of art.

I hadn't noticed that Christine hadn't followed me into the room. As I exited, I questioned her about her decision. "I didn't feel comfortable in there. I wish you hadn't taken that sword either," she complained while keeping her distance from me.

"Like you said, nothing happened, so don't worry about it," I countered. "Let's go find Firewind," I suggested.

We ran into Firewind back at the fork. He had found a sword in a room at the end of his path as well. We left the cavern. It was getting past noon, so we decided to head back to town. We went to the local tavern for a bite to eat.

We ate a meal of mutton, bread, and beans. We were joking and laughing when Braveer, Firewind's older brother, came in. We beaconed him to join us. When he did, Christine showed off her new ring. I broke out the sword I had found knowing that Braveer would appreciate it more than the ring. Firewind pulled the sword he had found to show it off as well. I don't know what came over me, but I made a snide remark about his sword and his manhood. He retorted in like fashion. We both sheathed our weapons and walked off. I stormed out of the tavern, opting to take a walk to cool off.

The further I got from the tavern, the more I cursed myself for a fool. I had started a fight with my best friend over something petty. I decided to go back to the tavern and apologize for being an idiot. As I walked through the door, I couldn't believe my eyes. Christine and Firewind were sitting in a corner locked in a passionate embrace.

"What in the hell is going on here," I demanded. They looked up at me and laughed.

"What's it looks like," Christine giggled. I felt my anger growing with each passing heartbeat. Firewind stood up and pushed me back.

"Why don't you go find someone who cares," he belittled me. I pushed him back. He grabbed his sword hilt. I grabbed mine and drew the sword from its scabbard.

It was over before I realized what I was doing. Firewind lay dead at my feet. Christine's body lay across his, neither recognizable as human. I ran from the building half in shock at the sight of what I had done. I turned back to the building to see Braveer standing in the doorway staring at me in disbelief. I shook my head and ran off into the night.

It had been a little over thirty-five years since those events unfolded. When I joined the company close to a decade later, Braveer was third in command. He filled me in on things that happened that night that I was unaware of. Christine had attacked me, wielding a power that Braveer had not been aware she possessed. After they were both dead, a power emanated from my sword that destroyed her ring and Firewind's sword utterly and leaving their bodies mostly a pile of ash. The after shockwave shattered everything in the tavern and knocked all but me off of their feet. He forgave me for killing his younger brother, something I still can't do for myself.

I reached out and retrieved the medallion from the chest and put it on, after removing the ring I had fashioned to mask my power and make me appear to be a non-initiate. The medallion was more than just a symbol of my power. I had enriched it by casting spells upon it when I forged it with the aid of my master, Cyclone, when I was thirteen. Under the medallion were my spell books, the accumulation of all my knowledge of the arcane, some written by me. I had never gotten around to reading all of the spells that I had acquired in my youth. I was hoping that somewhere in one of the books that I had acquired would be a spell to cure lycanthropy. I had to find it or suffer the consequences.

"What are you gonna do," Braveer asked, with genuine concern in his voice.

"Somewhere among this collection is a book that belonged to the wizard who brought this scourge upon the world. Hopefully, the spell he used to create the curse is in it. If so, I should be able to undo the spell," I told him.

"How long do you think it will take you to find out," he asked.

"Not long. I've got my medallion on. It helps me read quicker, and all I'm really doing is scanning through the spells looking for anything useful or better yet the spell, though as you can see there are a large number of tomes to go through."

"I'll see to it that you're not disturbed," he assured me as he left me to my studies.

It was well after noon by the time I finished scanning through the last book. The spell I needed wasn't among the books in my collection. I staggered to the mess tent to grab a bite to eat.

As I made my way through the camp, my comrades gave me a wide berth. Braveer had let it be known that I was Phoenix, and no one wanted to test my powers. I was kind of hurt that these men that I had fought side by side with didn't trust me, yet not in any mood to complain. With the burden I was currently carrying, it was probably best that everyone just leaves me alone anyway. I guess Braveer knew what he was doing.

After eating, I found the tent that had been set up for me. I went inside and lay down. I was tired, yet my mind was racing too much for me to sleep. A woman's voice called out from outside the tent. "Slasher, may I come in," she called.

"Come," I replied. The nurse came in carrying a tray of bandages and potions.

"Those won't be necessary," I told her.

"Doctor's orders. I'm to change your dressings and make sure you drink the whole potion. If you refuse, I was told I could get help making you comply," she warned me sternly. I laughed but could tell she was serious. Apparently, no one had bothered telling either her or the doctor what had come to pass. She was rather attractive, even while glowering at me, so I couldn't help but acquiesce.

"Well in that case I'd better do as you say," I chuckled.

She looked shocked as she examined the area were the wound was, probably from the fact that it was all but gone. Wounds as deep as that one was don't usually heal almost overnight, even with the aid of magic potions.

"I guess you won't be needing this bandage," she stammered.

"No, I guess not," I agreed.

"Well, drink the potion anyways," she ordered. I did so, regretting it immediately. It was the same foul-tasting concoction I had drank the day before in the medical tent. I shouldn't have drunk it.

Once again Chooser came to me in my dream. This time, having revived my own power, I could feel the magic emanating from the spell she had used to get there. I still marveled at her beauty.

"You must come to me," she commanded, her voice steeped in magic.

"I think not," I replied.

This took her aback. She wasn't used to her spells failing to captivate her targets. "You resist. Why," she implored.

"Quite simply because I have no intention of becoming a slave to you or any other mage," I told her.

"Once the changeling disease takes a hold of you, no one will be safe in your presence. Not even those you hold most dear," she warned.

"And you have the cure for the disease, I suppose," I asked knowing full well she didn't.

"No," she replied sternly. "No one has found a cure yet. I don't think anyone ever will. But I can prevent you from running wild killing those you hold dear," she said confidently.

"I think I'd rather find a cure. Thanks for stopping by," I said. I made a gesture and she vanished from my dream. The nice thing about wielding power was the ability to prevent unwanted guests from staying in your mind.

In the morning I awoke refreshed. I wasn't sure if it was the effects of the doctor's potion, or the growing effects of the disease coursing through my veins, nor did I care. I headed towards Braveer's tent.

Braveer and his right-hand man, Shameer, were standing outside the tent as I walked up. Shameer was visibly shaken as I approached. "Relax, I'm not gonna eat you, yet," I said jokingly. He looked confused by my remark as he walked off. "You didn't tell him about the changling disease, did you," I asked. Braveer just shook his head in reply. That explained Shameer's confusion.

"I have to leave," I informed him. "The spell I need isn't in my books. I'm gonna try the Library of the Magus in Graveer."

"You really think you can find it?" he asked, genuinely concerned.

"Don't know. But I sure as hell have got to try. I don't like the alternative," I told him.

"Well, do me a favor. If you do manage to find it, when you come back if we're dead, avenge us. Will ya," Braveer quipped.

"Don't worry. I plan on having a little talk with Chooser before I leave. I figure wizard to wizard she might get the hint to stay out of our crumby little dust bowl," I replied.

I went to retrieve a horse from the quartermaster. He didn't have any objections to me taking my pick. By now everyone had heard about my true identity. Fear makes men behave differently. Normally, as Slasher, I would have had to argue for an hour before he would have given in. I had grown accustomed to that sort of treatment over the years. A part of me was going to miss our witty banter. I then went to my tent and finished packing my personal belongings, leaving only the tent behind. Cyclops and Hermit came over as I was loading them on the horse.

"Are you really who Braveer says you are," Cyclops asked, before noticing the glow of an initiate I now allowed to show in my eyes. I nodded the affirmative, though the way his face paled told me I didn't need to.

"Did you really wipe out an ogre herd with one spell," Hermit asked incredulously.

"Yeah, but it was a small herd," I admitted. "I was a lot younger and more impetuous back then."

Ogres are big brutish things standing on average nine feet tall. They travel in family packs we call herds. An average herd number around eight or less. Their arms are thick, muscular, and powerful; their hands have three fingers and a thumb and are strong enough to crush a man's skull like an egg. Two large tusks protrude from their lower jaws, male's tusks tending to be larger than females. Thick hair covers their torsos and arms, while they tend to wear animal hide wrapped around their waists, bearskin being the most common hide used. Males are called boars, while the females are called sows. They seldom used weapons but have been known to rip up trees to use as clubs.

Twenty of them or so attacked a caravan I was traveling with before I had completed my ring of nullification. I released a chain lightning spell I had learned a few weeks before fleeing my village. It was the first time I had used the spell in combat and was surprised myself when it destroyed the entire herd. I had hoped to scare them off but didn't fret when it killed them.

"What's it like wielding so much power," Cyclops asked.

I finished lashing a bundle onto the saddle, thought about it for a second, then asked, "Do you remember the first time you unleashed a fireball from your fingertips? Think of that only a hundred times over." The awe in their faces was like that of a small child seeing his first falling star. Only instead of cute cherub faces, theirs were scarred and wrinkled. But the awe was there just the same. "Take care of the company while I'm gone," I told them.

"Where are you going," they asked nearly in unison.

"The library of magus to find a cure for the changeling disease," I answered.

"The library has been lost for centuries," Hermit chimed in. I merely grinned in reply. I mounted the steed and I headed down the mountain towards Chooser's camp.

Chooser's sentries attempted to bar my path as I approached. I was in the mood to put on a display of power, so I used a spell to form a lightning ball in my hand, one of the most powerful spells a ninth circle initiate could cast.

"Unless you want to try playing catch, I suggest you get out of my way," I told them. They looked astonished as they stumbled backwards out of my path. I rode on toward Chooser's command tent. A large crowd gathered and followed, though not too close to me, as I rode through the camp playing with the ball unfettered. When I reached the command tent, I dispelled the magic then dismounted. Two more sentries were barring the entrance to the tent.

"Tell Chooser that Phoenix wishes to see her immediately," I ordered. They glanced at each other before the one on the right slipped into the tent. He soon emerged followed by Chooser and her staff of generals. "We need to talk. Alone," I told her boldly.

"We can talk in here," she said gesturing to the tent behind her. I entered the tent followed closely by Chooser. Her general of highest rank attempted to follow. "He said alone, Drakar. Leave us," she ordered.

"But your majesty," he tried to complain.

"I can take care of myself," she assured him, sounding slightly annoyed. He obediently backed off.

"To what do I owe this surprise," she asked once we were alone inside the tent.

"Twofold," I started. "First, I've come to let you know that I am going to the library in Graveer to find Valtar's original spell. I intend to undo the magic he did that created the disease that I've been inflicted with, thanks to you. Secondly, I came to warn you against taking any action against Asmeria, in particular the company of men now guarding the pass through the Dragore Mountains. I am rather fond of these men and have come to regard them as brothers. Upon my return I would decimate those who would harm them in my absence," I finished.

"Let's say for the sake of argument that you really are Phoenix," she said, sounding condescending. "Then let's assume that you find the Library of the Magus at Graveer, which of course has been lost for centuries. What makes you think you can actually undo the power of Valtar," she inquired somewhat more condescendingly.

Despite her beauty, I was in no mood to be spoken to in such a manner. I quickly muttered a few words of the ancients causing the tent to go flying away. A few more words of power and I assumed the form of my namesake.

"You would be well advised not to trifle with me, young lady," I reprimanded as I hovered over her. "I was never known for my patience or sunny disposition. I will find the cure. I will be back. And woe be unto any who run afoul of my friends!" I undid the magic and returned to my natural form. "Heed my warning. I won't be nice if you don't, and you would lose everything including your life," I said as I made my way to my mount.

The entire camp had gathered round at my display of power. I glowered at the lot before turning my steed toward the northwest. Their jaws were open as they watched me ride off. The tent that I had so easily tossed aside with a spell had been secured with a spell to prevent just such an occurrence. Those with power now knew that my powers were real and quite strong, even stronger than Chooser's own immense powers.

As I rode on toward the untamed lands, I thought about what she had said about the library being lost. It was true that no one had reported being there in centuries. That is no one reported being there. Cyclone, my mentor from my youth, had told Firewind and myself how to get there. The way was treacherous and not recommended for those without the knowledge of the eighth circle of power, or a well-equipped armed force.

As darkness approached, I decided to set up camp. As a wizard I could set up spells to protect me while I slept. I was just about finished setting my wards when a noise to the south caught my attention. I looked to see Chooser and four changelings heading toward my perimeter. My hand went to my sword hilt while the words of a spell lingered on my lips. Chooser I could handle. Four changelings I could handle. Chooser and four changelings would be a stretch even for me to handle.

"May we enter," Chooser inquired. I glared back in response.

"To what do I owe the honor," I asked, my voice dripping with sarcasm.

"I don't blame you for being angry with me. But hear me out first," she implored.

I loosened my grip on my sword. "Come," I said blandly. "You. Not them," I stated bluntly as she and the changelings came forward. She motioned to the changelings and walked toward me as if it were a matter of walking into a state dinner.

"I apologize for my behavior earlier," she started. "You have to realize that I deal with Destroyer on a regular basis," she finished.

"I heard you two were allies," I remarked. "I didn't know that that was justification to be insulting to others." I could see that my remark cut her to the heart.

"I deserve that I guess," she replied obviously hurt. "I should have given you the benefit of the doubt. I didn't. I'm hoping we can start fresh," she added.

"So you come here to apologize with four changelings at your side and I'm supposed to believe that your intentions are on the up and up," I asked sarcastically, still prepared to cast a spell should the need arise.

"I wish you'd hear me out before you make your judgment," she implored.

A part of me told me not to trust her. She was admittedly in league with one of the worst villains the world had ever known. Yet another part of me told me to trust her. Against my better judgment I decided to trust her for the time being and give her a chance to explain.

"Your plea of innocence would be stronger if you hadn't brought those changelings with you," I informed her while motioning towards the changelings.

"Actually, they're the main reason I'm here," she replied. She went on to explain that she was a young girl, only three, when Destroyer invaded her kingdom. He had entered the kingdom on the pretext of peace. When the king, her father, decided to turn down his offer of an alliance, Destroyer unleashed a couple of changelings on the royal court. He used his magic to occupy her father's wizards while the changelings decimated the royal court. She alone was unscathed by the assault. The four changelings she brought with her had once been her older brother and three cousins. Destroyer had used his magic to speed up the disease and make the transformation almost instantaneously instead of the weeks or months it usually would have taken.

"Okay. So, you brought your family. Why? So, I can cure them after I cure myself," I asked somewhat perplexed.

"That, and to make sure you didn't try to kill me," she joked. "I'm also hoping that maybe you can help me rid myself of Destroyer."

"I crossed spells with him when I was a teenager. We were pretty much evenly matched. While I've retained my strength, I'm afraid I wouldn't be much of match for him right now," I admitted regrettably. "Thirty-five years ago, I swore off using magic after I killed my fiancé and my best friend. I'd like to say it was an accident, but it wasn't," I told her.

We stared at each other in silence for what seemed like an eternity. I could tell she was waiting for me to elaborate on what I had just told her. Instead, I excused myself and went to turn in. "I'm trusting you and your family not to kill me in my sleep," I said as I lay down.

CHAPTER 3

The Lost Library

ONCE AGAIN, I was visited in my sleep by the same woman who had been haunting me of late. I still had no idea who she was. Try as I might, I couldn't find her. Whenever I tried to follow her voice, it would come from a different direction. When I woke, I had a feeling of being perplexed. I had to find out who this woman was who was haunting me. It bothered me that she knew that I was Phoenix before I revealed myself.

I got up and rekindled the fire. I put on a pot of coffee and started some breakfast cooking. It had been sometime since I had had to cook for myself. I glanced over and caught a glimpse of Chooser's sleeping form. Incredibly, her angelic face was even more beautiful in the morning light than it had been the first time I had seen her. I stared at her until I heard the coffee boiling over. I turned my attention to the kettle and when I looked back, she was sitting up. And I couldn't believe that she was now even more beautiful still. Not good for my sense of self-control.

"Whatever it is you're cooking, it's burning," she informed me. I snapped back to reality and turned my attention to the bacon I was frying. I managed to save about half. As I fumbled with the pan, Chooser came over and volunteered to cook the eggs I had found. She did so with an ease that belied her status as a queen. She noticed my stare and felt compelled to explain. "When Destroyer made me his charge, he insisted that I be taught how to cook and clean, so when it was just us together, he wouldn't have to. I find I actually enjoy cooking my own meals on occasion," she explained, "though I don't often get to."

We continued Northward toward the untamed region. The changelings paced along with us. I noticed that Chooser would have to cast a spell to keep them in check from time to time. It occurred to me that she seemed to always know when they needed to be reined in. I thought about the incident that put us on this journey. I decided to put off mentioning anything about it until a later time when I'd have a better idea of what I was going to say.

We didn't stop until the sun was setting, eating our midday meal while riding. We made camp, Chooser cooked us a simple meal and the changelings went off hunting. I tried to think of the words that wouldn't get me in trouble with her yet would express my curiosity about the night I was attacked. After much consideration I decided to hell with being diplomatic.

"I noticed that you always have them under your spell," I started, nodding towards the four changelings. "So, I can't help but wonder what happened that made you decide to let them loose. Did you know we were there? Did you need some more? Why am I infected," I finally demanded to know?

She sat there taken aback by my seeming callousness. Her face flushed as she thought about how to respond. She stared at me apparently struggling for the words. After an unimaginably long silence, she spoke.

"I've been meaning to apologize to you for that. I didn't just let them run wild. It's just that I can't control more than four at a time. Or rather, I can't keep absolute control on more than four. I've kept them with me at all times. This was the first time they had gotten away from me," she said.

"The two I killed, who were they," I asked.

"Ironically, they were the ones that had killed my parents. Whoever they were prior to that I don't know. I don't think Destroyer knows," she replied, "though I could be wrong."

I sat there staring at her trying to determine if she was being honest with me, or just trying to pull the wool over my eyes. Had I thought about it before I burst out, I would have cast a truth spell before giving her a chance to answer. Of course, with her level of power it wouldn't be accurate, but it would have been better than taking her words at face value, especially considering the effects her looks were having upon me.

"We need to get an early start in the morning so I'm going to turn in," I said. I didn't know if there were more to her stories that I wasn't catching. I kept a grip on my sword hilt as I lay down in my bedroll.

"Phoenix. Phoenix," she called from the darkness. "Wake up!!" I leapt from my bedroll, sword in hand. As my eyes focused, I scanned the area for signs of danger. The changelings were surrounding Chooser. They seemed nervous which in itself was disturbing. A motion off to my left caught my eye. I turned in that direction, sword at the ready.

I began to feel like a marionette as my sword and body parried and twisted in defense against an unseen opponent. I had no control over my own body. I could feel the power emanating from my sword as it commanded my muscles to move this way and that in defense of an enemy I couldn't even see! I could feel my blade make contact with something that I could only describe as otherworldly in nature.

Suddenly the entire area was illuminated as if the sun had risen, Chooser had cast a light spell. Woeful cries of pain and disdain raced off into the night. Cries I had only heard once before when my master had destroyed a group of wraiths that had haunted a small neighboring village near where I grew up. I felt myself being able to control my own actions once again.

Chooser and I stared at each other, neither quite knowing what to say to break the ice. I sheathed my sword, knowing that the wraiths wouldn't return as long as the light shone on us. I went back to my bedroll, lay back down, and tried to get some more sleep, a useless gesture. My mind had too many questions to allow me to sleep.

We were on the trail again shortly after sunrise. We were getting into the thick of the untamed region. Signs of ogres, orcs and other vile creatures could be seen on a regular basis. Several small trees had been uprooted, a favorite pastime of young male ogres. The stench of orcs permeated the region, their dens dotted the entire area. Our changeling companions would keep most of them away. Those that were too dumb or thought themselves too strong to be dissuaded from attacking us would soon learn the folly of their ways. A ninth circle wizard had nothing to fear from anything that roamed this region, add a second such wizard and the journey was considered mundane. That is unless a large mature dragon had somehow happened to wander into the area. The odds of which were slim.

We rode in silence for the most part, neither knowing what to say to the other. There was a definite tension between us. I found it difficult at times to be near her. She was so attractive it almost hurt. She was also powerful and in alliance with a great evil, though she claimed to want to break from that alliance. I couldn't tell where I stood with her and wasn't sure I really wanted to know.

After three more days of riding through thick forest, we reached a clearing and could see mount Delthore, home of the Library of Magus. A road led to the ruins of a once large thriving metropolis in one direction, disappearing into thick forest in the other. The ruins of the once magnificent metropolis littered the area, while plant life had overgrown most of the streets. Partial columns covered in climbing vines of ivy reached upward only to be broke off before achieving their objective. Large building stones lay strewn everywhere, the remnants of the city of Graveer, destroyed by the dragon Dragore.

We picked our way through the rubble toward the road that led up the mountain, which was seemingly untouched by whatever power had decimated the surrounding area. From where we were, we could see that one building still stood unscathed. Undoubtedly it was protected by powerful magic. If my master had been right, which he certainly would be, we would have to face a trial in order to enter the library. He never elaborated on what the challenge consisted of and I had failed to inquire what exactly was entailed in the trial. He had said that failure meant death. I didn't intend to fail.

I stared back down the mountain at the ruins of the once great city. At its peak it had over a hundred wizards of the sixth circle, or greater, living there. I couldn't help thinking of the regular denizens thinking they were safe from the world due to having so many powerful initiates residing there. What must have gone through their minds as Dragore descended upon them in her righteous retribution for the fate that had befallen her offspring at the hands of a human wizard? Looking up at the library above us I wondered still how it could escape unscathed. Another fifty feet closer and I could feel the power of the spells that were protecting the library and had the answer to at least one of my questions. The changelings too could feel the power and balked at going any further until Chooser cast a spell to calm them. She seemed to genuinely care about the creatures, and I remembered that she had said they were her only living relatives.

It took us the remainder of the day to make the ascent to the library. We opted to camp outside for the night rather than face the trials while as tired as we were. In spite of the power emanating from the library I set about putting up my own protection spells, including the wards to protect against the undead like the wraiths of the other night. Chooser watched me apparently amused at my undertaking. I smiled at her and said, "better safe than sorry."

For the first time in many nights, my dreams weren't haunted by the mysterious woman's voice. I figured the power emanating from the library was my savior and was thankful for small favors. I awoke more refreshed than I had been in years. I also had a greater appetite than I had ever had before. Chooser watched me eat my food ravenously and I caught a hint of concern in her eyes. I remembered why I had undertaken this mission to begin with and became concerned myself.

As soon as we finished eating, we approached the entrance to the library. The entrance to the library turned out to be two large golden doors. On either side of the doors were two enormous statues, each holding a sword longer than an ogre. Runes and glyphs were carved on the doors, columns, and walls from floor to ceiling. On the door, in the language of the magi, was a warning about entering. 'All who seek entrance must know themselves first.' Seemed simple enough.

I reached out a hand and pushed on the left side of the double door. To my surprise it opened easily. I cautiously entered the foyer. As I passed through the doorway, I found myself in an arena. To my right was a dragon. To my left and slightly in front of me was a griffin. To my left and behind me was a minotaur wielding a sword. Chooser was nowhere in sight.

Before I could move, the minotaur charged. Instinctively my hand went to my sword. I was rewarded with a painful jolt from the hilt. I dodged to my right allowing the minotaur to charge on past me. The words of a lightning spell formed in my mind and I unleashed a powerful jolt into the beast before it could recover and charge at me again. It vanished as though it were never there.

I didn't have a chance to relax when the griffin leapt into the air and began circling me. Almost instantly the words to spell formed and I unleashed gale force winds in the general direction of the griffin. Surprisingly, it too vanished. I turned to face the dragon. It slowly raised itself off the ground and yawned. My mind raced, yet I couldn't think of a single spell to cast. It occurred to me that dragons have the knowledge of human language. I decided to try to engage it in conversation rather than battle.

"I don't ever recall meeting a dragon of your splendid coloration before," I said opting for flattery.

"Have you met many dragons," it asked with a slight lisp.

"To be perfectly honest, no. You are in fact the first dragon I've happened to come across," I replied.

"Are you afraid of me," it asked glaring down at me.

I laughed in my reply. "To fear you would be to fear death which is not in my nature. Everyone dies eventually," I explained. The dragon seemed to smile at me just before it vanished. I found myself standing in the foyer. A minute or so passed before Chooser appeared with me.

A set of double doors opened in front of us revealing the interior of the great library. Inside numerous wizards scurried about. They seemed oblivious to our presence. I was taken aback when I recognized my master Cyclone. He was far younger than I remembered him, but it was him, nonetheless. As I looked around, I began to see other wizards that I knew were no longer among the living. I half stumbled as I looked around at all the different faces of those that had been powerful when my ancestors were living!

A librarian witnessed my amazement and came over to assist me. "What may we do for you fine folks today," he asked politely. I was still gawking at the myriad of long dead wizards, so Chooser spoke up.

"We're trying to undo Valtar's changeling spell," she replied.

"Hmm, Valtar...yes, he's on level nine. Go up those stairs, down the hall then take the stairs on the left. I believe you'll find him in room 9a," he informed us.

As Chooser led me toward the staircase I asked, "Did he say he was on the ninth level?"

"I believe he did," she replied.

"Valtar, here," I asked again.

"Mmhmm," was her reply. I followed along stunned. I hadn't heard about this aspect of the library. Either Chooser had, or she was too interested in finding a cure for her family to find our surroundings strange.

In no time at all we were standing in front of room 9a. I looked at Chooser than decided to knock on the door. There was no reply, so I knocked again. Still we were greeted by silence. I decided to enter anyway. The room was full of bookcases as one might expect of a room in a library. In the center sat a rectangular table. At the table, sitting on a chair at the halfway mark, sat a rather small nondescript man getting on in years. I thought he looked remarkably well for a man that had died four thousand years before I was born! Again, I stared as Chooser spoke up.

"Pardon us. Are you by any chance Valtar," she asked timidly? The old man never glanced up as though he couldn't hear her.

"Maybe he's deaf," I suggested. Chooser shrugged, and then stepped forward as if to put her hand on his shoulder. He leapt from his seat, staff in hand as if to defend himself from an attack.

"We mean you no harm," I said all the while keeping my hand on my sword hilt, this time not receiving any jolts. "We just need some information that you have," I continued. He eyed us up and down, muttered a faint obscenity then sat back down. After a short moment he glanced up at us again.

"Well what is it? You Futures always act like you have an eternity," he grumbled.

"Very well," I said gaining my composure. "You cast a spell creating a disease known as changeling lycanthropy. I have recently been infected with the curse and have no desire to fall victim to its debilitating effects. I require the original spell you used that I may reverse it. Unless of course you already have a reversal spell."

He looked at me for what seemed like an eternity then started laughing. He continued to laugh for several minutes. Finally, his laughter subsided, and he regained his composure. "Don't take that personally," he giggled. "You see when I cast that spell it was for a bet with Drelcarth. He swore I couldn't come up with a curse that no one would be able to break. Sorry son, there just isn't a cure."

"Not yet there isn't. However as soon as you give me the spell you used, I'll create one," I countered.

"That's not going to happen," he said glaring at me. I realized that he wasn't going to help me. I began looking at the volumes he was reading. Most were of transmutation spells. I began to suspect that he hadn't yet cast the spell, at least not from his viewpoint. If he hadn't yet cast the spell, then he couldn't tell me the spell. He didn't know it. Somewhere, amongst the many volumes of spells in the room, laid the answer to my quest. I simply had to find it.

I took Chooser aside and told her of my suspicions. She nodded in agreement that I had a point and was probably correct in my assumptions. I suggested we begin reading through the numerous tomes in the room. I chose to start with the volumes on the table. I started with a volume that Valtar had just finished making notes out of. He looked bemused at my action, but I ignored him.

I totally lost track of time. It seemed as though I had been reading spell books for an eternity. I finally finished reading the last book on the table to no avail. I got up from my seat, stretched then looked around the room for the book that held the key. I felt certain that it was in this room for it was filled with spells pertaining to lycanthropy. We just had to keep looking no matter how long it took.

After reading what seemed like a thousand books it dawned on me that I wasn't feeling as tired as I should. In fact, I should have been fatigued after hours and hours of reading book after book. The magical properties of the library were astounding. Although I wasn't feeling the fatigue that I knew I surely must, I decided to take a break and explore the library a little. Maybe what I was looking for would turn up somewhere else.

I asked Chooser if she'd like to join me in my exploration of the library. She said she'd rather continue the search where she was. We each had our motivations for wanting to find a cure. I left her with Valtar and went out on my own.

I looked down the hallway. It seemed to go on forever. I walked a little way down until I came to the next door. It was labeled 9e. I went inside to have a look around. It was set up the same as the room I had just left. I went to one of the shelves and retrieved a book.

Opening it I soon learned that this one was dedicated to fire. Being Phoenix that piqued my curiosity. I took the volume in my hand and sat down at the table and began to read a myriad of spells on creating and wielding fire. There were at least a thousand spells in this book. I began to wonder just how many ways one could use fire in spells that would require this much space to hold them all.

My curiosity wasn't stronger than my need to find a cure for myself. I left after reading only two volumes of spells. I retained the truly potent ones for my own repertoire. I then went on to the next room.

The next room was dedicated to ice. I studied a few volumes from this room then moved on. The next room was dedicated to wind. I repeated my efforts in each room, determined to learn a little from each even if it had nothing to do with my true mission.

I had gone through what seemed like a hundred rooms it seemed when I chanced upon something different and startling. I opened a door that led into a room filled with changelings. They were standing around talking to each other in a civilized manner. One of them looked up at me and motioned to the others. They all began to gather round me. 'Are you truly Phoenix,' they would each ask, as they got close. I assured them that I was. They reverted to their animal behavior and attacked me. I felt their claws and fangs begin to sink into me, yet felt no pain, this conflicted with what I knew should be happening.

I awoke to find myself outside of the library. About ten feet from me, lying on her bedroll and seemingly asleep was Chooser. I attempted to get up and wake her, feeling incredibly weak. We were both covered in a light coating of dust. Her eyes were open and lifeless, yet I could feel a pulse beating within her. The library still held her in its sway.

I began to search the runes written on the walls of the library to try and learn what spells were there. Maybe I could undo the magic that held her enthralled. I was feeling a little weak from my own experience. No telling how long we had been laying there without eating or drinking, though I knew it had had to have been more than a day due to the dust that still covered Chooser. I grabbed some hardtack from the pouch on my side. I drank from my flask, all the while searching the runes for the key to saving the young lady who had caused me to come here in the first place. On the wall next to the door to the library, I found the answer to my quest. I spoke the words of the ancient language aloud. Magic crackled in the air electrifying the area. A loud explosion followed, and the doors swung open.

I stood there looking into the library proper. Chooser began to move, signifying my success. The interior of the library was dusty. No one had cared for it in thousands of years.

I looked around at the volumes of spell books strewn all over the place in disarray. It looked almost the same as I had seen it before, only this time we were alone.

"Where is everyone?" Chooser asked.

"Dead. Long dead," I replied. "We were apparently under the library's influence the first time. I happened upon a situation that my mind didn't expect which allowed me to escape. I then found the runes controlling the spells and disarmed them and here we are. You'd better eat something. I'd also suggest drinking some water. I don't know how long we were out of it, but it was more than a day or two of that I'm almost certain," I informed her.

I felt a strange tingle in the back of my neck. I turned to find nothing there. A nagging feeling told me to follow the feeling. It led me up the stairs, back to the room I had thought Valtar was in while under the library's influence. Upon the table I could see a piece of parchment with notes scribbled on it. Chooser and I stared at each other in bewilderment and disbelief. I picked up the paper to find the answer to what I had come for. Valtar had written his spell in this very room on this piece of parchment all those years ago. The library had simply shown us where to find the answer we sought. We just had to be strong enough to escape its grasp to do so.

We took the parchment and headed back downstairs. Chooser headed toward the door, I headed toward a flight of stairs heading downward. "Where are you going? We should get out of here," she suggested. I shook my head in reply.

"My master, Cyclone, had told me of a safe room designed to allow wizards to try out their new spells without risk of destroying the world. I think we should go there," I explained.

"If that's true, you're right. Lead on," was her reply, or words to that effect.

Valtar's spell was remarkably complex. He truly designed it to be unbreakable. However, armed with the original, any spell could be undone, including the one that made the universe, provided the being trying to undo the spell was of sufficient strength to do so. It would take time to undo the web of spells he wove together so intricately. First, I would have to familiarize myself with his distinctive patterns. I would then have to try various inflections of the different syllables, until I found the right inflection of each one. It would take time, but I knew I could do it. I just hoped I would have enough time to do so before the disease itself made it impossible.

After two days and dozens of attempts, I finally happened upon the correct inflection of ancient words to undo the disease trying to ravage my body. I almost regretted it, as the curse was being undone. First, I doubled over as the dark powers coalesced in my abdomen. Then I fell to my knees and began vomiting a thick tarlike substance that was the essence of the disease. I gasped for breath as the last of it escaped my body. I staggered back away from the dark mass, which Chooser disintegrated with a fire spell.

As we left the library, her changeling-infected relatives awaited us outside the library entrance. She enthusiastically cast the spell that freed each of them from the curse. Slowly they reverted to their true human form, convulsing, and finally vomiting the diseases essence as I had. Once human again, they seemed oblivious to what had befallen them. They hadn't aged a day since becoming the beasts that they once were. It would take some time to get used to the world situation as it was. They had no idea who we were, though Firestorm confusedly asked Chooser if she were his mother, a woman she was said to resemble.

CHAPTER 4

Back to the Border

I LEARNED that her brother was a wizard as well when I looked him in the eyes and saw the flame of a fairly powerful initiate. He had reached the eighth circle before Destroyer had wrecked his world. Standing outside the library he was anxious to enter and study the spells that would propel him to the next level and allow him to seek his revenge on Destroyer. Chooser talked him out of it, explaining that the library had almost taken our lives and we were ninth circle wizards. The disappointment was evident on his face. With a hint of an, 'I will return' look in his eye, he grudgingly left the library.

"Look at it this way, with an eighth circle and two ninth circle wizards, I don't see Destroyer defeating us," I suddenly blurted out. Chooser's face lit up. It was then I realized that I had committed myself to freeing her from Destroyer. She smiled delightfully at me. I returned the smile, though not as delighted. At my age I should know better.

As we journeyed back out of the untamed lands, we had to do battle more than we had on our journey to the library. We were no longer in the company of four changelings. It became painfully obvious that while Chooser was an enormously powerful ninth circle initiate, her training was seriously lacking. Her brother and female cousin cast spells proficiently enough. The other two young ones, both boys, required constant supervision. They were initiates into the realm of magic, but lacked the discipline required to become powerful at the craft, at least for now. Not being in line to rule, their parents had overindulged them before Destroyer had come into their lives.

Destroyer had taught Chooser what he wanted her to know, but definitely not enough to challenge him. I decided to take it upon myself to further her education, especially since I had managed to commit myself to liberating her from Destroyer. Fortunately, the denizens of the untamed region gave us lots of opportunity to hone her craft. Her brother and cousins paid attention as well, learning what I was willing to teach. By the time we reached our destination they all showed great improvement, with Chooser being closer to my equal than she had been.

We returned to the routine of setting up protective spells and wards at night. Chooser would place sleep spells on the two younger ones to keep them from possibly wandering off. I thought she was being a little overly precautious but could understand where she was coming from. She had looked after them almost the entire time they had been under the curse. She couldn't give up her motherly instincts now.

The journey back took longer than the journey there. We only had the two horses, so we allowed the younger two to ride while the rest of us walked. I didn't mind. Chooser and I talked more than we had going there. Our demeanor was far more pleasant this trip, the gravity of the original trek having been allayed.

I talked at length with her brother as well. His name was Firestorm. He needed to talk about his experience and recollect his life prior to Destroyer's entrance to it. He had been an avid explorer. He had wanted to travel the world seeing all the sights and wonders thereof, but his father insisted that he prepare to rule Anthgolia instead.

"She's quite taken with you," he said nodding toward his sister as we journeyed through the wilderness.

"I'm becoming rather fond of her myself," I replied.

"No. I mean she's in love with you. I can see it every time she looks at you," he explained. I glanced over in her direction. She smiled at me then quickly turned away. She was by far the most beautiful woman I had ever laid eyes upon, but she was also less than half my age. She was a queen; I was a wizard turned mercenary swordsman, turned wizard. Still, the notion was very entertaining.

We were about a day from our journeys end, sitting by the fire and eating, when Firestorm came over to talk to me as was becoming the routine.

"It just struck me who you look like," he said. "You resemble Destroyer. Have you ever met him?" I hadn't told him about my experiences with Destroyer. I had only told Chooser about my one encounter that ended in a draw between us. It was time to come clean.

"He's my cousin on my mother's side," I told him. He visibly paled. "Don't worry. We're not a close family," I assured him.

I explained how in our youth Destroyer would take delight in killing animals just for the sake of killing them. I would always have to stop him whenever Christine would catch him messing with her pets. He took a special delight in killing her pets. I think it was to goad me into a fight. One day he succeeded. We ended up laying waste to half an acre of farmland by the time we were through. Cyclone's intervention brought a halt to the battle and that was the last time I had seen him. As I told the story, the others had gathered round and listened intently. Firestorm's complexion had returned to normal.

"We can't control who we're related to," Chooser said afterward. "It's how we live that counts." She snuggled up next to me and leaned her head on my shoulder. A medallion was dangling from her neck and brushed up against my chest. Jolts of pain and recognition shot through me. I pretended nothing was wrong as I got up and excused myself appearing to be answering a call of nature. I apparently wasn't very good at the pretense though, for Firestorm had followed me. Once we were far enough away, he asked what had happened. I stared back at him judging whether or not I should tell him.

"The medallion your sister is wearing was given to her by Destroyer," I explained. "I've seen that medallion before, or one just like it. He tried to ensnare my fiancée with it," I replied. I further explained how insidious a devise it was. We then tried to formulate a plan to save her from Destroyer's devise, all while acting as though relieving ourselves. Once we decided on what action to take, I sent him off to explain to his cousins.

I went back and sat down next to Chooser. I meditated on the runes of the library, concentrating on the ones that had ensnared us in their grip. Once I had them, I formulated the spell that would hopefully incapacitate Chooser. Her brother and cousins came toward us causing a loud distraction that allowed me to start the chant undetected. By the time she realized I was casting a spell, it was too late. She fell back into a slumber. I quickly reached out and caught her before her head could hit the ground. I then lay her on the ground where upon I grabbed her by the shoulders while Firestorm tried to remove the medallion. The shock sent him flying across the camp. Miraculously he had managed to hold onto the necklace and medallion. He tossed them aside.

I began to chant the spell that would revive Chooser when a bright light distracted me. It came from where the medallion had landed. I stood up quickly, drawing my sword as I did so.

"Long time no see, cousin," Destroyer snickered grinning.

"Not long enough," I replied, as I put away my sword. He wasn't real, just a sending, an image of himself able to be received by the medallion. No doubt a last-ditch effort to retain control on the one enslaved by the medallion.

I made several gestures and muttered a few words sending a bolt of power at the medallion. It exploded in a golden flame then vanished, taking with it Destroyer's visage, even as he tried to speak a spell to prevent it. He wasn't going to like it, but tough. It wasn't the first time that I had spoiled his plans and I didn't intend to make it the last. His control over Chooser was broken. We merely needed to find out which of her generals were his and dispose of them thus averting a potential war between her and my friends in the company.

I finished casting the spell to revive Chooser. She woke startled and feeling betrayed. Her cousin Lindeth explained why I did what I did. She accepted it though she still looked hurt. It tore me up seeing the look I was receiving from her. I figured she'd forgive me in due time. I turned in for the night allowing them to talk it over like family.

For the first night since I left the library, I heard a voice call to me in my dreams. I could feel a presence close to me. Try as I might, I couldn't find the source. It was enough to drive me crazy. The only thing that could be seen as a saving grace was, I awoke thoroughly refreshed.

We decided it would be best to circle around Chooser's forces and try to enlist the company's aid. We arrived at the company's camp around four in the afternoon. Recognizing me, the company sentries weren't sure how to behave as we strolled on into camp. They opted for the better part of valor and they kept quiet, as they backed away. We walked straight to the command tent. Chooser and her family assumed their royalty mode and acted as regal as they could, as we marched through the encampment. I opened the command tent flap and invited her inside. No one in command knew what to say as we entered. Braveer glared at me in half amazement. I gave him my slimmest, slyest smile. I could see the immediate relief on his face.

I introduced Chooser, Firestorm, Lindeth, Mildeth, and Rockner to the commander. Braveer welcomed them into his camp. I asked him to clear the tent. Once all personnel had left, I cast a protection spell on the tent. I explained about Chooser, Destroyer, and my plan to help free her and Anthgolia from his grip. Braveer had never liked my cousin, something we all had in common.

Shameer listened intently. As second in command he had needed to stay with Braveer. I could see a hint of astonishment in his steely face. He could usually stare down a troll and not flinch. He had never been around powerful wizards as Braveer had. Chooser alone could unnerve any man. Add the rest of our group and I was the one amazed at how well he was taking the situation.

"So, what you're suggesting is a housecleaning of Chooser's camp with company men as guards, is that the gist of it," Shameer asked.

"That's why he's my second," Braveer retorted. "If I hadn't grown up with you, I'd think you were crazy. Having done so I know it's just me."

"Shameer, Chooser was under my cousins' control. Otherwise we wouldn't be here. I don't want to have to fight ten thousand troops either," I was explaining.

"A hundred thousand," Shameer interrupted, correcting me while not taking his eyes off of Chooser.

"But with you guys buying us a few seconds our spells will take them down harmlessly," I continued as though not having heard his correction. "Besides, if anybody tries to hurt you, Braveer will protect you. He's good at that sort of thing," I chided.

Braveer sent word to the cook to prepare a proper meal for our visiting royalty friends. Shortly after sunset a feast was brought into the command tent. Several junior officers were invited to meet our guests. I sent for Cyclops and Hermit. I felt a certain loyalty to those two, and if good eating was going to be done, then the men whose hunting and cooking skills had saved my pallet were going to be involved in it.

The impromptu formal party lasted several hours. The small talk was all politeness. My sidekicks ate ravenously, while at the same time keeping their eyes locked onto Chooser and her family. It did my heart good to finally be able to repay that debt.

It was getting late and everyone was feeling fatigued. I commandeered the medical tent for Chooser's party. No one else was using it. I had been the only one unfortunate enough to require its services in the last three months. Chooser pulled me inside and kissed me.

"I never thanked you for all that you've done for me," she said staring into my eyes. I hesitated only momentarily before I leaned forward and returned her kiss. Not since Christine had died had I felt for a woman the way I felt for Chooser. She had a quality about her that I couldn't resist. I apparently had a likewise quality that she couldn't resist either.

Her cousin, Lindeth had already drawn the curtains around the rest of the family giving us privacy that we hadn't had on our trek. Chooser untied the straps holding up her dress and allowed it to fall to the floor. She was now in a flimsy slip. She stepped toward me and removed my sword belt. I hastily undid the toggles on my tunic and flung it off. Chooser's delicate hands undid the belt that held my trousers up. She let them fall to the floor leaving me naked. I reached out with both hands and slipped a finger under each of the straps of the slip she wore. I pulled them up and off her silky shoulders. I let the slip slide to the floor revealing to me her voluptuous body. I leaned forward and kissed her passionately. I kissed my way down to her breasts. I took one, then the other of her ample breasts into my mouth allowing my tongue to linger on her nipples.

I kissed my way back up to the nape of her neck. We were both fully aroused at this point. She pushed away from me gently, took me by the hand and led me to a nearby bed. We made love like neither of us had ever been with another before. We climaxed nearly simultaneously. We fell asleep in each other's arms.

It wasn't quite near daybreak when I awoke. I had a strong feeling that something wasn't right. I quietly got up and got dressed before I woke up Chooser with a kiss. I placed a finger over her mouth to keep her quiet. She sat upright holding the blanket over her breasts to hide them. I thought the gesture quaint considering we were alone and had been very intimate a few short hours before. She seemed to sense the same thing that I was sensing and got up to dress equally quietly.

We left the medical tent and began scanning the camp, trying to place the feeling of abode to a single location. It was emanating from all around us, yet nowhere. It didn't make sense. The company horses and other animals could feel it too. They were braying and snorting nervously. They scraped the ground with their front hooves, further signifying their distress. The sentries were wandering about looking for something amiss but finding nothing to report.

Suddenly, the sky overhead lit up with the brightness of a flame. Everyone awake looked up as the form of a large dragon flew over. I could hear the wind rush from under its beating wings as it soared above us. The moon Crathos' light caused its shadow to engulf the entirety of our camp. The horses broke down the corral holding them and began to flee into the darkness terrified of the visage they had just witnessed. A couple of sentries tried to impede their progress to no avail. I felt the crackle of a spell and they were stopped in their tracks. Firestorm had also been awakened by the same feeling as Chooser and me, witnessed the horses and took care of the situation as only a wizard could.

I looked at Chooser dumbfounded. I didn't want to believe what I had just seen. If it was truly Dragore, we were in trouble. The dragon didn't stop, nor did it attack either camp. It flew northward over Anthgolia toward the mountains of Dylph. Dylph was the rumored current home of all of planet Asmodora's dragons. I couldn't imagine this being a good sign no matter how I looked at it. Dragore had nearly destroyed all of mankind, after the wizard Garthandal had taken her eggs from her. It took the combined power of the council of wizards, plus every initiate of the sixth circle and up to finally defeat the beast. If my interpretation of those events was correct, they weren't able to destroy Dragore, just bind her magically. Her powers were such that destroying the beast would have destroyed magic altogether, something even the council was unable to accomplish, nor had they a desire to do so.

I quickly made my way over to where the horses were still standing. I climbed on the healthiest looking one, spoke some words of magic releasing it from Firestorm's spell, and rode off toward the dragon's lair. I had to find out if the dragon we had just saw truly was Dragore. I spoke more spells as I rode, enabling the beast to ride full gallop in the limited light without stumbling. I spoke more words of magic to speed up the beast's pace. The sun was just peering over the horizon as I crested the mountain. I rode down the path, turning on the path that would lead to the cavern of Dragore. In a matter of minutes, I completed a journey that normally would have taken hours. I dismounted, casting another spell on the horse to keep it where it was, while allowing it to cool off without ill effects.

I burst into the cavern, expecting to find it empty. Instead, I stared up at the largest living creature ever imagined. Its smallest scale could cover a small mansion. The dragon that had flown over our heads was fully one third of this one's size. My heart began to race as I slowly backed out of the cavern hoping not to arouse the beast before me. As I was just about out of the cavern, my heel clanged against a chest of gold when an immense eye, the size of the moon Prothos, opened. Its pupil focused immediately upon me. I let my left-hand clasp the hilt of my sword.

"Surely you don't expect her to come to your aid," Dragore asked with a laugh. 'She knows better than to try me.' I somehow knew she was referring to my sword. I didn't know what to say. 'Why do you dare to disturb me,' she asked perturbed. The words pounded my brain. I began to realize that I wasn't hearing her with my ears, but with my mind. Dragore was telepathic.

"Well if you must know, I didn't expect to find you here," I answered honestly.

'Why should I believe such drivel,' she demanded

"Because it's the truth," I responded.

'Why wouldn't I be here? The games not over yet,' she yawned. I wasn't sure what she meant by that.

"I saw a large dragon fly overhead shortly ago. I assumed it was you," I replied.

'That was my great, great, great grandson,' she answered chuckling. 'He hasn't fully finished growing yet.'

"Sorry to disturb you," I said continuing to back out.

'We'll meet again,' she told me smiling slyly. It's a disturbing sight that, a dragon smiling slyly. Your blood seems to chill instantly.

I remounted the horse and slowly began the trek back to camp. I ran into friends just as I crested the mountain.

"It was Dragore wasn't it," they asked. I simply shook my head numbly. I was still in shock from my latest encounter. A being of that much power can change your thoughts of your own position in the scheme of things. They looked toward the entrance of the cavern. I looked at them solemnly, shook my head, grabbed the closest one by the arm and led them back toward camp. No one would be prepared to meet that beast. I could shield myself from some of its power and I was overwhelmed.

"You mean to tell me that humongous beast wasn't..."

"Wasn't fully grown," I finished raising my eyebrows to emphasize the statement. They exchanged astonished glances with one another. "Let's not disturb her anymore, shall we," I suggested. Everyone nodded his or her heads in agreement. We made our way back toward camp. I began to wonder about the story of the council of wizards taking her down, and for the first time doubted the tale I had heard had any basis in fact. I couldn't see a thousand wizards matching the power I had felt from her, thus a few hundred doing so just didn't add up.

It was past midday when we finally started toward Chooser's camp. I imagine it was quite a sight to behold. The queen of this huge army being escorted back to her own camp under guard by what had, until now been an opposing force. Her forces were in further disbelief when she ordered them to remove all upper body clothing. I hadn't thought it to be such a simple task, but it was. Those ensnared by Destroyer's medallions had no idea that they were. His devices were only active when actions contrary to his orders were taken. Exposing the medallions didn't appear to be in conflict.

Those wearing the medallions were quickly isolated and subdued. Their medallions were systematically removed and destroyed. I knew that there would still be those loyal to my cousin by magical oath, but we would just have to deal with them when and if they showed their true colors.

Once her camp was clear of obvious Destroyer slaves, the company headed back toward Asmerian territory. The commander, Shameer, Cyclops and Hermit were invited to stay for dinner. I of course would be staying with Chooser. Braveer and I spoke at length during the course of the evening. He could understand my attraction and seemed a bit envious. He also understood why I had to help her with my cousin. Of course, he left an invitation to rejoin the company anytime I wanted. I smiled and patted his back in reply.

Drakar, a pure military and ranking general, stared in disbelief at Firestorm. He had been one of his closest friends and advisers prior to Destroyer causing him to be cursed. Drakar had been sworn to protect the royal family and was devastated at his failure to do so. He had pledged loyalty to Destroyer only as a means to stay close to and protect, Chooser, the only unaffected member of the royal family. He fell to his knees before the restored prince, a gesture not missed by the rest of those present. Firestorm grabbed his arm and pulled him back onto his feet

It was strange, exciting, and inviting staying with Chooser in her lavishly furnished tent. "Enjoy it for now," she whispered seductively in my ear.

"Why you are planning on throwing me out," I asked in jest.

"Of course not," she exclaimed hitting me with a pillow as if insulted by my words. "It'll be my brothers once he assumes the throne, silly! You're unbelievable," she said hitting me again, as I laughed. I reached up and grabbed her by the waist pulling her on top of me. We kissed in a lingering embrace. Enjoying myself thus was easy, and she seemed to equally enjoy the situation we were in.

That night I had another visit by the mystery woman who had been haunting my dreams. Again, she called to me. When I called back, this time I received a one-word reply, divine. Once again, I awoke confused, yet refreshed. Women have that effect on me it seemed.

The encampment was busily going about the business of breaking down tents, loading up wagons and preparing to move out. Chooser had given orders that she wanted to be heading back to the capital shortly after sunrise. She grabbed me by the arm and we quickly made our way to the mess tent. It would be the last tent taken down. We joined Firestorm and Lindeth at a table. Mildeth and Rockner were there as well. A servant brought us each a plate of eggs, potatoes, ham, and biscuits. We ate ravenously. Lindeth asked if we had slept well. Chooser giggled and said, "yeah, but not much!" I think I blushed. Firestorm grinned a knowing grin. Lindeth kissed him on his cheek.

The journey to the capital would be a lengthy one. A hundred thousand troops could only march so fast. After the first day's progress proved how slowly the pace would have to be, I went out of character and suggested a new strategy.

"I think it would be wiser to take the cavalry and ride on to Blendell," I volunteered as Chooser and I watched the last wagon roll into camp. Firestorm was mounted right beside her and asked, "why?"

"By now Destroyer knows you're breaking your ties with him and attempting to free your kingdom as well. He'll probably try to secure the capital in order to retain a hold on the country. Let's face it, you're expendable, he can always put another puppet on the throne," I explained. General Drakar overheard and agreed. His approval was all that was needed for my idea to be implemented.

Chapter 5

A Sword is Forged

CHOOSER AND I enjoyed another night of passion. I couldn't tell you which one of us was enjoying the situation more. We both had a lot of stored up energy, and neither of us was holding back at releasing it. It almost seemed unimaginable that I could be feeling this strongly for someone again, especially someone I had only known for such a little while. I had spent a great many years not allowing myself to get this close to anyone, partially for fear of getting hurt and partially for fear of hurting them.

As I slept with Chooser in my arms, I dreamt of another woman. This one I knew nothing about. Yet she called to me as if beaconing me. When I tried to find her, she vanished as if never there. This time I was left with a lingering thought, divine.

I awoke the next day and got dressed as usual. When I went to put on my sword, I received a nasty little jolt. Immediately the word divine popped into my head. I somehow understood this to mean that I was to divine my sword. I had never tried to determine magically what my sword was capable of. I knew now I had better listen to that small voice screaming inside my head, or risk it getting louder. I suspected the next shock I received would be much stronger if I failed to listen.

I explained to Chooser that I had some important personal business to tend to, though I didn't elaborate exactly what. I was glad when she didn't ask me what business; instead, she simply bid me a hasty journey. I assured her that I would rejoin her before she made it to Blendell. She grabbed my shirt, pulled me close, and kissed me goodbye. Then she stared me in the eye. The lustful look in her eye ensured that I wouldn't linger long from her side.

As I rode off toward the northeast. I wasn't planning on traveling far. Just far enough away from everyone so that I wouldn't be disturbed while working my magic. The divining of any magical item required concentration. The more powerful the object being divined, the more danger involved in divining it, an object as powerful as my sword could not only kill me but could take half the kingdom with me should things go wrong! I wasn't about to take any unnecessary chances.

It was midmorning when I found what appeared to be a suitable location. I began by breaking out my magical supplies stored in my old chest. Once everything was properly arranged, I began to weave the magic that would unravel the secrets of the sword. When done properly, the divining spell takes the caster back to the very forge where the magic was imparted unto the object. I had divined about two-dozen items in my past; none were even on the same page, let alone in the same chapter, as this sword. In fact, they weren't even in the same book. Its spells were more powerful than even I could cast. I had heard of wizards whose powers were such that they became like gods, but I had never run into any, and hadn't really believed they truly existed, though this sword would tend to prove that they did.

I cautiously began the ritual spell that would guide me back to where the sword was forged. In seemingly no time at all I was standing in a forge watching a burley one-armed man working metal into the shape of a sword. Five men and five women were magically bound in the corner, each watching with fear as the blade took shape. Two more powerfully built men and a beautiful woman stood around the hearth chanting, while a dark figure in the shadows nearby repeated their chants. They each took turns inscribing a rune on the length of the blade in gold and silver ink. Each rune would then float away into the metal, becoming part of its very being. I didn't recognize a single rune. I could only watch in bewilderment as the final rune was inscribed on the blade and those creating the weapon spoke the words of power that went with it.

I wasn't expecting what happened next. One of the young women who were bound in the corner began to float, then vaporize and be wisped into the blade. I found myself being pulled into the blade with her.

I couldn't explain what happened. I found myself in a room filled with throw pillows. Upon the pillows was the beautiful young lady I had just witnessed being encased into a sword, my sword.

"Welcome Phoenix," she called in by now an all too familiar voice. The lady of my dreams it turns out, lives in my sword. She seemed to sense what I was thinking and laughed out loud.

"So, I'm the lady of your dreams," she asked amused.

"At least the lady that haunts my dreams," I confessed.

"Relax, Phoenix, you're safe in here. I've placed an almost impenetrable shield around you in the outside world so we can talk," she said matter-of-factly.

"I'm all yours," I stated humbly, awestruck by the power radiating from her.

"What you just witnessed was my internment into this cell and my entry into the game," she informed me.

"Okay, I'll bite, what game," I had to ask. She laughed again and I could have sworn I heard birds singing. Her voice was very soothing as she explained in great detail about the game that the immortal ones were playing with her and others of her race. In the realm of magic, counted as we did by circles, she would be considered an initiate of the twenty-fifth circle. Those who had enslaved her would be on the fiftieth. In my naivety and arrogance, I hadn't realized that there were any above the ninth. I could feel the immense power emanating from her and could feel the greater power that encapsulated her into this sword. They were staggering, beyond imagining.

All at once I found myself back in my own body. I was cradling the sword in my lap. I would never be able to look at it in the same way again. I also had the answers I had long sought about the night I had killed my fiancée and my best friend. It had been a part of the game. Their lives had been forfeited at the whim of a being of power. To what end this game of theirs was for, only they knew, and they weren't sharing that with anybody. Whatever it was, I was now a part of it, and had been, like it or not.

I made myself a snack to help regain my strength. I was far weaker than I had expected to be. Of course, I hadn't expected to meet a goddess. I would need some time to fully absorb what had just happened. Without really thinking about it, I set up protection for a camp, then lay down and rested, even though it was only slightly past midday. I fell asleep almost immediately.

For the first time in I don't know how long, I wasn't called to in my dream. Soulbinder, the lady in my sword, didn't need to visit me there anymore. Since I had found her, she could call on me anytime she pleased.

She told me how remarkably simple our minds were and how easy it was to manipulate us. I was the fourth to wield her. The others had all died of old age, not really furthering her position in the game. In the thousands of years since the game had begun, more than half were still in the game. To be taken out of the game meant death. Soulbinder had no desire to die. She wouldn't settle for anything other than victory and the freedom that she hoped would come with it.

The following morning, I proceeded toward Blendell, and Chooser. I worked magic on my steed to increase its speed and endurance. Doing so, I realized that Soulbinder had been doing the same thing to me. The time I took on the two changelings for example. It was her manipulation of my limbs that enabled me to take them out, and again against the wraiths that night in the untamed lands.

Soulbinder began a constant communication link between us. It was greatly unnerving being controlled by a sword, though her intentions seemed honorable enough. I guess I'd do the same thing if I were in her sandals.

Chapter 6

Changing of the Guard

I RODE straight on through the day and night and half the day again finally rejoining Chooser's party. She reacted like we hadn't seen each other in months instead of just days. I've often heard that the beginning of a romance was always the most energetic. Holding her in my arms again took a little bit of the edge off my discovery and trek here. She called a halt for a meal break while I took the time to sleep. My body wasn't rested enough, but somehow, I made it through to the next rest break. Chooser saw how tired I was and understood when I fell asleep on her. In the morning she awoke early and woke me to make up for lost time.

For posterity's sake, Chooser would retain control of the title and command of the troops until a proper ceremonial changing of the guard could take place in Blendell. After that, we would stick around making certain that Destroyer didn't attempt any more tricks to regain control of Anthgolia. I knew that the only way to keep my cousin out of the picture was to take him out of the game.

I felt a trace of humor sent to me by Soulbinder after my last thought. Yeah, I thought back, life really is nothing but a game with ever changing rules. But it's the only game we have, and like her, I didn't want to lose.

We continued on toward Blendell at a fast trot. At our current pace we would be there in two more days or so, according to General Fortwall. There was no way of picking up the pace with four thousand cavalries. We would just have to be prepared to face whatever Destroyer would throw at us.

The day seemed to drag on as we pressed on. Finally, the evening shadows told us it was time to rest. We ate a hearty meal of stew. Chooser and her generals discussed strategy while I ate and listened. Their main concern was how to limit casualties. The soldiers they were most likely preparing to face were her subjects being manipulated by Destroyer, though some would be loyal to him for other reasons. Just as they seemed to have it all figured out, Firestorm came in, looked at the map, and suggested another option they hadn't pursued. I continued to sit there listening and finally I had to laugh. My laughing didn't go unnoticed. Slowly everyone else quieted down until everyone was staring at me. I looked up at them shaking my head.

"You people can sit around conjecturing a million possibilities and still wind up totally wrong. None of us can truly see the future. That's because there are too many different things that could change everything," I began sounding amused. "Tell me this, what good is all this conjecture going to do if everything you didn't think of goes wrong? None. I suggest rest, lots of it. That advice is from a twenty-five-year mercenary soldier, who has fought a thousand or more battles, not a ninth circle initiate."

Lindeth, who had just arrived, agreed somewhat bemused herself. With that, Chooser dismissed everyone from our area. We snuggled up in a bedroll together. We made no secret that we were removing our clothing under our cover blanket. No one in the camp would dare look in our direction for fear of angering a powerful wizard or two. I lay there holding on to her thankful for the warmth of her touch. I had only received a little of this type of attention from the last woman I genuinely loved before the game got a hold of us.

"Can you keep from slaying all my citizens should we have to go to battle," she asked tracing a finger around the curvature of my chest muscles as she laid to the right of me my right arm under her head. I had my arm around the back of her shoulders, so I pulled her in closely to kiss her yet again.

"Beautiful, don't worry about a thing. I have the perfect disabling spell in mind should a battle erupt," I assured her.

The remainder of the journey to Blendell was uneventful. We were about an hour or so from the city, so I suggested to Chooser that she might want to send a scout ahead to warn us in advance if we should expect trouble. She sent a junior wizard, one capable of spurring on his mount without being missed should he be killed upon arrival at the city. As we crested the last hill, the scout approached. He had found no evidence that Destroyer had set up an ambush for her return.

Securing the city turned out to be an easy task. Chooser's top wizards, along with Chooser, Firestorm, Lindeth and myself, were able to identify and nullify all of Destroyer's medallions. There were only five in the city. Evidently Destroyer figured his hold on Chooser and a few others was sufficient to hold the country under his control and had been until now. He hadn't planned on my coming along and falling in love with his puppet and curing her relatives of the disease he had purposefully inflicted them with.

The next morning plans were made for the transference of power from Chooser to Firestorm, the true and rightful heir. The ceremony would be held in two months' time, allowing the rest of the troops to make it back to Blendell. In the meantime, Chooser set about filling her brother in on all the pertinent details he would need to be an effective ruler. I listened in intently, especially when she started explaining about Destroyer's war with Hellfire.

Hellfire was another wizard of the ninth circle. His true age was unknown, unnaturally long thanks to the dark powers he possessed. He was said to be ancient when the ancients were young. His only care in the world is power. He couldn't care less about living creatures. To him, they were mostly obstacles in his way. He was said to kill children for their blood to use in certain potions. He ruled an area with very few human inhabitants even though; humans had originally settled the region. Those who remained there usually ended up as food for one of his pets. The land was also where a vast number of gems could be found. Gems used for casting magic. That was Destroyer's interest in the place. He also ruled a land said to have scarce human inhabitants. His army was made up of ogres, orcs, changelings, and hobgoblins. They turned out to be an equal match for Hellfire's forces of goblins, trolls, ogres, and hobgoblins. That was why he had wanted Chooser to cross Asmeria. She would have forced Hellfire to defend two fronts.

As I listened, I began to wonder if helping Destroyer might not be such a bad idea. I didn't voice my opinion knowing the arguments that would surely sprout up from such a suggestion. I decided to play the wait and see game. If others started voicing similar beliefs, then I'd of course play devil's advocate. Otherwise my relationship with Destroyer might tend to make my motives suspect.

Nighttime had become my favorite time. With a woman like Chooser sharing my bed, it was a given. However, I should probably refer to it as my sharing her bed. It was her castle after all. Nevertheless, my nights were finally filled with a passion I hadn't ever imagined since Christine's passing. I began to fantasize about having children. I could see Chooser making a wonderful mother. I couldn't imagine what kind of father I'd make. I had been a bachelor for a great many years.

It was only two days until Firestorms coronation as the rightful ruler of Anthgolia. I was lost in my thoughts, staring out toward the northeast, towards Destroyer's domain. I tried to figure out what in our youth turned him as dark as he was. He hadn't been abused or mistreated. I couldn't figure it. 'Some people are just naturally evil,' Soulbinder sent bemused. I really wasn't expecting an answer. I found it disturbing at times the way she would just chime in with her thoughts. I was back in my thoughts when Chooser came up beside me.

"Thinking of me," she asked playfully.

"Of course. What else," I replied, as I took her in my arms and kissed her.

"I don't know. Destroyer perhaps. At least that's what I've been thinking about lately," she replied as though she had read my thoughts. I was a little unnerved by that thought until Soulbinder assured me that she hadn't. "I think it might be wise to help him defeat Hellfire. Hellfire is the greater evil, by all accounts," she continued unaware of my little chat with Soulbinder.

"Funny you should say that. I had that same thought the other day when you were assessing the situation for Firestorm," I told her.

"Why didn't you speak up then," she asked.

"Several reasons, not the least of which is the fact that Destroyer is my cousin, like it or not. Had I suggested that course of action, my motives would have been suspect," I replied.

"I wouldn't have judged you, especially since you saved not only me, but my kingdom," she remarked, obviously perturbed.

"Not by you, but by others. You're biased when I'm the subject, just as I'm biased toward you. But I'd question the loyalty of your generals and advisers, if they didn't question my motives," I said smiling at her. Even scowling she was sexy. Damn that wasn't good for my sense of self-control.

"Not to worry. I won't let anyone else take control of you," Soulbinder sent.

'I imagine you wouldn't,' I sent back. I received laughter back.

"Doesn't matter now. Firestorm will assume control over Anthgolia tomorrow next, and we'll be free to do as we choose," she chimed.

"And what will you have me do after that," I asked whisking her into my arms.

"What you will, my love," Chooser said staring deeply into my eyes while leaning in for a kiss. We kissed passionately allowing ourselves to linger in the exultation of it. As we allowed ourselves to break away, I had a strange feeling about me. I half reached for my sword before it dawned on me what was happening. Soulbinder had sent her essence over to Chooser. They were now in communication. The feeling passed almost as quickly as it had appeared.

Chooser stared at me in half disbelief. I sort of shrugged knowingly. 'Mind telling me what just passed between you and Chooser,' I sent. I didn't get an answer. I reached out and took her hand, bent down, and looked her in the eye.

"She's one powerful lady," Chooser finally gasped. I nodded my head in agreement. "Where did she come from," she asked in amazement.

"She resides in my sword. I never asked her where she originates from, she's stronger than me and I'd hate to press my luck," I explained trying not to sound too wimpy, though not feeling it.

Chooser reached out and grabbed the hilt with her other hand. I could see the instant transformation take place as her consciousness was transported into the sword. I tried to join in the conversation and found myself locked out. So, I kept a look out until Chooser returned to herself.

"How is it that I've held this sword for over thirty five years and had to divine it before I could speak with her, yet you come within a foot and she's gabbing away with you," I asked her feeling somewhat slighted.

'It's because you divined me that I'm now able to interact with your race,' Soulbinder sent. 'As for our conversation, had I wanted you to know what was said, you'd know.' I could see this was going to get interesting, though wasn't quite sure if it were a good thing or bad.

After dinner, we joined Firestorm and Lindeth in their private chambers and discussed the world situation and our fears. Chooser, it turned out, was a terrific orator.

She could sell her ideas to anyone. The four of us debated the situation between Destroyer and Hellfire at great length. Finally, it was decided that Chooser and I would lead a mission to try to reach an accord with Velouth on helping us defeat, first Hellfire, then Destroyer. We would explain how this venture would be to our mutual benefit. A messenger was dispatched to Grendale, capital of Asmeria, asking for a meeting. We would leave the day after the ceremonies and await the reply at the border.

The coronation went off without a hitch. Chooser looked elegantly regal as she handed over the mantel of leadership to Firestorm. Lindeth was beaming as the Crown was placed on his head. It had been announced that they were to marry come the fall, which would be in two months' time. I had suspected those two had a thing for each other. They were well suited to each other. I had learned that they were cousins through marriage, not blood.

We celebrated with Firestorm and the rest of the royal court until well after sunset. I reveled in the attention lavished on me by Chooser. We retired unbeknownst to everyone else, wanting to linger in the luxury of the castle. We made love until all of our energy was spent. Some men my age relied on magical stimulants to enable them to perform, I couldn't imagine needing such items with Chooser as my partner. Her slightest glance in my direction tended to arouse me. I suspected that it was just the newness of it all but hoped it would never end.

Chapter 7

Diplomatic Quest with a Side Trip

WE SET OUT toward Asmeria shortly after daybreak a week after the wedding. We had an escort of forty troops. It seemed as though I had just gotten over the ride to Blendell, and here I was in the saddle again. I never could understand why anyone would desire to ride for days on end. The only good thing I could say about riding, was that it was faster and easier on the feet than walking.

There was no real sense of urgency surrounding this trek, as there had been the last time. We stopped at least twice a day to give our derrieres a break. I would stretch, and then stare at Chooser at each such break. Eventually she would see me and come put her arms around me. I tried to remember when I felt such joy as I did in those moments but couldn't. Even when Christine was still alive and we were at our happiest, I didn't feel the elation I did when Chooser held me.

I was surprised to find the company still camped out at Dragore Mountains. They hadn't received any new orders, so they were taking advantage of the time to relax. Chooser and I rode into the camp unfettered. The sentries knew me and were afraid of her. I could hear a few snickers from the crowd along with a few crude remarks. I turned in the general direction, and asked boldly, "jealous?" Obviously, from their remarks, they were. Most blushed and turned away, though some did just out of fear.

Word of our approach had reached him and Braveer was standing in front of the command tent grinning ear to ear as we rode up. He slapped me on the back bidding us to come in.

"We're on a diplomatic mission to enlist Velouth's aid in defeating Hellfire, then Destroyer," I explained.

He cocked an eyebrow, then asked, "you really think you have a chance at recruiting his aid?"

"Realistically, no. But it is worth taking the chance, of course. What's the saying you're so fond of, nothing ventured, nothing gained," I asked.

Chooser had been listening to our banter, but finally spoke up. "I think I can persuade him that it would be in his best interest to do something about them now, rather than waiting until they turn their full attention onto Asmeria." It was a simple statement, but it carried with it a sentiment that was deeply profound to the military man standing before her.

"Will you marry me?" he asked her. Her jaw dropped. The question was totally unexpected.

"Trying to steal my lady," I asked trying to sound offended.

"She's amazing," Braveer remarked. "It's truly an honor to be in the company of such a wise and may I say beautiful young woman." Chooser blushed, stirring in me my animal instinct.

"We have a small honor guard with us. Where should we have them set up our camp," I asked Braveer.

He hesitated to take his eyes off of Chooser, then said, "Have them pitch your tent near mine. You're both completely welcome in my camp. You needn't post guards unless you want to."

"Don't take it wrong, but I think we'll post guards. I don't want them getting lazy just because we're among friends," Chooser replied.

"I'd have questioned your actions had you said otherwise," Braveer remarked.

"As would I," I added.

We sat around talking at great length, Braveer telling Chooser all about our wild youth. He took great pains to recollect all of my most embarrassing moments. I smiled politely, promising him I would get even with him, should he ever find a woman foolish enough to consent to be with him. Chooser assured him that somewhere there was such a woman. I thanked her for giving me hope.

We retired to our tent sometime around midnight. I stretched out and fell asleep seconds after my head hit the pillow. Soulbinder met me in my dream again.

"I thought we were over this stage," I stated puzzled.

"Sometimes I like to look at you face to face," she replied.

"So, we're back in the sword," I inquired.

"No. We're no longer on the plane we were on. We're actually on my home, a thousand lifetimes in the future," she replied. I let the statement sink in. We were surrounded by nothing. No planet, no space, no darkness, no...nothing.

"Okay, I'll bite. Why here," I had to know.

"I wanted you to see what lies in store for us. I can't tell how our journey together is going to turn out. There are some things you need to be aware of," she explained. I waited for her to be forthcoming with the important news. She stared at me for what seemed like an eternity. All at once we were in the middle of a field. A butterfly flittered in front of my face, then off to the nearest flowering plant. Off in the distance a bird was singing melodiously.

I found I couldn't take it anymore, I had to speak, "What is it I should know," I asked trying not to sound impatient.

"Your upcoming opponents are wielding two of the dark swords of the game. They are both aware that we're traveling together. They may in fact be planning on destroying us by luring us into a trap, disguised as a war amongst themselves," she explained in a matter-of –fact tone.

"You've known this fact for how long now? And you wait until I'm committed to defeating them, don't ya think the time for that was before," I implored. She laughed sounding genuinely bemused at my tirade. "Okay, so what do we do about this little predicament," I asked.

"First, we'll have to deal with the scouting party you encountered earlier," she instructed.

Of course, being the interested and astute person that I was I merely had to ask, "which scouting party would that be?"

"The one in the tunnel of course," she said condescendingly. "Why did you think I made the blade glow?"

"So, I could see," I replied truly not knowing the answer. She looked baffled, which I thought was disturbing because of how powerful she was. She turned her attention back to me. Finally, she laughed. "You have an odd sense of humor," she told me. I decided to go with discretion.

"Do you think they're still where we saw them last," I asked in earnest.

"They will still be in the tunnels. Where exactly I can't tell you."

"When should we get started," I asked.

"Now," she said. I found myself wide-awake instantly. I sat up, turned towards Chooser, and gave her a gentle shake. I looked upon the face that had captured my heart as she opened her eyes and stretched. She went from the stretch to wrapping her arms around my neck. We kissed passionately.

A half hour or so later we were making ready to move out. I went straight to the command tent and made a report to Braveer. In all the excitement of the past few weeks, I hadn't had a chance to talk about the tunnel we had fallen into. Cyclops and Hermit had almost forgotten about the tunnel and the hobgoblin. It came rushing back to them when I mentioned it.

"I had honestly forgot about it myself. We need to check it out," I suggested.

"We," Braveer asked.

"Once a company man, always a company man," I assured him. He smiled back.

The messenger hadn't returned with news of a diplomatic meeting yet, so I informed Chooser of the need for investigating the tunnel. I suggested Chooser go on without me for the time being, should the meeting be agreed upon. I would be traveling with the company's investigators to eradicate a hopefully small scouting party of nasty creatures. We would meet at the Gates of Herald, Twin cities on top of two mountains overlooking Grendale, the capital of Asmeria.

Soulbinder was still being somewhat standoffish. I couldn't figure her out. She would seemingly keep constant tab on my every thought, now a massive vagueness.

Braveer assigned thirty men to investigate. We reached the ruins where we had encountered the scouting party. Shameer, currently in charge, had a party of six men uncover the entrance we had accidently made. We filed down in groups of three. Once in the tunnel, I drew Soulbinder from her scabbard. I received a couple of odd looks. By now, everyone present knew that I was a powerful wizard, yet there I was, holding a sword.

"She's stronger than I am," I stated flatly. They gave each other looks of inquiry shaking their heads at one another and shrugging their shoulders.

I took the lead, heading in a direction towards Asmeria's interior. I enchanted two torches enabling them to stay lit longer than would be normal and emitting a brighter light than would be naturally emitted. We followed the tunnel for quite some time. When we began to feel fatigued, we stopped to rest. We took turns as watch, allowing everyone a chance to sleep. An hour or so before we were to leave, I awoke, my alertness at full. I scanned the area beyond our torch light, trying to see something in the darkness. The flickering torchlight seemingly made every shadow move. I clutched Soulbinder's hilt. I had a strong feeling of death in the air. It passed through me; on its way to who knows where. 'Did I just imagine that or was that my dead soul that just passed through me,' I sent to Soulbinder.

'That was you,' she said sadly.

"'Am I going to die here?" I asked her.

"'No. I didn't give you permission to die." she proclaimed.

I fumbled with my thoughts. I had witnessed my death in these tunnels, or something like it. I decided not to take a chance; I cast a light spell into the darkness. Vaporous images of a battle shimmered momentarily, then disappeared. The watch witnessed the apparition and stumbled toward me.

"What was that," he asked me dumbfounded. I shook my head and shrugged my shoulders. I had sensed something odd in the darkness, what I saw in the light, served to confuse me further. Especially since the battlefield we had just witnessed looked more like Blendell then this tunnel.

My light spell awoke the rest of the squad. They were almost instantly at the ready to fight then started asking us what happened. We looked at each other, looked back at them shaking our heads. Drelldore, the butt of many of Cyclops' jokes, asked me, "Throwing around light spells for fun Slasher, I mean Phoenix?" He had an irritating sarcastic tone to his voice.

"Drelldore, that threat that Cyclops likes to use about turning you into a toad, I really can," I informed him. Cyclops looked at him, nodding in agreement. The look on Cyclops' face convinced Drelldore that he was approaching a boundary he shouldn't cross. Though he still mumbled something under his breath, he let the matter drop.

"Let's move out," Shameer barked.

After numerous hours of traversing the tunnel we were in, we came upon a fork. It was suggested that we split into two groups to speed up the search, which

Shameer rejected. I could understand how tactically his was a sounder approach to the situation. We still had no idea how large a group we might encounter. We could see tracks leading into both tunnels. I suggested the one that seemed to head southward more towards Grendale, Asmeria's capital city. It seemed good enough for everyone, so that's the direction we started in.

We had only gone about twenty feet, when a heat wave rushed past us. Hermit and I looked at each other, remembering our last adventure in the tunnel. I pushed my way through the squad, taking the lead once again. Whatever created that heat had something to do with our mission. My mind began to imagine the various creatures that used fire as a weapon. We proceeded steadily yet cautiously down the tunnel. I began to hear noises coming from up ahead. I signaled to the squad to halt. I quickly muttered a spell that doused our lights. I spoke the words of another spell, and suddenly I was able to see in the darkness as if it were daylight. Not having that spell in my repertoire before, I knew it had to come from Soulbinder.

I continued into the tunnel, staying close to the walls in an attempt to stay hidden. As I rounded a curve, I could see about twenty hobgoblins. They were sitting around a large round rock inside a large chamber. On the rock were the remains of a human. They were taking turns ripping pieces of flesh from the corpse and eating them. It was too far devoured for me to determine whether it had been a man or a woman. It really didn't matter. Whoever it was, they were dead.

I backed out the way I had come from. Once I reached the squad, I informed them as to the situation ahead.

"'Can we enchant the entire squad to see in the dark,'" I asked Soulbinder.

"Yes, but I wouldn't recommend it."

"Why not?" I asked.

"If any source of light appears, you will be blinded." Somehow, I knew how to reverse the spell that had enabled me to see in the darkness.

I cast a spell of silence over our party that would prevent the hobgoblins from hearing us as we approached. We linked hands and headed toward the hobgoblins. I began to see a faint glow, as we got closer. I hadn't noticed it on my first approach due to the spell I was under. I formulated the words to a light spell. As we rounded the final curve between the enemy, and us I unleashed it into their mix.

The spell temporarily blinded the hobgoblins. We tore into them. Before they could gather their senses, it was over. All but their leader lay dead on the floor. The leader was wounded, but still very much alive. A rumbling from further in the tunnel caught my attention.

With Soulbinder in hand, I proceeded toward the source of the rumbling.

It turned out to be further into the tunnel than I had imagined it would be. I found myself staring at the ass of a giant fireworm. Once I realized what I was looking at, I quickly backed away. A noise coming from inside the creature made me start running. I was about twenty yards back up the tunnel when I could start to feel the heat. I fell to the ground, covering my head with my arms while muttering a protection spell. An intense heat wave rushed over me, singeing my hair. Fortunately, it was a short burst. Fireworms are so called because they eat the earth and give off a highly volatile explosive gas. Except for this gas, they're harmless, though I had never heard of one larger than a man's forearm. I got up and continued quickly back to the squad.

"Big fireworm," I explained as I got back. Shameer was busy interrogating our captive. I glanced over to the rock, and seeing the mangled remains, felt disgust rising up in me. From this vantage point, I could see the partial face of a young girl, probably no more than fifteen. I walked over, muttered a prayer, then the words to a fire spell. Almost instantly the remains were turned to ashes.

"'Let me interrogate the prisoner," Soulbinder sent. I walked over to the prisoner and grabbed him by the neck. I stared deeply into his eyes. Soulbinder used her immense powers to enter his mind. Once she had all she wanted, she left him a lifeless corpse. I staggered backward, allowing him to fall to the floor. Being the conduit through which she operated in this realm; I was drained of quite a bit of energy. Shameer bent over and checked for life.

"Way to go. He's dead. Now we'll never find out what he knew," he berated me.

'The main party is down the other path,' Soulbinder sent. I stared at Shameer defiantly.

"The main party is down the other tunnel," I remarked stoically.

"How do you know that," he asked.

"You really don't want to know," I replied.

We made our way back to the other branch of the tunnel. Shameer sent two scouts in front of our lights. We trekked for several hours. I suggested to Shameer that we take a rest break. No sense in wearing ourselves out before we have to battle.

As I relaxed against the tunnel wall, I tried to remember how far a fireworm traveled in a day. As I thought about it, I realized I had never studied fireworms more than in passing. I'm quite certain that my old master knew. I was more interested in above ground magics. "How about you?" I asked Soulbinder.

"Sorry, no fireworms where I'm from."

"Being a worm, I can't imagine that it travels amazingly fast," I sent.

"Where magic's involved anything's possible," she sent back.

Time seemed to pass quickly. I had barely fallen asleep when it was time to move out. I checked with Soulbinder to see if they were keeping a fairly accurate watch. She told me she wasn't a timekeeper, in no uncertain terms, seeming perturbed by something.

We continued following the tunnel for a couple of more days. On the third day, we began to feel a faint trembling. My mind went instantly back to that day that we discovered these tunnels in the first place. Just for kicks, I pulled Soulbinder from the scabbard. The blade was glowing faintly. It had a sort of greenish tint to it. 'What's with the glow," I asked her.

"It indicates another is in the area."

"Another as in an enemy of yours?"

"Yes, though I can't discern whom," she explained.

"You mean to tell me you know all of the others," I asked incredulous.

"Of course, they're my brothers and sisters," came back to me.

"And you're trying to kill each other?" I asked her incredulously.

'There will be only one winner, besides, you're going to try to kill your cousin,' she defended. I tried to explain that it was different, but couldn't overcome her logic, which was strictly female.

Our scouts stopped suddenly and signaled that something was ahead of us and getting closer. I realized that if Soulbinder could sense the other, than they could sense her. I prepped a spell. Hermit and Cyclops each prepped a spell of their own. Cyclops let loose a light spell into the darkness ahead of us, bathing the approaching band of hobgoblins in its brilliance, temporarily blinding them. Their leader was wielding a relative of Soulbinder. I unleashed a massive ice storm with gale force winds ripping towards the band of hobgoblins. When it finally subsided, the entire band was frozen in a block of ice, with only Soulbinder's sibling protruding. Soulbinder, glowing brightly with multiple colored rays encircling her length, walked me to her sibling and swung herself with all of my might at it. It shattered into a thousand pieces. The explosion that accompanied the shattering knocked everyone but me off of their feet and shattered the ice and hobgoblins with it. I had Soulbinder anchoring me and was unaffected.

When I found myself once again in control of my senses. I spun around and asked if everyone was all right. They shook themselves off and timidly nodded that they were okay. I suggested to Shameer that we set the guard and rest. He willingly agreed. I could tell he was intimidated by my presence now more than before. After the display that Soulbinder put on through me, I couldn't blame him. I was intimidated by the display she put on, only I couldn't show it. Everyone would think I was powerful and crazy; no one would talk to me and then I would go crazy. Besides, it's more fun watching people that once tried to intimidate you realize how lucky they were.

I checked in with Soulbinder to find out if she could tell what lies ahead. I was embarrassed to find her crying on her pillows.

"I'm sorry, I'll come back later," I told her.

"No. Stay," she sobbed. I stood there, not really knowing what to do. Like any man, a woman crying strikes a nerve in me. But this wasn't just any woman. This woman had powers that scared the hell out of me. Still, the sound of her gentle sobs tugged at me strongly. I slowly stepped ever closer to her. Once at her side, I knelt down and asked if there was anything, I could do for her. She turned and hugged me laying her head on my shoulder and continued to sob uncontrollably. After a long while, when the sobbing stopped, she began to tell me the story.

"She was my younger sister. We had been inseparable. I hoped that one of the others would find her first, and they didn't! She had been bound and made to serve a...non-magical...a hobgoblin!!! I had to. I couldn't bear to see her suffer anymore," she rambled on. Most of what she said was in fractured sentences. It really didn't matter what I heard; it was the shoulder that she really needed. This proved to me she was a real being with feelings. Though I hadn't seen mine in decades, I had sisters that I cared a great deal for, I couldn't conceive of being forced to kill them.

I don't know how long I held her. I suddenly found myself back as myself in a tunnel. I was surprised to find that I was fully rejuvenated. The last watch was beginning to wake everyone up. After we ate, we would resume heading further into the tunnel. The trembling had continued nonstop since we first felt it. Whatever was causing it lay further ahead, and I fully intended us to find the cause. About a half day marching the trembling began to grow stronger. We still couldn't hear anything, but we could definitely feel it. We rested and ate again. The trembling subsided a little while we relaxed. Shameer ordered us to advance.

The tremble was stronger than ever. Our scouts were having a hard time advancing. The tremble kept knocking them off their feet until it became apparent that the only one capable of advancing was, me. I let them know that I would continue on my own to see what there was to see. Soulbinder somehow was managing to keep my feet steady as I advanced into the darkness of the tunnel. I recast the spell enabling me to see in the darkness once I was well enough away from the light of the torches.

As I rounded a curve, I spied the oddest-looking creature that could ever be imagined. The back looked like a rhinoceros, the mid-section was multilegged, and the head resembled a worm. Like the fireworm we had encountered in the other shaft, this thing was eating earth at an incredible rate. It was stomping its many legs with each bite. It was larger than the fireworm, being equal to two or three of the creatures. I contemplated what to do with this oddity. I didn't get the sense that it was an unnatural creation. I decided to use my powers to reduce its size to a point it would no longer cause tremors. I made my way back to the group. Although I had never seen such a strange creature before, I couldn't see harming it simply because it was being followed by hobgoblins.

As I reached the group, I described what I had seen to the party. None of the others had ever heard of such a creature either. Shameer questioned my decision not to destroy the creature. I really didn't care. In my opinion, the creature wasn't a threat to either us, or the nation. I wasn't going to kill something just because I didn't understand it. Too many creatures are extinct because they were misunderstood by so called intelligent creatures. With proper conservation some delicious animals would still be around for us to enjoy.

It took us just as long to get back out of the tunnels as it had for us to progress into them. Fortunately for us it was nighttime when we reached the surface. We were spared being blinded by the sunlight. This way our eyes would adjust to the morning light without causing us pain.

After we were all up, awake and had eaten, I cast a spell collapsing the sides of the tunnel leading towards Asmeria, then we resealed the hole leading to the tunnels. I was glad to see that we hadn't lost anyone on this trip. I would be even more delighted to catch up to Chooser's party. Now that I wasn't thinking about saving my skin and wondering what danger lay ahead in the darkness, my mind kept envisioning her and the nights we shared, and the nights we would share.

As we resumed our journey toward the capitol, a light rain began to fall. Like everyone else, I reached into my saddlebags to retrieve my raingear. Hermit and Cyclops began their usual banter about rain. This time Hermit was for it, Cyclops against. They were like young brothers in this respect. They would argue for hours on end, neither conceding a thing to the other. Anyone listening would mistakenly think they were worst enemies instead of the closest of friends. The rain continued for the next several days. The drought that had plagued the region had finally ended. Hopefully, it would remain a light rainfall and not a deluge that could cause a flood.

We trudged along at a brisk yet leisurely pace. I seemed to be the only one eager to rejoin Chooser. Admittedly I was the only one with a reason to want to see her. To the rest she was still the enemy. I couldn't really blame them. They didn't know her as I had come to know her, intellectually speaking of course, I'd never allow them the opportunity to know her any other way. Hermit and Cyclops wouldn't give her a chance because they were used to avoiding wizards of Chooser's and my caliber. Over a twenty-five-year period they had come to know me without my powers. Now that my powers had been revealed, they were hesitant to trust me. We still managed a few words of witty banter here and there, but nothing like it used to be. I thought of sitting them down and discussing it with them, but I knew it wouldn't do any good. I could tell them I was still the same old me a hundred times, and maybe they might relax a little, but then a situation would come up where I would have to use my powers and the distrust would return.

After five days of traveling in the rain we came upon a small village with a large inn. We took a vote, and it was decided we would take a break from the rain. This was a very modern inn the proprietor assured us. As it turned out, there was a bath in every room. Turns out the spells I had created in my youth for my families benefit, had become well known throughout the region. I inquired as to whether Chooser and her party had passed through yet, knowing they would have had to have passed by this way on their way to Grendale, Asmeria's capital. I was told a party fitting that description had passed through just before the rain began to fall.

Like everyone else, I went straight for the tub the moment I got in the room. The water was warm and thoroughly relaxing. The stress of the trip washed away with each passing minute of soaking up the warmth. I stayed in the tub long enough for my skin to wrinkle then figured I had enough.

I slept more peaceful than I had in what seemed like forever. I awoke with a start, about an hour before dawn. I couldn't tell what, but the feeling of something amiss was strong and wouldn't be ignored. "I sense your anxiety, but I can't discern a cause," Soulbinder sent. That should have relaxed me, but it didn't. Something was wrong, I still had no idea what, but something definitely was.

I got dressed and made my way downstairs. I kept a hand on Soulbinder's hilt. I scanned the entire great room in a matter of seconds. Nothing seemed amiss, so I continued right on out of the inn and into the street. The rain had finally subsided. I scanned the entire area, though nothing seemed to be wrong here either. I was just about ready to relax when the earth below my feet began to shake violently. Without hesitation and almost subconsciously, I muttered the words to my transformation spell. I quickly transformed into a phoenix and flew upward away from the rapidly forming hole. A giant fireworm rushed out of the hole. I was already flying higher than the creature could leap. The words to an ice spell formed in my mind. I unleashed a spell of the magnitude of the one I had used back in the tunnel, though this time I did it on my own without Soulbinder's help. I then flew back towards the door of the inn. I resumed my human form and I looked over at the creature I had just slain.

"Someone was controlling that thing,' I sent to Soulbinder. 'Someone very powerful and very dark."

"I got the same impression," she replied.

"That's not an impression, I can see the darkness surrounding the corpse," I replied. Even as I thought it, the power dissipated without leaving a trail.

The rest of the company came rushing out of the inn to see what had happened. Seeing the frozen fireworm caused them to pause in contemplation. Shameer, the first on the scene, stared at me inquisitively.

"Chooser has a week's head start on us. I suggest we leave," I stated.

"That thing attacked you," Cyclops said astounded.

"Yes, and I froze it. What's your point," I asked in reply?

"It tracked you down and tried to eat you," he said incredulous.

"You think so? How did it track me? I think it just happened to be in the area and decided to pop up. I merely reacted instinctively brought on by fear and finely honed reflexes," I lied. He stared at me a moment longer, then Shameer ordered everyone to pack up and move out. I left the inn- keeper a little extra to help cover the expenses the fireworm's removal would cost, though I couldn't explain why I felt the need to do so.

We set a fairly quick pace. If Chooser stayed with the plan, they would be waiting for us at the Gates of Heralding. If they were keeping the normal pace, it would take them another day and a half before they would get there. At the pace we were setting, it would take us four days to reach the gates. For me, that was four days too many. As noon approached, it occurred to me that my presence wasn't needed with the group and I was Phoenix, which is a bird after all. I bid farewell to my brothers in arms and transformed into the flaming bird that was my namesake.

It had been many years since I had flown for any distance. Hovering was simple enough. Actual flight took some thought and work. I flew upwards to an extreme elevation and then I flung myself forward, gliding downward and towards the Gates of Heralding. As I descended, I occasionally flapped helping to build up to an incredible speed. I leveled off just above the tree- tops. I reveled in the thrill of it all. I had forgotten what it was like. I never really knew how much I had enjoyed this type of experience. I had had so many and believed there would be many more, not foreseeing the events that changed my way of thinking.

The landscape zipped by rapidly. On two occasions I swooped down on a game animal, frightening them near to death, before climbing to an extreme height. As the sun began to set, the Gates of Heralding loomed below. I had taken a route I hoped was out of Chooser's ability to detect. I wanted to surprise her by getting here first.

The Gates of Heralding were two cities on twin peaks. A wizard of long since past had joined the two by way of a bridge suspended by magic. The peaks overlook the Asmerian Planes, sight of the seat of power of Asmeria, and Velouth's home, the city of Grendale. I landed near the northern city. The best lodgings were to be found there, though the road to Grendale was in the southern city. The nightlife was in the southern city. The bridge between the two had a toll of 1 silver coin.

I hadn't been in the northern city before, though the company had spent many nights in the southern. I had some fond memories of that place, none of which I'd care to share with Chooser. I made some inquiries into which establishment was the best for lodging. I was assured by nearly every merchant, that the Green Dragon Inn was the best the city had to offer. I got the directions on how to find the Green Dragon Inn and made a beeline toward it. I found it fairly easily, and upon arrival received a surprise myself. Chooser and her entourage were making their way into the inn. They had obviously changed their pace, and I had a feeling Braveer had something to do with the decision to pick up the pace.

"What are you doing here, and where are the others," Braveer asked as I approached.

"I'm here to see this beautiful young lady of course. The others are about three days away," I replied, taking Chooser into my arms, and kissing her.

"How'd you get here so quickly then," Chooser asked putting her arms around my neck.

"I am Phoenix," I replied kissing her again. I could see from the puzzled look on her face that she didn't understand. "Bird of fire," I suggested. She still looked confused. Suddenly I realized that she was linked with Soulbinder, and I began to feel stupid. Abruptly Chooser started giggling. I imagined that Soulbinder had informed her of my embarrassment. I was correct. It dawned on me that I was outnumbered and out powered. It just didn't seem fair.

The dining hall was huge and fairly packed. We were all famished from our journey, and the food smelled inviting, so we joined the rest of the patrons in line for the buffet. It turns out we had become somewhat recognizable and everyone seemed more than willing to allow us to go ahead of them. Braveer eagerly filled a large plate. I helped myself to a rather healthy portion as well. Chooser surprised me by imitating us. Our escorts cleared us an area so Chooser, Braveer and me could sit away from everyone else.

"That's a pretty large amount of food for such a petite woman," I quipped.

"Yes, it is," she agreed. "It helps that I'm eating for two," she added. I sat there stunned. I had considered the thought of having children, but only in passing. Few in my trade actually do so. Most are so wrapped up in gaining knowledge and power they never start a relationship. Now, apparently, I was going to be a father. I sat silently for several minutes that Chooser swears were an eternity.

"Are you sure," I finally asked after a long awkward silence.

She punched my arm and retorted, "Am I sure?"

"Once this diplomatic mission is over, we'll hold up in Blendell. You'll be needing plenty of rest," I finally said matter-of-factly.

"I never would have guessed that you'd be the motherly hen type," Braveer quipped. I felt myself blush a little.

"I've never been a father before," I defended myself.

"I've never been a mother before," Chooser chimed in.

"True, but I can tell you're going to make a great mom," I assured her. She kissed me in appreciation.

We ate our fill then headed to our rooms. Once again, our escorts took up a defensive position. Alone in our room, Chooser and I expressed our love passionately. I rejoiced in her touch and the feel of our skin brushing against each other. I was in seventh heaven, until I fell asleep.

The grim realities tend to creep into your mind via your subconscious. I was standing on a mountain overlooking a fertile valley next to a small boy, my son. Without warning, a great fire swept over the valley leaving only ash in its wake. I looked down to see if my son was injured. Instead I found a young Destroyer. The evil in his heart was apparent even at such a young age. I stepped backward in revulsion and fell off a cliff. I was falling uncontrollably, unable to utter a sound. I looked down to see the rapidly approaching ground and just before I hit the ground I woke up.

I sat up and scanned the room quickly. Chooser was still sleeping peacefully beside me. Looking down on her angelic face filled me with a sense of calm. The longer I looked at her, the less I remembered from the dream. In no time at all, the nightmare was a distant memory. The one fact from the dream that had remained was that Destroyer was evil from a very young age.

As we prepared to depart the inn to begin the final leg of our journey, a large group of royal guardsmen began to file into the great hall where we had eaten the night before. Braveer came to our room and informed us of the situation. I doubted that anyone knew who I was. I hadn't done anything noteworthy in more than two decades. I did however still wear company markings. I suggested to Braveer and Chooser that they stay put and let me do some negotiating on my own for a couple of minutes.

I entered the great hall, scanned for, and quickly found the commanding officer. I walked straight toward him. Two guards, with drawn swords, used their swords to bar me from getting too close. I couldn't help grinning at the notion that they could stop me, but I played nice anyway.

"Commander Braveer wishes to extend his greetings," I stated loudly enough for the commander to hear while staring down the larger of the two. He was quite assured of himself, for a non-initiate.

"Let him enter," the commander ordered. And like two trained dogs, they snapped back to their more relaxed postures, and let me pass. I was more than slightly startled when I suddenly noticed that the commander was reading a spell book.

"Do you have any magical knowledge..." he started to ask as he swung around to look me in the eye. His eyes transfixed on my medallion and he stood their mouth gaping.

"I think I might know a thing or two," I replied. His eyes rose to look into mine. I could see the flame of power burning within them. He could undoubtedly see the raging fire that burned in mine revealing me to be a major power.

"Braveer sent you," he asked his voice wavering. I shook my head.

"I simply said he sends his greetings. I never said he sent me," I replied. "He and I have been friends for more years than either one of us want to admit," I explained further.

"You're with Chooser then," he half inquired. "She's under my protection," I confirmed.

"Protection," he asked amazedly. I let a ball of electrical magic gather in my hand. The spell caster in him realized the power and skill it required to perform such a simple seeming task. He shrank backward in fear and respect.

"You and your men may inform Velouth that we should be arriving for an audience soon," I instructed him. He started to balk. The better part of valor quickly won out. He barked at the troops under him to move out. They hesitated at first then realized that they had just been given an order and began following it immediately.

I continued to play with the ball of power for a few minutes. I turned and started walking back towards the rooms. I looked over toward the swordsman that I had had the staring contest with. The understanding that was taking place in his mind showed on his face. As I stepped toward the hall, he backed away, almost stumbling. I controlled myself until I was beyond his vision before allowing myself to grin. Several company men had been in the great hall eating breakfast when the royals had arrived. They were smirking broadly after witnessing my little display.

As I reached the hallway to the rooms, I let the ball of power dissipate. As I entered the room, Chooser and Braveer stared at me inquisitively. Having learned over the years to never volunteer information that wasn't requested, I remained silent. It was Chooser who finally decided to ask the question that was on their minds.

"How'd it go," she asked.

"Fine. The captain of the guard will inform Velouth that we should be expected to request an audience soon," I replied. I could see that my answer wasn't quite what they were expecting. Perhaps they were expecting greater detail. If so, they were in for disappointment. I was no longer Slasher information officer; I was Phoenix ninth circle initiate and escort protector of Chooser and father of the child she now carried in her womb.

We took the time to eat in the dining hall again. It was getting close to mid-morning when we finally set out from the Gates of Heralding. We paused momentarily on the bridge between the cities to gaze down upon the beautiful planes of Asmeria. Even Braveer was struck by the beauty of the scenery, I was somewhat surprised by the old warrior's appreciation of the view. He caught the puzzled look I was giving him and became somewhat indignant.

"I can appreciate beauty like anyone else," he growled. Chooser giggled. She too had been taken aback by Braveer's reaction. He just didn't appear to be the type that could be struck by nature's beauty.

We began the trek down the mountain towards our meeting with Velouth. I was hopeful that Chooser could convince him of the urgency of our needing to take the actions we were recommending. Having met him once some fifteen years or so ago, I was doubtful that he could be swayed. He came off as extremely weak. He was cocky when surrounded by his personal guards, but that façade tended to disappear when in the presence of true power. Braveer had intimidated him on that occasion.

We reached the mountains base shortly after sunset. It was still a good distance to Velouth's castle from that point. The captain of the guard had apparently let it slip that Chooser and I were traveling together. Everyone got out of our way and bowed in respect as we passed. Chooser, in all her splendor, nodded back in acknowledgement of the greeting. An extremely comfortable inn lay halfway from the mountain base to the castle. We rested there for the final night before our meeting.

The following morning, children clamored around as we passed though the cities gates. I had never wanted or had the opportunity to show off for an audience before, but I took advantage of the current situation. I began simple enough by making an apple that one youth had turn into a pigeon. The others stood around smiling as I stepped up the power and moved onto some pretty powerful magic. The children were dazzled and amazed at the images I made appear and disappear. My display wasn't only witnessed by the children and those in the street, Velouth and several of his advisers watched from a window on an upper floor of the castle that overlooked the portcullis. As a finale I transformed myself into a phoenix. The children weren't the only ones awed by the transformation. Velouth's wizards staggered backward from the window as I rose up to look them in the eyes. Velouth seemed to be able to steel himself better than his magical advisers. He stared back at me intently. After I resumed my human form, we continued on to the castle's main entrance. Braveer approached the nearer of the guards at the double doors that made up the main entrance.

"We'll be needing lodging for visiting diplomats," he informed him. The guard acknowledged Braveer and disappeared behind the doors. He returned soon accompanied by some castle functionary. The functionary stared first at Chooser, as if sizing up the danger she presented, then at me. When his eyes caught sight of my medallion, he noticeably paled. I couldn't help thinking that my reputation must have greatly suffered during my hiatus. Everyone seemed to know and fear me. It really was only a small herd of ogres, no more than twenty.

We were led deep within the castle to a large guest quarter. The area was encased in glyphs and wards in the way of runes inscribed in the walls and ceilings covered by murals. Apparently, the inscriber failed to inform the royals that powerful initiates of the upper circles can see the power emanating from the magical writings. One rune in particular caught my attention. It was designed to prevent anyone from using transformational magic while in the room. Very few wizards were capable of transformational magic. It required one to abandon one's own being, with little regard for regaining it. I have utmost confidence in my image of self. I found out early on that although being a phoenix was enjoyable, being a human was so much better.

"You should try being a dragon sometime," Soulbinder sent me.

'You were a dragon,' I asked intrigued.

"In many ways, I still am," she replied. That was an odd thought to conceive, a woman encased in a sword, saying she's a dragon.

Getting back to the runes, I began to recognize the signature of the rune writer. Magical drawings radiate an energy pattern that can be recognized by someone familiar with their works. In this case, I recognized the signature of my master, Cyclone. I smiled wryly as I glimpsed his personal disarming key. Enabling these runes, in the proper order, rendered the remaining runes harmless for a cycle of the sun. They were intricately woven into the fabric of the main spells such that their removal would render the rest useless. The typical house wizard wasn't of any real significant power for fear of usurpers of the throne. Outside wizards were often hired to place the various spells in the castles of rulers. Only the most powerful wizards could accomplish these tasks, and their labors carried hefty prices. No two rulers will knowingly hire the same wizard that a rival had, though most of the time there really was no other choice.

We had just settled in when a new functionary knocked on the door. He was flanked by two of Velouth's personal guards. He had an invitation to dine in the royal banquet hall with various other visiting dignitaries. I was curious to find out who else would be dining with us. Chooser accepted the invitation and thanked the functionary. I had half expected her to ask with whom we would be dining.

Dinner was still several hours away, giving Chooser and me a chance to cleanup. Caressing her soft skin gave me a feeling of peacefulness I had never imagined. Even surrounded by all these runes of power, she set my soul at ease. After drying off, we held each other close. She rested her head upon my shoulder, one arm around my neck. Finally, Chooser broke from the embrace and dressed in her most elegant dress. It managed to show cleavage while still looking regal and domineering.

We followed a functionary to the main banquet hall. Numerous guests were already milling around. A fair portion of these would be the local bureaucrats; those charged with seeing to the actual running of the daily operations of governing. There were several different delegations from little known kingdoms, city states eager to make trade agreements with prosperous countries. I only recognized the representative from Dreclornia, a fairly large city in the southern region just beyond Asmeria's borders. They produce a large quantity of iron ore and honey. The residents were friendly enough but could put up one hell of a fight when pushed, something that bordering Hellfire's domain forced them to do quite often.

Velouth entered the hall accompanied by a large entourage of bodyguards and sycophants. There were two in the midst who caught my attention. One was a general, General Mythryl. He was renowned for his victory over the Brextrill rebels. All favorable accounts have him slaughtering a force of twenty thousand with a mere fifteen hundred men. The problem I have is with the omission of the fact that nineteen thousand of the rebels were woman, children, and the elderly. He's Destroyer's most trusted military advisor. The fact that he was in Velouth's entourage, filled me with a sense of intrigue and foreboding.

The second person who caught my attention was a young wizard of quite some power. I had been out of the loop for too long as far as wizards were concerned and didn't recognize him. I immediately recognized the weapon he wore on his hip. It was one of Soulbinder's siblings. I grabbed her hilt. I could sense her presence and her power but couldn't get through to communicate. Chooser squeezed my hand and nodded in his direction as though to clue me to his presence. I nodded my head slightly to signal that I had already seen him.

There was a large commotion to my left. A waiter had slipped and dropped a large tray of food. He quickly scampered to clean up his mistake and vacate the hall. The guests resumed making small talk. Velouth reached the main table. Chooser and I were ushered to that table. I placed myself between Chooser and the two guests that I had noted earlier.

Once all guests were seated, servants began dishing out plates of food. Velouth was, of course, the first person served from the food cart. A food taster quickly stepped forward and sampled the fare. When he showed no ill signs, Velouth began to enjoy the meal. I ingested a small tablet and sipped some wine just as the servants began to fix my plate. It had a magical quality that rendered poison harmless. I offered one to Chooser. She accepted. We became the only two to not use taste testers.

Dinner was delicious. Everyone in the hall seemed to be on their best behavior. Everyone became involved in conversation except me. I was content to merely observe the other guests. Occasionally I'd inject a statement when it became apparent that the speaker was referring to me. Soulbinder remained silent the entire night. I noticed that every time I looked in the direction of the gentleman wielding the other blade, he would look away. I found such behavior annoying. I managed to ignore his obvious insolence. Before I knew it, it was time to retire. Chooser and I were the first to leave.

Back in our room, I immediately went over to the command runes and inactivated the spells that limited my power in this room. Chooser was slightly astonished that I could so readily disarm the protections that Velouth's family would have paid a hefty price to have installed.

"Did you inscribe this room," she asked, her voice sounding incredulous.

"No, but my master, Cyclone, did. I recognized his signature the moment we stepped into the room," I informed her, as I made my way to the door. It took only a couple of seconds to find and activate the runes of repulsion. These would be the first runes inscribed in the room to prevent anyone from entering and distracting Cyclone while he worked. Some wizards remove these runes once the job was complete. Cyclone simply added an off rune to the mix, thus eliminating the need to remove them.

With the runes activated in the manner that I wished, I felt more at ease going to sleep. With Chooser snuggling up closely, I managed to drift off to sleep rather quickly. Her presence somehow filled me with a sense of peace.

I had half expected Soulbinder to visit me in my sleep and catch me up on what was taking place between her and her sibling. In the morning, when that turned out not to be the case, I decided to initiate the conversation. 'Soulbinder, who was in that other sword,' I sent her. There was no answer. 'Soulbinder,' I sent again. Again, there was no reply. Not knowing what else to do, I began to enter the trance state that would allow me to project my consciousness into the blade. As I propelled my mind toward her residence, I hit a wall of power. I found myself immediately out of the trance, with a bit of a headache. It seemed that she wasn't ready to talk to me. Knowing how powerful she was, I chose the better part of valor and set about doing my morning hygiene regiment.

After we finished cleaning up, I reversed the runes. Once again, the revulsion was dormant, and the dampeners were active. Chooser was decked out in her most formal attire. Despite her beauty, she had an aura of authority that was undeniable. She had had some suits made for me to wear that I might be as presentable as she was. I was surprised at how comfortable they were.

"One can't appear to be in command if one is fidgeting in one's clothing," she informed me. I quickly grabbed her by the waist and pulled her close to me.

"One can't huh," I said seductively. She giggled and kissed me. It was while we were embracing that a castle functionary knocked on the door. I let her go and answered it.

"Breakfast will be served for the next two hours. After that Velouth will attend to in house business. After that, he will see you and the other delegates on all international affairs," he informed us. I thanked and dismissed him. Turning, I slowly began to walk back to Chooser.

"It appears we have some time to kill," I said suggestively looking toward the bed. She smiled and put her arms around my neck.

"What ever shall we do to pass the time," she asked coyly. I leaned down to kiss her. I fell to my knees. The pain shooting throughout my body was excruciating. I pressed the palms of my hands against my temples in a vain attempt to dull the pain.

Chooser ran over and followed the procedure I had used to inactivate the runes that dampened our powers. She then began to chant the words to a shield spell. It took several minutes for the pain to finally subside.

"Soulbinder, what the hell was that," I asked out loud. Still she didn't answer. I looked at Chooser determinedly. "She's not talking to me. She hasn't since last night after we saw her sibling in the banquet hall," I told Chooser. "I'm going to divine her again to see if I can break through the wall, she's got around her. Do me a favor, keep me safe while I do."

"You had to ask," she asked somewhat slighted.

"Of course not. Just thinking out loud," I replied in way of apology.

Unlike the first divining I didn't need to unweave every spell cast upon the sword. I had successfully navigated through the patterns and left a trail I could easily follow. Everything was going perfectly until I woke in my own body. Soulbinder, or someone of equal or greater strength had prevented me from getting to her.

"She's not receiving visitors," I told Chooser.

Without warning, the room began to fill with a brilliant light. The sheer intensity was overwhelming. I felt as though the light was flowing through me exposing every shadow within my soul. As suddenly as it started, it ended. It took several moments for us to compose ourselves enough to talk.

"I feel as though I have been peered into and thoroughly examined," I remarked.

"Any idea what that was?" Chooser asked.

"The gamekeepers," Soulbinder replied. I couldn't tell if I was more surprised to hear her remark with my ears or see her standing behind Chooser.

"How did you get out here?" I asked.

"There has been a breach of the rules of the game. The gamekeepers have suspended the game while they decide what actions to take," she informed us.

"What was the infraction?" Chooser asked.

"Even if I knew, I couldn't tell you. That would constitute another breach, which would result in my death. I'm not ready to die, ever," Soulbinder replied firmly and convincingly.

I stared at her in awe and amazement. With Chooser standing beside her, I began to realize that although she was stunningly beautiful, I really had no feelings of sexuality for her. She did her mind reading thing and gave a vocal explanation. It turns out she radiates a strong spell to prevent men from becoming walking boners.

"Chooser of course wanted men walking around perpetually horny, or she too, would learn to control her pheromone output," she went on to explain. Chooser's mouth gaped open after hearing this.

"Perhaps she was unaware of her effect on men, or didn't realize that the cause could be controlled," I suggested in her defense.

Soulbinder shrugged, "never-the-less, that is why you don't find me as sexually attractive as you do Chooser."

"Thanks, I never could have solved that all-consuming thought had you not explained it to the universe," I shot back. She looked at me amused.

Soulbinder wandered about the room examining every little detail. I watched her studying the myriad of inanimate objects astounded that she could be so wrapped up in ordinary objects of everyday use. I felt a twinge of hunger and realized that we hadn't eaten yet. I asked Chooser and Soulbinder if they would care to join me for some food. Soulbinder laughed.

"You realize that you can't leave this room," she stated. I looked at her confused. "The gamekeepers have suspended the game. No one can move until they decide to restart the game. I wasn't involved in the breach, they rewarded me by allowing me this time with you," she explained.

"Well, in that case, why don't you tell us about yourself, I mean the you before you became a game piece," I suggested.

She stood there, staring back at me, as if assessing whether or not I was worthy enough to hear her life's story.

"I'm not much of a storyteller," she replied. I figured that would be the end to that endeavor. "I can however show you my youth if you so desire," she added. Without waiting for us to answer, she made the slightest gesture and all at once the room began to coalesce, then vanish to be replaced by another.

"No one can see or hear us," Soulbinder explained. "These images are merely my memories taking physical form. This is the school where I was educated." She pointed to a man standing in the front of the room. "That's my teacher. He also happened to be my father," she added. Her teacher/father began writing an equation on the wall, which the children in the room began to copy onto parchment immediately. It took me a few minutes to recognize the equation as being the formula for creating lightning bolts. The children appeared to be around five or six years old, way too young for any children of our realm to comprehend such complex equations. Yet these children seemed to have no problem grasping the concept. They even pointed out the mistake the man had made as quickly as he made it. He smiled and praised them for their keen observation.

He followed that equation with another. He then added three more. He then turned and waited on the children to finish copying before finally asking what the formulas had in common. They appeared to be totally unrelated. Each was for a different type of spell. A young girl in the corner at the back raised her hand immediately. The man ignored her, waiting for someone else to raise their hand. A boy in the middle of the class raised his and the teacher immediately acknowledged him. "Yes Crathort, what do you think it is?"

The girl in the back was visibly upset at having been ignored. It was obvious that she had an idea as to what the common thread was.

"Electricity," Crathort answered.

"No, I'm afraid that's not right," the teacher corrected. "Anyone else care to guess," he asked. No one else raised their hand. The little girl that had tried so desperately to be picked earlier now sat crossed armed, angry at having been overlooked.

Having failed to get any volunteers for the right answer, the teacher turned his attention to the girl. "Soulsta, would you be so kind as to give us the answer," he asked her.

"Elementals," she grumbled.

"What about elementals," the teacher prodded.

"They're all base elementals," she snapped obviously still annoyed at having been overlooked.

"That's correct. Can anyone else tell us why these formulae are so important," he asked the remaining children.

"Had I known then what my fate was to be, I would have been less angry with him for slighting me," Soulbinder interjected with a sorrow in her voice that was undeniable. It occurred to me that Soulsta was her name, it was the sword that was named Soulbinder.

The scenery shimmered and changed. We were now outdoors. The first thing that struck me was the green sky. It was far different from the blue I was used to. The children from the class were all present, only older by a few years. Crathort and another boy were squaring off to battle. Soulsta was standing nearby with a girl that looked to be her twin, only slightly smaller. Crathort unleashed a bolt of power that made my own seem powerless. The boy on the receiving end deflected the bolt with ease. It started straight towards the smaller Soulsta. The larger Soulsta quickly shielded her sibling.

She was visibly angry over the carelessness that had almost hurt her sister. With a slight gesture she sent waves of power at the two protagonists. Their forms shimmered then changed into swine.

An adult from nearby witnessed the incident and came rushing over. She made a gesture of her own and the two reverted to their earlier forms. The woman grabbed Soulsta by the ear and led her away. We followed although we didn't have to walk, the scenery moved around us. Soulsta was taken to her father. After the woman explained the situation, Soulsta was allowed to plead her side. Her father dismissed the woman assuring her he would take the appropriate disciplinary action. Soulsta looked downtrodden hearing those words come from her father.

"But dad, they almost hurt Krella," she implored her father as the woman left the room.

"But they didn't, now did they," he asked in the way fathers have when correcting an errant child.

"No sir," she admitted.

"I'm not saying that what you did was totally uncalled for, young lady. But I want you to think about what consequences your actions might have caused. Crathort and Baxlar aren't as wise or as powerful as you are. Their acts were the acts of undisciplined boys. Being your father, I know that you were raised better than that. Now go sit in the corner and contemplate what I've told you," he ordered.

The scene shimmered again and changed to another outdoor scene. We were in a meadow full of wildflowers in a variety of colors and sizes. Soulsta, now almost a full-grown woman, was walking with a young gentleman, holding his hand. The looks on their faces made it evident that they were smitten with each other. I was taken aback when I recognized the gentleman as Crathort. They stopped and embraced in a lingering kiss.

Without warning, a powerful bolt slammed into Crathort. His head was ripped from his body. Shocked and very visibly shaken, Soulsta turned to see who had committed such an atrocity.

Just as suddenly, we were back in the room of Velouth's castle. Soulsta was nowhere in sight. 'The game has resumed,' she sent me. She was back in the sword.

Another in the long list of functionaries at Velouth's command knocked on the door. To him and almost everyone else in the world, nothing had happened. It was still early morning and breakfast beaconed. We were once again led to the banquet hall. This time the food was served from a line. There wasn't any choice for breakfast. Scrambled eggs, bread and bacon were the staple of the castle. Foreign dignitaries that so desired them were offered fresh fruit.

I scanned the room and noticed that the wizard with the sword was absent. Perhaps I would see him later. We took our plates and proceeded to take the seats reserved for dignitaries, such as ourselves. We ate slowly and held conversations with the other guests at the table. The castle residents began to file out of the banquet hall toward the hearing chambers, sometimes called the throne room.

'Soulbinder, I haven't seen your sibling this morning. By the way, which one was it,' I sent her. The excruciating pain was back. It didn't last long, subsiding almost as fast as it appeared. 'What was that,' I implored her.

"That was a warning not to ask too many questions about things that don't concern you," she snapped. I now knew what part of the infraction had to deal with, or at least an idea of what. Her sibling.

It was merely a blink of the eye before Velouth was receiving foreign dignitaries. Several ambassadors offered to let Chooser speak her peace first, but she politely bid them go first. I knew it was because she planned to take up the rest of the day to plead her case should Velouth not be receptive of our plan from the start. I noticed that Destroyer's envoy was nowhere in sight. I felt better about our chances for success but couldn't help wondering where they were.

In the center of the hearing chamber was a scale model of the region. All the major powers were represented. Chooser walked over to it when it became her turn to address Velouth. She studied the model for a few seconds then made a gesture with her hand while muttering the words to an illusion. Forms began to appear on the model. Armies began to take shape. Destroyer's troops began to amass in boats on Lake Arness, north of the Plains of Dread. Another gesture and Hellfire's minions could be seen amassing in both the Mountains of Krell and on the border to the Plains of Dread. By this time Velouth and his staff were straining to see what she was going to do next. As if reading their thoughts, she began her speech.

"It's not what I'm going to do that decides what appears next, gentlemen, but rather what you decide. You see, Destroyer and Hellfire have begun their separate quests for world domination. You can sit here and try to ignore it and pretend that it doesn't exist until one of them comes out victorious and then turns their attention and the power of both kingdoms on you. Or you can join Anthgolia in a plan we believe is in the best interest of both our kingdoms," she explained. A simple twist of her wrist sent the armies at each other until they merged into one. This one army then swept over the region that is Asmeria ashes appearing in its wake.

"It is my belief, and that of my brother, King Firestorm, that we should seek out a pact of mutual protection. The functional aspects of the pact should be hammered out in private. After all, the affairs of our nations are our concern, not the worlds," she finished.

One of his advisors leaned down and whispered in Velouth's ear. Velouth nodded, then leaned toward another that I recognized as Grindolph, an aging wizard of the seventh circle. While only of the seventh circle, he was dangerously experienced and cunning. He too whispered something and again Velouth nodded. Velouth then whispered to an aide standing nearby. He then stood up and walked out of the hearing chamber, followed closely by his entourage.

"His Majesty King Velouth is conferring with his advisors and promises to get back to you the moment his decision is made," the aide informed and dismissed us. Chooser stood there dumbfounded. She had never been dismissed so offhandedly before. I think her hormones from the pregnancy may have also added to her reaction.

"Can you believe that," she exclaimed shocked. I took her by the hand and led her out of the hearing chamber. "I've never been dismissed like that before," she remarked incredulously.

"Don't take it personally. It is a major obligation you're asking of him. Why don't you go back to the room and relax in a warm bath, I'll be there soon. I need to talk to Braveer," I suggested. She nodded and headed toward the room, muttering in astonishment at having been treated like a commoner, rather than a queen.

I found Braveer involved in a discussion with a royal officer. They were nodding and shaking hands as I approached. The royal walked away just as I arrived.

"I want an audience with Velouth, now," I stated to Braveer.

"Why tell me," he asked dismissively.

"Because you have the connections to make it possible," I replied. He stood there staring for a few seconds.

"I'll see what I can do," he said, then added, "I'm not promising anything, remember that."

"I need this, or rather we all need this," I said flatly. He walked away and I began to mingle about the banquet hall.

It took Braveer about ten minutes before he returned. General Greythorn accompanied him. He looked me up and down as if determining whether or not I posed a threat. I assessed him similarly.

"I'll get right to the point, General. I'm Phoenix. Chooser is carrying my child. I pose a threat only so far as I could level this castle with a single spell, and none of the resident wizards could prevent it. I'm telling you this, so you'll know where we stand. I think it's also fair to inform you that I happen to be related to Destroyer, although I rather wish I weren't," I informed him. He stood there silently assessing what I had just said.

"What is it you wish to convey to Velouth," he asked me.

"The importance of stopping Hellfire and Destroyer now rather than waiting until their strength is beyond us," I replied. It took a moment before he acquiesced.

"Come with me then," he commanded.

I followed him out of the banquet hall and down a corridor that led us deeper into the castle. We passed several doors on either side of the corridor before reaching what I presumed was Velouth's command chamber. There were two guards on either side of the entrance. They snapped to attention as the general approached. "Right in here," the general said, gesturing toward the door. The guards barred the entrance with their lances.

"I'm sorry sir, I have strict orders that no one is allowed to enter. This order comes from Velouth himself," one of the guards informed us.

I looked at Greythorn inquisitively. He shook his head in disbelief. "You wait here, I'll take care of this," he instructed. "Out of my way if you value your life," the general barked at the guards.

"I'm sorry sir, I can't do that," the guard replied. Greythorn was visibly upset by this turn of events. He was about to throw a tirade, but I grabbed him by the shoulder, and shook my head. The sentry was obviously following his king's orders and was not at fault. To mistreat him wouldn't be right.

"If you aren't under specific orders, can you tell us with whom Velouth is meeting," I inquired of the sentry.

"I have no orders against it. He's meeting with Grindolph, Riverseige and a visiting general named Mythryl," he informed us. Greythorn's facial expression became a scowl. Mythryl was not well liked by any real military men.

"Forgive me," I said as I made a gesture invoking a sleep spell on the guards. I reached out and opened the door as they hit the ground. "After you," I suggested to Greythorn holding open the door and standing aside.

General Mythryl was standing over a map similar to the model in the hearing chamber. He had three of

Destroyer's apprentices with him. Grindolph and Velouth looked up startled at our entrance. "What's the meaning of this outrage," Velouth demanded.

One of the apprentices began a chant. I made a quick gesture that silenced him. I kept my eyes fixed on Grindolph.

"I wouldn't suggest testing my skills at this time old man," I stated boldly keeping a grip on Soulbinder's hilt. "Mythryl, while Velouth may govern this land, it's still my home. Go back to Destroyer and tell him the people of Asmeria rejected his offer. Tell him Asmeria's premier protector, his cousin, is back at the task he regretfully neglected for too long," I said taking charge of the situation.

"Sentries escort our visitors to the exit," Greythorn barked.

Grindolph and I continued to stare at each other. I drew Soulbinder from her sheath and laid her on the map table. "I want you to look at this weapon and see the power contained within it," I told him. He continued to stare at me a moment longer assessing whether I was threatening him or not. Finally, he allowed his gaze to go to the blade. The runes swirling about the blade struck him like a sledgehammer. His face became bewildered as I sensed Soulbinder link her mind with his. It was only a momentary connection, but enough to convince him that he was greatly overpowered.

I turned my attention to Velouth. "I had a feeling that my cousin's emissary was holding sway over you," I told him. "I meant what I said about being a protector of Asmeria. I won't allow that evil bastard to in anyway influence the future of this the land where I was born."

"So, you'd rather we become a puppet of Anthgolia instead," he snapped back.

"No, I'd prefer Asmeria to stand with Anthgolia as allies. King Firestorm is no threat to Asmeria. In all probability, Chooser and I will set up our home near the border. Whether it's on the Asmerian side of the border or Anthgolia's doesn't really matter. We will act in the best interest of the people, the biggest asset a nation has," I informed him.

Velouth began twitching as an angry man sometimes does when he doesn't know what to do next. "Your majesty," Greythorn said placing his hand on his shoulder, "I think it best if you relax and listen to the entire argument that Lord Phoenix has to make."

I stood there waiting for a sign that he would be receptive of my comments. Not readily noticing one, I began anyway. "You probably aren't aware of what's at stake. Destroyer, Hellfire, Chooser nor I are really the powers behind the events unfolding around us. Like yourself, we are but pawns in the grand scheme of things," I informed him.

He looked at me trying to assess if I were being dramatic or if I really felt like a pawn. I reached down and retrieved Soulbinder returning her to her scabbard. Velouth watched my every move intently. I looked up into his eyes. I could see the concern and a hint of fear before he steeled himself back to his normal regal composure.

"The powers I'm speaking of are gambling on the outcome of the upcoming wars. We are the final determining factor. We can act as decent caring humans and defend our race and those that seek peace. Or we can sit back and watch as our world collapses around us," I continued.

I looked around the room. There were several paintings on the wall depicting the royal bloodline from Velouth back nearly three thousand years to the first of his line to rule Asmeria. I couldn't help but notice the children surrounding him in his portrait.

"Do you love your children," I asked rather bluntly. The outrage on his face at being asked such a question told me he did. "Mine isn't born yet. Already I know that I will do everything in my power to protect my child. I get the impression that you would too. That's another reason to join us. But I'll be honest with you. I don't need you to join us. Your army knows what's at stake and are willing to follow us. I think it would be better if you were to lead them," I bluffed giving Greythorn a sideways glance.

"You do not already have my army willing to follow you," Velouth said calling my bluff. "You see, I know my cousin just as well as you know yours. But it was a good try. Something I might have tried were our positions reversed. In any event, the way you dispatched Mythryl left me little choice now did it. Besides, I really couldn't stomach the thought of having goblins and orcs on our land," he finished beaming a broad smile.

I gave a glance at Greythorn, who asked, "What? You didn't think we were seriously considering Destroyer's offer, did you?"

"I must admit, your arrival was quite timely, young man," Grindolph chuckle as he took my arm in his hand. He led me away from Velouth and Greythorn, chuckling all the while. Once we were out of their earshot, he warned me not to take too much stock in any protections my evil blade may have promised. He had seen such blades before, in his youth his master used to craft such things using wraiths and minor demons to power them.

"Thank you, I'll be careful," I assured him. I couldn't break it to him that Soulbinder was more of a goddess than a demon.

"What do you mean more of," Soulbinder demanded.

'Can't I have one thought that's my own,' I implored.

"Of course, all of your thoughts are your own. Just be careful of who you're calling a demon," she replied.

I exited the chamber through the same door I had entered. I made a gesture, and the sentries were immediately alert and back on guard. I could hear them questioning one another as to what had happened as I made my way back through the corridor. Braveer was waiting in the banquet hall when I arrived.

"Mythryl and his escorts are still here. Maybe a couple of company men should shadow them until they are safely out of our hair," I suggested.

"Good idea. Why don't you and Shifter take care of that. You two are the best that are currently available," he replied with a sly grin.

"I would, but I must attend to Chooser. I did promise King Firestorm that I would look after her after all. You wouldn't want me to renege on my promise now would you," I retorted. We both chuckled. "I'm going to see how my lady is fairing. I'll see you later," I said heading off toward the room that I shared with Chooser.

As I made my way down the hall, I thought about how lucky I was. Undeniably the most eligible woman in the known world was in love with me. A part of me couldn't help feeling as though I didn't deserve such a beautiful, charming, intelligent, and graceful woman. I quickly quashed those feelings. After all, I was considered to be quite a catch myself, being a powerful wizard and all.

"You are damn lucky to have her and don't think twice about it," Soulbinder sent.

When I got to the room, Chooser was preparing to cast a spell. From the preparations, I could tell it was an astral sending, most likely the spell she once used to visit me in my dreams. She was already beginning to meditate and was starting the chant. I grabbed her by the arm and broke her concentration dissipating the magic that was starting to coalesce around her.

"Are you out of your mind," I demanded. "You can't astral project while you're pregnant!"

"For your information I've cast this spell hundreds of times and never had any problems," she snapped back.

"But you weren't pregnant, then were you? No, I can't let you risk injury to yourself or our child. I'll do the sending," I insisted. We argued for several more minutes before she finally relented. We kissed to seal the deal, and as she pulled away, she reminded me.

"I let you win this time, but don't expect things to go your way every time." I couldn't help grinning. "Go ahead, enjoy yourself for now," she said as she turned her back on me and walked over to the desk, where she sat down and proceeded to brush her hair. After a moment, she grabbed a quill, dipped it in ink and began to scribble something on a piece of paper.

I picked up the spell book and read through the procedure. I had only cast this spell twice before and that was long ago. After refamiliarizing myself with the spell, I set about with the precasting preparations. Chooser watched as I meticulously set about doing the prep work. She would make little sounds letting me know that she didn't agree with what I was doing, or when she would have done things in a different manner. I managed to ignore her and finally was ready to cast the spell.

"Is there anything in particular that you wanted to say to your brother, or should I just wing it," I asked off handedly. She got up from the desk and carried the piece of paper that she had been writing on over to me.

"Here, this is all I wish to convey to him for now," she said handing me the note. I quickly scanned the note.

Once finished, I shook my head, "this won't work. I'll just wing it." Chooser's temper flared.

"First you refuse to let me cast a spell that I've cast hundreds of times…"

"For the sake of our child," I interjected.

"…then you refuse to inform my brother of the situation at hand. What's next?" she demanded in a snit.

"I'm not refusing to inform him of the situation at hand," I replied calmly. "But this is not the situation that currently exists," I added shaking the note for emphasis.

"What do you mean," she demanded. I was about to explain how I had gotten into see Velouth when I recognized the look on her face. Seems Soulbinder beat me to the punch. I found out immediately when the contact was broken.

"How dare you summarily dismiss me and then go and meet with them behind my back," she demanded infuriated. I was about to respond when "she's pregnant" burst into my mind. My experiences around pregnant women, my six sisters to be precise, I realized that women behave erratically when they are pregnant.

I steeled myself and spoke rationally and calmly as I explained, "you have to remember, I was born in Asmeria. I will always fight for what I believe is best for her future and the future of her people."

I walked over and took her in my arms. She resisted, although not too hard. I pulled her tightly against my chest.

"The other thing to remember, darling, it really doesn't matter who took the lead, so long as the goal was achieved," I reminded her. She pulled away and looked into my eyes. "Forgiven," I asked playfully, hoping the worst had been avoided. She scowled in response, we kissed, and I set about preparing to cast a spell that I hadn't cast since I was an apprentice.

Once I had refamiliarized myself with the procedure, I began the chant that would help me shape the powers needed to project my essence onto the astral plain. I lit an incense to help get my mind into the right frame of thought to complete the transference. I soon found my mind floating over my body. I turned and raced toward Blendell, to contact Firestorm. In less than seconds, I was floating around the private chambers of the reigning king of Anthgolia. He was performing the royal duty of trimming his regal beard. I took the place of his reflection in the mirror, making contact with his mind.

"Ouch," he said as his beard got snagged in the scissors when my image replaced his in the mirror.

"Careful," I replied with a smile, then added, "if anything were to happen to you, I'd never hear the end of it." He took a step backwards.

"So how goes the mission? I trust that the journey wasn't too arduous," he inquired. "And why are you here and not her," he added.

"First, the mission is a success. Asmeria and Anthgolia shall work in their combined best interests. As to the second part, the journey was as I expected it to be with rewards I hadn't really expected," I said pausing as I collected my thoughts. "As to why am I here, simply because Chooser is unable to at this time. I'm quite certain that she will explain it to you in person upon our return," I finished. "Any news you wish to relay to her," I inquired of him. He grinned from ear to ear. He nodded his head in agreement.

"Tell her Lindeth is pregnant," he blurted, adding, "I'm gonna be a dad."

I knew I was in trouble. I now had to inform Chooser of her brother's expectancy of child. I bid farewell, lost in my thoughts of what I might say to soothe the situation. I remember my one sister being pregnant and being told by her husband of her younger sister's pregnancy. I still feel sorry for that poor man for the tirade she hurled upon him. I shudder to think of it. Though I'm not suggesting that Chooser was in any way like any of my sisters.

Chooser was brushing her hair as I returned to myself, and the land of the conscious. "Oh, you're back," she chimed cheerfully as I shook the cobwebs from my head. "How is everything? How are my brother and Lindeth?"

"Pregnant," I blurted.

"I know I'm pregnant, I told you," she replied.

"No," I said dragging out the o, "Lindeth is pregnant," I finished trying to gage what her reaction was going to be.

"Oh, that's wonderful," she cheered throwing her arms around my neck. I hadn't really prepared for this type of situation and was pleasantly surprised. I hesitantly put my arms around her then twirled around with her in my arms.

"Honey, you really shouldn't twirl a pregnant woman around like that," she explained as she ran to the necessary room. "So, what did he say when you told him that I am pregnant too," she asked upon her return.

"I didn't tell him," I replied cautiously.

"Why not," she replied her tone telling me that she was secretly pleased to hear that I hadn't.

"I figured that was something that you wanted to tell him face to face," I explained.

"I think you're being silly," she remarked as she went back over to where she had been brushing her hair.

Remembering my sister's pregnancy reminded me that I hadn't seen or heard from my family in over thirty-five years. I turned toward Chooser. "I think it would be nice if you were to meet my family," I stated.

"I thought Braveer was your family," she remarked somewhat stunned at my statement.

I shook my head as I replied, "he's from my home village, but he's not really family. His brother and I were the best friends growing up. The family I'm talking about is my parents and six sisters."

"You have six sisters," she asked incredulously.

"Yeah, they still live in the mountains between Asmeria and Anthgolia. It would be nice to see them considering that I haven't done so in well over three and a half decades," I answered.

"You mean to tell me that for thirty-five years you haven't once returned to see how your family was fairing," she asked making it sound like a bad thing.

"I never had the right opportunity," I defended, though feeling guilty at not having tried to see my parents and sisters.

"Well we are definitely going. I would kill for the chance to have you meet my parents, but I know that I can't bring them back. So, you'd better believe that I won't pass up the opportunity to meet your family," she informed me, then asked, "Are you sure they're still alive?"

"My mother is, I can still feel her life force," I replied referring to the connection all initiates feel to their birth mothers. As long as she lived there would be a connection, a physical feeling letting the child and mother know that each lived. Even if the mother were a non-initiate, as in the case of my own mother, each would know if the other had passed away. It's a sensation Chooser hadn't known since she was three and her mother was killed.

It took a couple of days for the diplomats to iron out all the petty details of this joint venture. Mythryl was reported heading out of Asmeria and back to his master. I took the opportunity to converse with a number of the generals who roamed the castle. I discovered that Asmeria had the manpower to be a nation of high regard yet lacked the training necessary to be so.

The members of our company were all skilled mercenaries. Each had mastered their skills before becoming a member. Mine was an unnatural ability with a sword, and a great capacity for making detailed observations of my surroundings effortlessly. I spoke at length with Braveer about the problem and suggested that maybe he could help the royals out by volunteering the company to be drill instructors. It wasn't exactly greeted with enthusiasm at first, but when informed that the royals would become their subservient, they warmed to the idea.

Braveer expressed jealousy when I informed him that I would be taking Chooser to the village where we had been born. I suggested that he would be welcome to join us, but he rejected the idea lamenting about the monumental task he had before him.

Chapter 8

Going Home to a Wedding

THE COMPANY would remain in the capitol preparing the royal troops to be warriors. Those that showed skill were to be trained as leaders. If all went well, the armies of Anthgolia and Asmeria would be able to gel into one gigantic army.

I bought a carriage from the vendor that makes the carriages for Velouth. He had a method of suspension that gave the carriages the smoothest ride over the roughest terrain. I wanted Chooser to be as comfortable as possible. After all, she was carrying my child, something I was still getting used to.

My parents had given up hope of having any grandsons from me from the moment I began using magic. It was believed that magic made a man sterile or impotent. I figured that it was simply because most wizards don't often seek sexual gratification because the wielding of power gives the user a feeling of euphoria that nothing else can match, not even pleasures of the flesh. Once a wizard felt that euphoria, sex never enters their minds. I had achieved great power then vowed never to wield it again. I rediscovered sex during this period and couldn't imagine giving it up. I want my sex and magic too, and thankfully Chooser is of a like mind, though she never gave up her magic.

The road to the village of my birth had seen major improvements since my departure. A valuable mineral mine had been established in my absence creating a need for a better trade route with the capital. I recognized the mountains, especially the one containing the cavern where I had found Soulbinder. The buildings on the other hand were another story. Where once there was a humble little village, there was now a booming city-state. The one building I did recognize, the old tavern, brought painful memories flooding back to the forefront of my mind.

"It wasn't your fault," Soulbinder sent.

"I know. But that doesn't make it any less painful," I replied.

The local residents began filling the streets as news of the arrival of a person of importance quickly swept through the city. Our entourage wound its way through the masses. My pulse began to quicken as we passed through the city and approached the farmlands that I once called home. I had the driver stop the carriage in front of an old farmhouse. I felt a lump in my throat as I recognized the old woman in the front yard weeding a flowerbed as my own sweet mother. I climbed out of the carriage, not once taking my eyes off her, even as I helped Chooser from the carriage.

"That's Chooser," came the whispers of those that had followed us from the city

"I think the man is Phoenix," whispered another.

We ignored them as we walked up to and then through the front gate. My mother stood up when the carriage stopped. She dropped the spade she had been holding as she began to recognize her long lost son, me. She started walking toward me. Slowly at first as if unsure that she was really seeing what she was seeing. Picking up the pace as the realization set in. I ran to her in return. I hugged her in an embrace that seemed to make the years melt away. She seemed shorter and far frailer than I remembered. She had been in her late forties when last I saw her and was now in her early eighties.

My father had been working behind the house and came to investigate when he heard the noise of the crowd that was gathering in front of his home. He stood there in disbelief as his eyes met mine and he began to recognize me. I let go of my mom and stared back at him trying to figure out if he was happy to see me. I finally decided to take the lead.

"Hi dad," I said offering my hand for him to shake. He took my hand and pulled me into him. I could feel his body shake and realized that he was crying being so overtaken with joy at my return. I felt a great remorse at having waited so long to return. He pushed me away and smiling wiped the tears from his cheeks.

"Let me look at you," he exclaimed.

"There's someone I'd like you both to meet," I blurted, my voice crackling from the emotions that threatened to overwhelm me. "This gorgeous young lady is Chooser, the soon to be mother of my child," I said. Their mouths dropped open. I could see the disbelief in their eyes. Their only son, a powerful wizard was going to be a father. The mother of their future grandchild was a powerful wizard in her own right.

"I don't know what else to say except congratulations," my father finally managed to stammer.

"That's perfect," I said in acceptance.

"Let's not stand out here in the sun. It's not much, but please come in," my mother offered putting her arm around Chooser's shoulders.

"Thank you," Chooser said smiling in reply. My father grabbed me by the arm.

"Can you give me a hand out back first son," he asked.

"Of course," I replied. My father hadn't asked for my help since I first got involved in magic. "We'll be right in," I assured Chooser as I headed to the back of the house.

When we got behind the house my dad grabbed my arm again. "Do you know that she's in league with that devil of a cousin of yours," he asked with genuine concern in his voice. I couldn't help grinning. My father hadn't realized how powerful a wizard I had become before I fled that night so many years ago. He believed the stories of my power were just that, stories, with no basis in reality, as neither him nor my mother were initiates. I shook my head in amusement.

"Dad, it's okay. I freed her. Destroyer holds no power over her anymore," I explained. "Now, what was it you were wanting my help with?"

There was a stack of firewood that needed to be chopped and stacked. I picked up the ax and began taking care of the task at hand. "I thought you were a powerful wizard," he asked. "If so, why are you doing that by hand?"

"Because you never approved of my magic," I replied trying to defend my actions.

"I didn't not like your magic, I didn't like you never being around to help with the farm," he grumbled. "Now take care of this mess so we can get back in with the ladies," he commanded rather sternly for a man of eighty-seven. Actually, he was still rather strong and in remarkable health. His father's father had lived to be one hundred fifteen and died in his sleep. His own father died at the young age of forty-two due to his lifestyle. He fancied himself a swordsman and was defending the village from marauders when, his heart was pierced by an arrow. My father was ten at the time.

It took me a few seconds to gather the right spell in my mind. Once formulated, I waved my hand and unleashed the magic. In a flash the wood was cut and neatly stacked. "Now that's useful magic," dad remarked admiringly. He put his arm around my shoulders and squeezed in love and adoration. We walked back around to the front of the house.

"Quinny," a woman's voice questioned as we came around to the front of the house. I looked up to see my sisters Cyndar and Valleese entering the front gate. It was Cyndar who had posed the question using the version of the name Quintan given to me at birth by my parents, a name I was never really too fond of even though it had been my father's fathers name.

Word of my arrival had already reached them that quickly. I scooped them both up in my arms once we were close enough to do so. They looked the same as I remembered them, but with a few more wrinkles. While it was true, they were older, their eyes still had that familiar light. They hit me with a barrage of questions as we headed into the house. I could see mom and Chooser were standing in the front window. Using my extended arms, I corralled my father and sisters up onto the front porch and through the front door. As I was about to enter, the feel of strong magic being used along with the sound of approaching horses caught my attention. As I turned my head in the direction of the approaching horses, I drew Soulbinder from her scabbard, which by now was instinctive.

I leapt from the porch and into the middle of the lawn. Destroyer and an escort of thirty riders were coming up the road. I stood ready to battle the lot of them, alone if necessary. The Anthgolian guard joined me ensuring that I wouldn't have to.

"Relax, cousin. I am here as a family informant," Destroyer announced. "Is my aunt here," he inquired looking up as she came out of the door surrounded by my sisters, my father and Chooser. "Aunt Irene, you were always my mother's favorite sibling. It is my sad duty to inform you of my mother's passing. I've always respected you and felt that this matter deserved my personal attention. I hope you'll forgive this intrusion," he told her. I was amazed to the point of speechlessness. I had never seen Destroyer so cordial and polite in my entire life. My mother was stunned at first until the news sank in and she then began to weep uncontrollably.

"Until we meet again," he said looking me in the eye and giving me his best evil stare. I twirled Soulbinder around several times and deftly returned her to her scabbard without taking my eyes off his. I couldn't help smirking as I realized this was just another projection.

"Until then," I replied. He turned his mount back the way he had come from and rode off followed closely by his entourage. They vanished in a mist after a short distance. I could feel the waves of power emanating from where they had been. Destroyer truly was a powerhouse, and the projection was designed to give that very impression.

Another group of riders came from the opposite direction, in the direction of the city. The leader was a muscular man about six foot three. I did a double take as I recognized him as Spiderlegs, the skinny little boy from up the road. It turns out he was now the leader of the local militia and married to my oldest niece.

"Spiderlegs," I asked incredulously. His face turned a beet red as his men snickered.

"It's Beararms, now," he said offering his hand. "Was that Destroyer," he asked the concern in his voice showing.

"Yes, it was, though it was only a projection of his true self. I'd appreciate it if you could have some of your men help our guards stand watch tonight," I said to him.

"Consider it done," he replied slapping my shoulder, with a familiarity I wasn't expecting, considering how timid he had been as a child. He was fearless, but none too bright.

Chooser spoke at length with the leader of the guards. I attended to my mother along with my father and sisters. My mother was a wreck of mixed emotions. Her only son returned on the day she learned of her twin sister's passing. I was glad that I had returned to help her over the grief she was now feeling. My father held my mother tightly, rocking her back and forth trying to ease the pain, while I introduced Chooser to my sisters.

"Thee Chooser," Valleese asked in disbelief.

"Yes, thee Chooser," I replied half mockingly.

"Forgive me for saying this, but you're even more beautiful than the stories about you give you credit for," Cyndar said. Chooser blushed at the compliment.

"Thank you. I wish I could return the compliment, but your brother hadn't mentioned any family at all until recently," she remarked getting me in trouble with the lot in the process, not to mention the guilt I felt hearing the statement of fact.

"He probably associates us with some really bad memories," Valleese defended. I felt lower than I had.

"You don't have to defend me," I said. "Chooser's right. I should have told her about you, my family long ago. After all, she confided in me about her family. I ask now for your forgiveness. I should have returned long ago to check on you all to assure myself of your wellbeing. I didn't and that was wrong."

My family sat there flabbergasted. My mother even stopped her sobbing for a moment not believing what her ears were hearing. I was never one to apologize in my youth. In my arrogance my way was always right, damn whoever got hurt. Learning of Chooser's pregnancy, as well as the years I traveled with the company, had tempered my thinking. I may not be able to undo the sins of my past, but I could try to atone for them in the future.

My mother wept for several hours until my father insisted that she go to bed to rest. I prepared a potion to help her sleep. It would allow her to sleep for however long her normal sleep cycle was.

I was closer to Valleese and Cyndar than I was to my other sisters, but even so we weren't that close. Kathora and Karenthia the twins who were also the oldest, were out of the house and had families of their own by the time I was seven, Loralinda and Iris were too busy off chasing the local eligible young men to care about anything I did. Cyndar and Valleese were tasked with watching out for me when I was young and taught me how to properly form sentences during my earliest years.

Valleese, Cyndar and I began to rehash old memories. For every embarrassing moment they brought up on me, I brought up two on them. I couldn't recall us ever just sitting around joking like this before. It felt good. Finally, we called it a night well after the sun had set.

Chooser and I shared my old room while my sisters decided to stay in their old rooms instead of returning to their own homes, just a short distance away. I was surprised to find that my parents had kept my room the same as when I had left it.

"Your mother was certain you'd be back for your things and insisted that we not touch anything. Over the years it became sort of a shrine for her. Well, goodnight," my father said closing the door behind him and leaving me feeling guiltier than ever.

Many childhood memories flooded my mind as I scanned the room. As each item I had collected in my formative years caught my eye, the adventure that was required to retrieve it would jump to the forefront. In nearly everyone, Firewind was by my side. A smile crossed my lips as I remembered the time, he was chased by a nest of lightning bees. The honey we had collected then was still glowing in the jar I saved my share in. Realizing the joy, the memory gave me, made me smile even more. I hadn't remembered the fun we had had, just the pain of that last awful night. It was good to know I could finally see beyond it.

We weren't surprised in the night. Evidently Destroyer truly was grieving over the loss of his mother. I really didn't get the chance to know my aunt very well. My father and her husband did not like each other and made no bones about showing it. I know it bothered my mother losing touch with her twin sister, but neither would abandon their husband and families.

I awoke before the crack of dawn, as was my ritual since I first joined the company. The sound of clanging metal in the kitchen area told me mother was awake and getting ready to cook breakfast. I made my way to the bath, the first indoor bath in the region, and cleaned myself up. I smiled knowing the spells I had placed on the fountains still worked the way I had intended them to, after all these years. These were the spells others had learned to recreate in my absence.

Chooser was still sleeping soundly when I returned to my room, so I allowed her to rest. As I made my way to the kitchen, the first rays of sunlight were creeping up over the tree line and through the dining room windows. I helped myself to a cup of coffee that was sitting near the hearth. I startled my mother doing so.

"Since when did you get up so early," she asked sounding in good spirits.

"Since I left. Being a mercenary, you have to acquire light sleeping habits, and rise before the cock crows," I answered. She turned and looked me in the eye.

"We really didn't get a chance to talk yesterday. I want to hear all about your many adventures since you left. This girl you're with, I've heard that she was in league with your cousin. Can you really trust her?" she asked with all the concern of a mother.

"Destroyer murdered her parents and made her his puppet when she was a young girl. He caused her brother and three of her cousins to become like wild beasts, controllable only by the most powerful of magics that we know of. I freed her and them. Can I trust her? Yeah, I think so. Do I love her, with all my heart," I said answering questions both asked and not asked.

She smiled at me and cupped my chin with her right hand. She then turned and went back to preparing breakfast. I then began to regale her with stories of my adventures with the company and Braveer. She acted like she was slightly taken by surprised to hear that I had been traveling with him all these years, though I knew he had been in touch throughout the years and kept them apprised of my wellbeing. It turns out he was the one that had borne the news of the events of that fateful day. He had defended me right from the start.

It wasn't long before the others started waking up and filing in. I continued to recount the many adventures I had with the company. I must admit that I embellished the stories a little for dramatic effect, but I kept the facts accurate. Chooser entered lastly. I was still amazed at how beautiful she looked even first thing in the morning when she thinks she's at her worst.

My mother noticed my stare, along with the fact that I had stopped telling my tale. "He must truly be in love. I've never known him to stop telling a story, even with Christine," she commented while giggling.

"Story tellers appreciate true beauty when in its presence," I lamented. Chooser graced me with a smile convincing me that I was truly the luckiest man in the world.

"I remember when you used to look at me that way," my mom told my dad.

"I remember when you looked like that," dad joked back in reply. Mom hit him with a towel she was using as a potholder. I couldn't help but smile. My sisters smiled as well, as did Chooser.

"Tell us how you met," Cyndar asked. "What did you think the first time you saw her?"

"That's easy. I said to myself, 'there goes a goddess.' A woman of such rare beauty enshrouded in power. I sensed a gentleness yet strength about her as to intimidate me," I said reminiscing.

"Are you sure you're remembering the first time we met, because I got the distinct impression that you feared no one," Chooser interjected.

"She didn't ask about the first time we met, which by the way was in my dream when you informed me about the changeling disease. She asked about the first time I saw you, which was two days before that," I corrected her. My mother gave me a look warning me not to antagonize a pregnant woman.

"You wouldn't have seen me, I was too adept at camouflage," I added trying to smooth over my misstep at correcting a pregnant woman in front of her mother-in-law. I looked over to my father for some sort of support all I got was a knowing look and a smiling shake of his head.

We were eating the midday meal, when I figured the time was right to invite the family to Blendell for our wedding. "Mom, dad, Chooser and I would like to invite you to our forthcoming wedding in Blendell," I said.

"Honey," Chooser said tugging on my tunic. "I was thinking, and your mom and I were talking, what if we held our wedding services here," she suggested. "I've already sent a messenger to invite my brother and family as well as the company," she finished. I was speechless.

"Never mind," I said obviously out of the loop.

"Weddings are more for women than men," mom informed me.

Throughout the day, various local dignitaries came to the farm to meet the powerful couple whose arrival had so disrupted the normal routine of the humble farming/mining community. We graciously greeted each new visitor as was expected of someone of Chooser's status. The local mayor was a newcomer to the area, at least as far as I was concerned. He introduced himself as 'the smiling dragon.' Something about him was familiar, though I couldn't quite pinpoint what or why. It was getting on in the day when the last of the official visitors departed.

The entirety of my living family gathered at my parent's farm to reacquaint themselves with me, although for many, it would be a first meeting. It looked to me as if my sisters had each attempted to repeat our mother's feat of having seven kids, coming close by producing thirty-seven kids between them. I discovered I had twenty-three nephews and fourteen nieces, the oldest of these having several children of their own.

As the day wore on to night, I couldn't help noticing that there was a full moon rising. Several of those gathered began to fret about being away from their homes. Their behavior started a nagging question, a link between this and something from earlier in the day. After several minutes of unsuccessfully trying to figure out the link, I let my attention return to the family gathering.

"Is it true what they're saying about you, Uncle Phoenix, that you cured yourself of the changeling disease," my niece Jennell asked. I nodded in response.

"He was magnificent," Chooser spoke up on my behalf. "We had to journey through the wildest terrain you could imagine. There were all kinds of evil creatures, everything from ogres to wraiths. Your uncle rode on fearlessly, using his powerful magic to ward off the evil creatures. Many days we traveled, through dark ominous looking tangled forests, until finally we came upon a once mighty city, now nothing more than mere ruins. Looking up, above this fallen seat of power, stood an ancient building, gleaming in the sun as though carefully polished. This was the Library of Magus in Graveer."

"This bastion of magical knowledge stood alone, waiting for travelers to enter and absorb it's treasure, a wealth of knowledge surpassed by nowhere else in the world. Here, the great Valtar sat and devised a spell, a cursed disease, that would be incurable. He left his notes sitting on the table as though challenging all who dare to try to reverse his curse. He was certain that no one ever would, though he hadn't counted on your uncle, Phoenix to ever have a desire to do so."

"You knew Valtar," Renjyn, my four-year-old great nephew asked. Everybody laughed. I looked down smiling and placed my hand on his head.

"I did get the chance to meet him through his work and the words in one of his books that I managed to collect when I was young," I replied.

"Anyway, as I was saying, Phoenix found the library and made it past the deadly traps that the builders had used to prevent those that weren't truly adept at magic from dabbling in its most powerful of spells. Using his great magical skill, he released me from the traps that would surely have killed me had he not. We cautiously entered the main body of the library. During the tests, that had nearly overwhelmed us, the library had actually given Phoenix clues about where to find the answers he sought. So strong is his power, that bastions of power tell him how to wield them for maximum effect! He boldly strode through the dusty halls and straight up to the ninth floor." Chooser had everyone enthralled as she told her tale of our adventure to the library. I looked around and had to smile, seeing the looks she was getting. I lost myself in my thoughts for a moment admiring what a fine storyteller she was.

"...and then he let loose a bolt of power and Destroyer's medallion was gone for good," she finished

A howl ripped through the night from the woods. It was an easily recognizable sound. It belonged to a werewolf. It was baleful and drenched in an aura of magic. Everyone began to gather closer for protection. I looked to the captain of the guard. "Stay with my family and Chooser. Anything happens to them, I'll be coming for you," I warned him.

I transformed myself into my namesake and quickly elevated myself above the terrain. I looked down upon the land with magically enhanced vision. It didn't take long for me to spot my prey. The werewolf was heading directly toward my parent's farm. I dove down upon it with the fury of a true phoenix, my first attack knocking the creature to the ground. In a fluid motion, I transformed into my natural form and drew Soulbinder from her sheath.

The creature shook itself off from the effects of my first attack. I had already formulated a spell and unleashed its force in a massive lightning bolt. The bolt hit the beast in the middle of its chest, sending it flying backward. As the beast lay there smoldering, I quickly formulated the next spell, a spell of binding that would entrap the creature in a web of power immobilizing it.

The power that I wrapped the creature in forced it back into its mostly human form. The nagging question resolved itself. The creature was the mayor. It must have been the lycanthropy link that I felt. I used my powers to raise him off the ground and carry him back toward the house.

The entire family and most of the neighbors were waiting for me when I returned. They watched in curiosity as I placed the beast/man down and retrieved my notebook. The spell I used to cure myself would be in this book and I intended to use it on him. I would have to modify it a little, but it should still eliminate the curse from him, and hopefully anyone he would have infected.

As I flipped through the pages, Chooser inquired as to my intentions. 'What, you're not keeping her fully apprised of the situation,' I asked Soulbinder. Before she could answer, a bolt of power slammed into my web, dissipating it. I quickly reactivated it keeping the beast within entrapped. Chooser quickly wove spells of protection that engulfed everyone who had gathered on the farm for protection. A second bolt of power deflected off her shield, enabling me to trace its source.

I grabbed a horse from one of the guards, and rode off in the direction that the bolts of power had originated in. With Chooser's shield in place, my bindings would hold the werewolf until my return. Whoever was trying to free the beast would have to face me, and I intended to win no matter who or what I had to fight.

As I crested a hill, I felt the familiar gathering of magical power and took steps to protect myself. No attack was forthcoming. I spotted a flash behind some trees and felt a wave of spent power. When I arrived at the spot where the spell had been cast, I found only an area of bare earth. I had seen this kind of pattern before. It was what was left after a transportation spell was used. Very few wizards attempted such spells, because they required an intimate knowledge of the destination site to prevent the caster from ending up in a lethal situation, such as ending up inside solid rock.

I wrestled back the urge to cast a tracer spell that would send me to the same destination as the previous caster, that too was dangerous because even if the original spell caster arrived at his or her destination safely, they might not be out of the way and you could end up inside of them. I looked around for any evidence as to whom the spell caster might have been but found nothing that could help me ascertain their identity. It was someone of the seventh circle or better, I suspected eighth or ninth. I knew that from the spells that had been cast, but beyond that I was clueless.

I returned yet again to the farm. I dismounted and told the guards to set the watch. I doubted we would have any more trouble tonight but couldn't say for certain that that would be the case.

Once again, I retrieved my notebook. Once more I found the spell I had recently worked out and cast to cure Chooser's family and me. I read through it again, figuring where I would have to modify it to encompass the type of lycanthropy that ensnared the man trapped within my web of magic. Concentrating, I let the power flow through my entire body, coursing through my veins as if it were my lifeblood. Focusing on the desired results, I uttered the words that shaped the power enabling it to complete the task at hand. A brilliant flash occurred where the werewolf had been bound. As my eyesight returned to normal, I could see that I had been successful, for where the werewolf had been, now stood a man.

He stared at me as I approached. Part of him was afraid. Part of him was angry. He was totally confused. He was unsure how to react as I released the spell that bound him in place. He fell backward and was seized by the town guards.

"For the murders of sixteen citizens, I place you under arrest," one of the guards announced.

"He shouldn't be held accountable for crimes he may have committed while under the influence of a spell," Chooser said standing up for the man.

"She's right. The poor man was cursed, and his actions weren't his own," I agreed. "I realize of course that the decision is yours, but my humble opinion is that he should do a service for the village as restitution for the crimes he was forced to commit, but any punishment beyond that wouldn't be justice," I finished.

"My daughter had her throat ripped out and her entrails eaten! Are you asking me to let her killer go," the guard asked me angrily?

"The beast that committed those crimes ceased to exist once I dispelled the curse that had transformed this man. Nothing you can do to this wretch will bring your daughter back to life."

"We'll let a magistrate decide his fate," Beararms interjected. That statement summed up the situation. I hoped the local justice system would spare the poor wretch from any great suffering and allow him to atone for the lives that were shortened by his being cursed.

The weather was beautiful on the day everyone arrived for the wedding. The local inhabitants were out en masse as various dignitaries began arriving. First to arrive were Chooser's family. They brought with them an honor guard of nearly five thousand of their best troops. They arrived in splendor, a carriage gleaming in the sunlight surrounded by thousands of troops in dress uniform. They set up their camp on my parent's farm, which was the largest in the region.

Chooser rushed toward Lindeth. They hugged each other, then stepped back and stared at one another. "I'm pregnant," Lindeth exclaimed almost shouting.

"I know. So, am I," Chooser replied.

"You're kidding, that's wonderful," Lindeth stammered wide eyed while putting her hands in front of her mouth in surprise. They embraced again smiling broadly.

The company was the next to arrive, leading the royals and Velouth. Braveer rode up to the farm and dismounted, quickly being rush by my sisters. My mother got in on the act as well. They had a brief exchange, which I couldn't, and probably wasn't meant to hear. He shook hands then hugged my father. Finally, he made his way over to us.

"Chooser! Phoenix! It's good to see you again. Although I must say you're marrying the wrong man," he said winking at Chooser and hugging us both.

"Still trying to steal my lady," I asked raising an eyebrow in mock jealousy. "Honestly, can you blame me," he asked.

"You'll need to post a guard, especially now that so many high-ranking people are here," I told him.

"And who do you think is going to disrupt the ceremonies that would require posting a watch?"

"Destroyer. He was here three days ago, or at least a projection of him that felt real. Then there was a second power here trying to prevent me from curing a man stricken with lycanthropy. I managed to frighten that one off, though I am not sure who it was. It wasn't Destroyer, I'd have recognized his power signature." He stared at me in some disbelief then began barking orders to Shameer. Meanwhile Firestorm's top general had ordered his men to set a watch as well, the two sets of guards would compliment each other making it that much more difficult for any one of hostile intent to penetrate the area and causing trouble.

By early evening all who were invited to attend had arrived. The ceremony was set for the next midday. Chooser and I would each say some words of commitment, followed by some ceremonial words added by Velouth who had asked to officiate the ceremony. One forth of the gathered troops would be allowed to celebrate. The rest would have to stand ready just in case. Naturally, the company would be amongst the revelers, they were after all, my brothers in arms.

It was the dead of night when I awoke. I got up and went to the window. It was pitch black outside. Neither of our two moons was in the sky. It was a rare occurrence, and one that usually portended ill fortune. I softly muttered to myself, feeling the power that then enwrapped me in its grip giving my eyes the ability to penetrate the darkness and see what was there. I quietly made my way outside so I could scan the entire area surrounding my parent's home.

I could see the guards as they paced back and forth on their appointed rounds. Nothing seemed out of place. I was just about to relax when I felt the presence of something flying overhead. I looked up and saw a dragon circling. Its eyes seemed to be transfixed on me. A booming voice filled my mind. 'The great Dragore wishes to speak with you. Now,' it told me. The dragon then landed a few feet from me. 'Get on my back, I will take you to her,' it said. Knowing the power Dragore possessed, and feeling the power emanating from this dragon, I didn't see where I had much choice. I climbed onto the dragon's back hoping I wasn't doing anything that it found offensive. In seconds we were high in the air zooming towards Dragore's lair.

In what seemed an incredibly short time, we were landing at the entrance to Dragore's lair. I stepped inside, curious as to what might await me. I cautiously approached the dragon. Her eyes opened and transfixed their awesome gaze upon me.

'I must apologize for not recognizing you the last time we met. I had let my mind wander too far to realize who you were and when it was that we were meeting,' her voice boomed in my mind. 'Recent events brought me back to myself. Your world and your people are in grave jeopardy. You must travel a path that even to my great eyes is obscure and treacherous. You must learn to control your emotions and your instincts if you are to succeed,' she sent.

"I'm afraid I don't understand. What it is it you're trying to say," I implored the great beast. A glint sparkled in her eyes, as though a light had been flashed in them, only no light source existed from what I could see.

'I can sympathize with your plight, but due to constraints placed upon me I am unable to elaborate further. You already know your heart, follow it to those you can trust, but beware, not all is as it seems,' she sent. 'It is getting late. You must return to your people. Just remember what we spoke of. It will become all too evident soon enough.'

I once again climbed onto the back of the young dragon that had brought me to Dragore's lair. The trip seemed only slightly longer on the way back than it had on the trip there. I will be the first to admit that I had no idea what it was that she tried to impart to me. Once I had dismounted, it occurred to me that not one of the guards had noticed my departure or return. My spell allowing my eyesight to pierce the darkness was still in effect. I scanned the perimeter to ensure myself that we were still safe.

I turned back toward my parent's house and started towards the door. The veil of darkness was pierced by a bolt of power that ignited a patch of dry grass near where I had been standing. I quickly assumed the form of a phoenix and ascended into the sky. Another flash slammed into the ground I had just vacated. The origin of the power illuminated like a beacon in the night. I didn't know who it was that was attempting to assault me, but I was going to make them regret the act. I dove toward my protagonist, weaving my way so as not to give him an easy target. Power flashed by me searing the air. Before he could evade, I released a bolt of power myself. The power that slammed into his chest sent him flying fifty feet or so before he hit the ground.

I resumed my natural form as I landed, walking towards him, and drawing Soulbinder from her scabbard in stride. He was struggling to try to regain his feet. I quickly focused on a web to bind him then ensnared him in a magical binding. I gestured and the binding drew him closer to me. I placed the tip of Soulbinder's blade at his throat, just under his chin. "You are going to regret your unprovoked attack on me. Before you die, you will tell me why," I promised him. I headed back toward the farm, my bindings dragging my captive long behind me. While he could not escape, he could feel the sting of the branches that I drug him through. He was rather bloody by the time I got him back.

The sentries came rushing towards us. I dispelled the enchantment that allowed me to see in the darkness as the light from their torches began flooding the area. I didn't stop at their arrival, I continued on towards my parent's farmhouse, prisoner in tow. As we made our way, our entourage became a throng. It seemed that everyone that was awake wanted to know what was going on. Braveer met us about halfway back to the house.

"Sentries return to your posts. We can handle this," he commanded. Grudgingly they obeyed. Leaving only a smattering of followers with us.

Once we passed through the gates, I headed straight to the barn. We could conduct our interrogation there in relative privacy. I turned to Shameer and said, "post some guards. I don't want us being disturbed."

I opened the barn doors and flung my prisoner to the ground inside. He landed with a thud. A motion from my hand and he was suspended in the air a couple of inches off the ground. I walked over and ripped open his shirt. This served two purposes. First it exposed his flesh allowing access for instruments of torture should they prove to be necessary. The second was that it would expose any medallions he might be wearing whether for protection or obedience or power for that matter.

He wore no jewelry. He did have some odd tattoos. They seemed to be runes of protection, though none that I had ever encountered before.

"Who are you," I demanded. He looked me in the eye, unflinching. I sent a bolt of power into his abdomen. His body spasmed from the pain this inflicted. "Who are you," I demanded again, not changing the pitch in my voice. He attempted to spit. "Fine, I'll allow my friends to have some fun with you. If you still resist, I'll simply kill you and use necromancy to get the information I want," I said in a matter of fact tone. "Hermit, Cyclops, he's all yours. Have fun."

I could hear his screams as I left the barn. I motioned and chanted and quickly sealed the barn. His screaming might continue, but those of us outside the barn wouldn't have to hear it. My family and Chooser were standing in the doorway as I climbed up the steps to the front porch.

"What was all that wailing? It sounded like someone was in total agony," my mother inquired.

"A young wizard foolishly tried to kill me. I managed to capture him. He's being questioned to find out who he is and why he should want to assault me," I replied. "Chooser, I'd like to speak with you in private if I may."

"Of course. Do you think he might be Anthgolian?"

"No, it's not about him. Let's take a walk," I suggested.

We followed a path that I hadn't traversed in more years than I cared to count. I held her hand as we walked in silence. I kept glancing around to assure myself that we were alone. Finally, we came upon a large tree that had fallen a crossed the path. "This looks like a convenient spot," I said gesturing for her to have a seat. I sat down next to her.

"Forgive me if what I say sounds confusing, I still don't understand it myself," I started. "I had a visit with Dragore. I'm still not certain that I understand the message in its entirety. She said it would become all too clear soon enough. The one thing that leaps out at me was her apology for not recognizing me. There was a feeling of familiarity that pervaded the meeting, like we were old friends."

Chooser watched me as I prattled on about my encounter with Dragore. Finally, I explained about the attack on me. As I described my assailant, a look of shock, as if she is recognizing the man I was describing, came over her being.

I stared into her lovely eyes, looking for a clue as to what she was thinking. She continued to stare back, with a look of expectancy in her eyes.

"Having been tutored by Destroyer, I was sort of hoping that you could examine the tattoos he has to see if any of the runes are familiar," I asked.

"Naturally, I'll be more than happy to help you. After all, had he succeeded in harming you, our baby would have been deprived of his father," she replied.

"His," I inquired inquisitively.

"Or hers. It's a figure of speech, not foreknowledge, or hopefulness, so drop it," she retorted.

We made our way to the back entrance of the barn. As we entered, the screams of sheer pain reverberated around us. Cyclops and Hermit were perfectly suited for torture. They were probably the type of children that amputated the legs and wings off insects for fun. In spite of all the pain they had inflicted, our guest refused to divulge his name or why he had attacked me. Chooser came over and examined the tattooed runes that adorned him.

"I do recognize these runes," she said after her examination. "But not through Destroyer. No, I recognize them from the library of Anthgolia. They're the sacred runes of Tribelth, my great, great, great, great, great grandfather on my father's side. They are protection spells. They are said to ward off demons and devils. I don't recall hearing of them being used by anyone since Tribelth's death. He won't talk as long as their power remains in effect. We'll have to get Firestorm. He learned his magic from our family. I learned mine from Destroyer. He should be able to deactivate them," she finished.

Braveer sent a messenger to find Firestorm. He and Lindeth came with a small guard. Firestorm couldn't remember the sequence for disarming the runes, but Lindeth said that she could. She began circling the man chanting ancient words of power. As she did so, the various tattooed runes began to glow. A faint humming sound could be heard, growing in volume and pitch as more and more runes glowed. Just when I was beginning to think my ears would burst, there was a flash of light followed by silence.

"He'll tell you everything you wish to know," she assured us as she headed towards the door. She seemed weaker as she headed outside. Firestorm took her in his arms and helped out of the barn. Evidently reciting the runes took a lot out of her. He lifted her into his arms and carried her back to their camp.

Chooser and I followed them out of the barn. Hermit and Cyclops resumed their interrogation. I was certain that they would get him talking now. They'd probably enjoy it more if they knew that he was a seventh circle initiate.

It turns out that my first instincts weren't far from the mark. The wizard that had ensnared him was one of Destroyer's lackeys. A powerful enough wizard in his own right, but too weak to challenge Destroyer. He saved his own hide by swearing fealty to Destroyer. He was allowed to study Anthgolian's history, while keeping tabs on Chooser all the while. He had on numerous occasions confessed his desire for Chooser in front of our prisoner whom the wizard kept as an assistant. The spells the wizard had placed upon him when they first got together insured the wizard that his apprentice would never rebel against him. He was trying to remove me as competition for Chooser's affections.

The prisoner, called Tulacho, had never learned the wizard's name, calling him only by the term master. He was able to tell us where we could find his master, though I doubted that he would still be there if we were to head there. I decided that killing the man wouldn't really be justified but couldn't leave him as he was for fear that he might yet again try to kill me. I stared at the runes that adorned his body. A nearly evil thought crossed my mind. I could place runes upon his back that would cause any action against me to cause him to burst into flames until his body was totally consumed by them. The runes would also prevent him from using any magic above the second circle, thus preventing him from teleporting back to his master.

In the morning, Chooser had a bout of morning sickness. It was a rather severe case, quite possibly something she ate didn't agree with her stomach making it worse than normal. Lindeth and Firestorm came to check on us. I went to the barn to take care of the prisoner.

After finishing with the prisoner, I headed to the house to check on my soon to be wife. She was up and drinking the tea Lindeth had made for her. She again graced me with a smile as I entered the room.

"Is everything taken care of," she inquired as I approached her.

"Almost," I replied, leaning down to kiss her. "Some things will have to wait for another day."

A carnival like atmosphere took hold of the once quiet little countryside. Revelry was everywhere. Somehow nearly just as many women appeared as there were young soldiers. Everyone who wasn't on duty was dancing, dining, or drinking. Everyone I saw, congratulated me on my forthcoming nuptials. I made my way through to Velouth's command tent.

"Due to events earlier today, I'm afraid we're going to have to postpone the ceremonies until tomorrow," I informed the assembled staff. "Please make it known to all your men."

I continued to make the rounds, informing everyone that the ceremonies had been postponed a day, then headed back to the house. Chooser once again had the youngster's enthralled as she told another tale, this one about the great dragon Dragore and how an evil wizard nearly brought doom to us all. Seeing the look on their faces as she spun her yarn made me realize even more that our child was blessed to have her for a mother.

The remainder of the day passed uneventfully. I soon found myself lying beside Chooser, again feeling the elation of a man in love. I was amazed again that I could feel so much for one woman. I put my arm around her and pulled her into me, reveling in the feel of it, the warmth of it.

I slept unmolested. I awoke, went into the kitchen for a cup of coffee and was quickly ushered off with the rest of the men. The women had to prepare the bride for the ceremony. I begged them not to upset her, because I wasn't sure I could undo her wrath should they upset her. Lindeth admonished me for my bad sense of humor.

Due to the sheer number of guests that clambered to attend, the ceremony was being held in the pasture. The cattle were driven off to another area to graze. Troops quickly policed the path the bride was to traverse to ensure she didn't have any unwanted missteps. Braveer stood at my side as I awaited the start of the ceremony. I was remarkably calm, compared to the rest of the men in the area. Braveer kept fidgeting with his uniform. Velouth kept rehearsing his speech. Finally, Firestorm's royal trumpeters bleated the commencement of the wedding.

Chooser was amazingly beautiful. She seemed to glow as she beamed me a smile. I found my chest swelling with pride, that I had managed to win the heart of this remarkable woman. I couldn't take my eyes off her.

"Careful," Soulbinder sent. It had been the first contact between us for some time.

'I was wondering when you were going to speak up,' I returned. To be on the safe side, I scanned the crowd once quickly. I could see the security keeping tabs on the crowds. 'But I can't help but wonder of what it is I am to be careful about,' I asked, knowing that I wouldn't get an answer.

"Letting your emotions blind, you," she replied proving me wrong.

"I am pleased to be standing here uniting in wedlock two people that care greatly for their people. I have rehearsed the speech I was expected to give all night. Seeing the look, you two are sharing with each other tells me that you are right for each other. May your union be blessed with many happy years and children," Velouth adlibbed. I was taken aback momentarily. I glanced back at Chooser and smiled.

"Unless someone can show just cause that this union shouldn't take place, then I declare this union official, may the gods watch over you," he finished. There was an awkward silence. I leaned over and kissed Chooser. The assembled guests cheered.

The celebration broke out immediately. I danced one dance with Chooser, then led her off into the woods that I at one time knew like the back of my hand. Aside from some new underbrush, truly little had changed. These woods were ancient before I was born. We made our way to a little creek that had a nice sized swimming hole that was actually a hot spring. I had all but forgotten how great it was until this moment brought back those happy times.

"You'll love this, the waters warm all year round," I told her as I started to disrobe.

"You're not serious," She giggled putting her hand in front of her mouth.

"Of course, I'm serious! Come on, you won't regret it. I promise," I assured her.

"But what if someone should happen upon us," she protested.

"We're wizards, I'll blind them until we can get dressed," I argued. "Come on...no more excuses. Besides, we're married, no one's gonna care. Hell, they're expecting us to do something like this. Come on..."

Reluctantly she began to disrobe herself. Having already undressed, I slowly made my way into the soothing waters. I turned to see Chooser's voluptuous body being revealed as the last of her gown hit the ground. Her body, to me was flawless, even as her pregnancy began to show. I looked up into her eyes smiling. Unlike me, she quickly immersed herself in the water. I stopped and waited for her to catch up to me.

The feel of her silky skin underwater was a new thrill. We embraced with heated passion. We each desired the other intensely. I was fully engrossed in the moment until Soulbinder screamed in my mind.

"Look out!" came the warning. I looked up in time to see a bolt of power heading our way. I pushed Chooser back and tried to avoid a direct hit, I wasn't quite successful at the latter. The pain from the assault was immense and intense. I was blinded by it, for what to me, seemed like an eternity. I could hear Chooser chanting a spell but was too dazed from the one that had hit me to recognize what she was chanting. I shook my head to try to clear the cobwebs. I felt the sensation of a spell going off but couldn't discern what it was. I was in trouble.

My vision was the first of my senses to return to normal, followed by touch and hearing. Chooser stood about twenty feet from me. She was engaged in a bitter struggle with another wizard. As my strength returned, I focused on a powerful lightning bolt hitting this other wizard square in the middle of his chest. I gathered all the power I could muster. Without warning I unleashed my wrath upon this would be assassin. The bolt I unleashed picked him up and slung him against a giant tree, pinning him there as I continued to will it to do so. For him to survive such a bolt would be a miracle. I was getting tired of being attacked in my hometown. Enough was enough. I was going to make an example out of this one.

Chooser turned to me. "Are you all right," we asked simultaneously. My shoulder still smoldered where his bolt had hit me. "I'm fine," we both answered. I looked over at the corpse. "Any ideas who he was," I asked.

"Not a one. How good are you at necromancy," she asked?

"I've got a book," I replied with an evil grin.

'Thanks,' I sent to Soulbinder.

"I warned you about letting your emotions blind you," she scolded in an I-told-you-so tone.

'You could have been a little more specific,' I shot back.

"Careful," was all that she said.

We made our way back to the farm. We came up to the back door and crept inside. We made our way to the room we were staying in. Chooser began applying first aide to my shoulder. I was flipping through the pages of my spell books. It took three tries to find the right book. I set about memorizing the spell. Ironically, it was electrically based. I electrified him to kill him, now I'll be doing it to make him talk.

The ointment Chooser was rubbing into my shoulder was definitely doing the trick. I felt no pain whatsoever. It was when she started nibbling on my ear that I forgot the spell I had just memorized. But it was my wedding night after all, and I was allowed to forget about the rest of the world for a little while. As Chooser started kissing her way around my body, I chanted a spell of protection that would place a bubble around us. It would only protect us against one blow, but that was better than what I had let happen earlier by not casting it.

After an hour of teasing and pleasing each other, our energies were spent. I awoke a short time later. Chooser was sleeping peacefully. She must have spent a lot of energy battling our as yet unknown assailant. I dressed quietly, made my way outside and found the captain of the watch. I instructed him on where to find the body. I ordered him to send a few men to retrieve it and put it in the barn. With that taken care of, I went back inside and lay down beside Chooser once again.

When I awoke, I ascertained from Soulbinder that it had been ten hours since the assault. I would need this information to successfully question the dead wizard who had attacked us. Necromancy works best within the first twenty-four hours, after which it's more likely that a minor demon would animate the body than the soul of the departed. There was still a chance that the procedure would fail, but that's the risk you take with the arcane arts.

Chooser was still peacefully sleeping when I headed towards the barn. Once inside, I set about examining the body. Besides the charred area where my bolt had hit him, there were seven other battle scars. Judging from the wounds, Chooser spent a lot of energy. To withstand that kind of assault tells me that he had a lot of energy in him. That would severely lessen the likelihood of my success.

Cyclops and Hermit stood nearby as I examined the body. "You two feel like helping me with a spell," I asked unsure of what their answer would be.

"Only if it involves necromancy," Hermit quipped. I grinned at the humor of it.

"Good, gather up these supplies," I commanded handing them the book open to the component list for the spell I intended to cast.

"Um, Slasher, I mean Phoenix, where are we supposed to get ten pounds of silver dust," Cyclops asked.

"Check with Firestorm. Being a king and wizard, it wouldn't surprise me to find that he keeps a trunk full of it," I suggested. "If he doesn't, then see the smith in town. Take two royal guards with you, make him think Velouth wishes it." He grinned a wicked grin at the thought of using the royals as dupes.

While Hermit and Cyclops were busy gathering the components, I set about preparing the body and the barn for casting the spell. First, I removed all the clothing from the body, especially the jewelry. Next, I grabbed some oils from my private stash, a secret hole in the barn floor I had made as a preteen. The bottles were covered in the dust of thirty some odd years, but still sealed tightly. I was only slightly surprised that no one had found my little cubbyhole, but then again knowing my family they probably had found it but were too afraid to touch.

I had to dust off all of the bottles to see the labels. It had been so long that I couldn't remember which oils I had stashed. The first bottle I grabbed; I had labeled oil of bat. I didn't write the species because I was certain that I would run out before I forgot. Who knew? The second was rose and the third was the one I was looking for, oil of lilac.

Firestorm came in as I traced out the pentagram to be filled with the silver dust. I looked up as he approached. "Bring the silver dust," I asked nonchalantly.

"Yeah, I keep it strapped to my belt as spare change," he replied sarcastically. "However, I did send my men to purchase the dust with some gems I carry for just such an occasion. Did I hear them right, you're going to use necromancy to question a man you killed last night," he inquired.

I finished tracing the pentagram, turned, and looked him in the eye. "My wife, the woman carrying my child, exhausted herself defending me after this S.O.B.

blindsided us on our wedding day. I haven't a clue as to who he is or why he's after me. He's the third person in as many days that's tried to kill me. I'm beginning to take it personal. Yes, I slew him once I regained my composure, but I want answers and I don't care if he has a peaceful afterlife or not," I explained to him.

He looked me in the eye a little dumbfounded. "Um, great?! Mind if I watch," he asked obviously confused by my minor tirade.

"Actually, I was more hoping that you'd ask to help. I could use all the strength I can gather on this one. From the wounds I inspected, your sister spent a lot of energy on this bastard. He'll surely try to resist coming back to a defecated decaying shell," I said trying to entice him into joining his strength with mine.

"Okay, I'm in," he quickly volunteered. "You might want to lose that sword during the spell casting. I was taught metal interferes with the bridging of the gap between this life and the next."

I merely smiled back at him. He had no way of knowing how powerful this sword really was, and I wasn't about to tell him. There was no way I was 'losing' Soulbinder, and I doubt she'd let me if I tried.

It wasn't long before Cyclops and Hermit returned with all the ingredients on the component list, except oil of lilac. The only reason I had it was because I spent the entire summer when I was twelve making it. I sacrificed a childhood for my power. Very few are lucky enough to be born with a power like mine. Only seven people are born with a gift like mine every two hundred years or so. Chooser was among my peers. As were Destroyer and Hellfire, though the latter wasn't of my generation. Of the remaining three, Firestorm had been overcome and transformed, weakening his overall strength. Firewind was slain at an early age, and I never met the last, though I suspected that my would-be assassins were in fact working for him.

We began by wrapping the body in cloth bandages soaked in lilac oil. Once all but the mouth was covered, I scribed runes over the vital organs of the body, each with a different ink to imbue them with separate and distinct powers. While I did this, Cyclops and Hermit filled in the lines of the pentagram I had traced around the body. Meanwhile Firestorm mixed together a seven-herb incense and lit it. He placed one at each point of the pentagram, and several at various areas around the barn to permeate it with the smoldering fragrance. The smoke provided a relaxing atmosphere in which to concentrate on the spell. Upon placing the last rune upon the carcass, I carefully stepped away from the body and out of the pentagram. We stood side-by-side, arms out at a forty-five-degree angle palms facing the corpse. The book lay on a pedestal in front of me. I began to recite the ancient words, being sure to put the right emphasis on the right syllable. With each new utterance, a power started to coalesce over the cadaver. I could see it taking the shape of a man, yet featureless, as though it had no real form of its own.

The coalescing power finally began to take on features. Quickly the image of the man now wrapped in cloth became apparent. He struggled to break free from the binds that were attempting to reunite him with the shell he had occupied not so long ago. As I finished the chant, the spirit was still outside the body and doing all he could to break away and flee this place. I repeated the last verse. As I did so, the spirit sank further into the corpse. I started repeating it again, and Firestorm joined in. as our voices combined, the spirit was forced into the corpse. It gasped for air with dead lungs.

"WHHYY HHAVE YYOU DISTURBED MMY SSLUMBER." he complained. I glowered at the corpse.

"I'll ask the questions," I replied bluntly. "You assaulted me and my wife last night, Why," I demanded.

"MMY MMASTERS ORDERSS," it replied.

"Who was you're master," I inquired further.

"MMASTER…" Came the baleful reply.

The power surrounding the corpse disappeared instantly, like the light of a candle that has been extinguished. This caught me completely off guard. Spells of this nature normally lasted until the caster dispelled them. I was far from finished with my interrogation and had not dispelled the magic. The components of the spell were still in place. I recited the ancient words of power as I had earlier. Nothing happened. I tried again. Suddenly a brilliant flash of blue flames shot up from the pentagram. When my vision returned, the corpse was gone. Only smoldering ashes remained I glanced at Firestorm.

"Someone is going through great lengths to keep me from finding out who it is that's behind these attacks," I said flatly.

"Whoever it is, is surely a power to be reckoned with," he assured me.

"Maybe, but so am I, and I won't be intimidated by anyone not brave enough to face me," I countered.

"Still, for Chooser's sake I would suggest that you be ever alert, and possibly double your normal guard," he suggested. I grinned at the suggestion.

"And do you know what double of nothing is," I quipped in way of suggesting that I had no current guard watching over me. "However, I will have your men that are protecting Chooser doubled. I couldn't bear the thought of anything happening to her."

We left the barn and I went back up to the house to find Chooser. She was up and eating. She smiled as I walked up to her, kissing her on the cheek as she chewed. She swallowed the food in her mouth then asked, "where have you been?"

"The barn," I replied, trying not to divulge the nature of my business there. Chooser would have no problem with my using magic. Nor would my family, except that people tend to believe that necromancy causes buildings to become permanently haunted. I tend to take the more magically proven fact that ghosts and other such freakish beings, either have unfinished business, or died a horrific death and are seeking revenge on the living out of jealousy. Chooser must have sensed the deeper meaning for my vagueness, or wasn't curious enough to ask, because she didn't inquire any further.

The various visiting dignitaries began departing for their respected homes. Braveer and the company were given new orders to head for the Plains of Dread, so named because of the great spells that permeate the region causing those of weak wills to flee in fear. The plains lie between Asmeria and Ardole, Hellfire's kingdom. Knowing that my brothers in arms would be in harm's way tore me apart. I wanted to join them, and help keep them safe, but I now had other obligations. One of which was due in less than three months.

Chapter 9

Preparing to Leave

IT WAS HARD saying goodbye to my family again. The last time I left I had simply run off and never looked back. They had forgiven me for abandoning them under the circumstances. This time they held me tightly yet let me go with their blessings. I promised to return before another thirty years passed. Firestorm invited them all to Blendell after the babies arrive. They eagerly agreed to come.

As we rode off, it occurred to me that Soulbinder had been extremely quiet during all of this. 'Are you still in there,' I inquired.

"That's probably the stupidest question you have ever asked," she retorted, "but thanks for caring." The latter oozed with sarcasm.

'I don't suppose you could tell me what happened during my necromancy spell casting,' I asked.

"It failed," she replied. No further explanation was forthcoming.

'Thanks, that's extremely helpful,' I replied sarcastically

I put my arms around Chooser and pulled her close. Somehow holding her seemed to make all seem right with the world, even when I knew that darkness would soon be encasing it. I tried to imagine going back to my mundane ways and a chill went up my spine causing me to shiver.

"Are you okay," she asked looking up at me.

"Yeah. Just had a chilling thought," I said.

"What was it?"

"Nothing important," I replied letting the matter drop.

The journey to Blendell was uneventful. The carriage rode beautifully. Chooser and I made out like a couple of teenagers almost the entire time. It almost seemed all too soon that we heard the city trumpeters announcing our arrival.

All of Blendell was in the streets to greet us. Firestorm and Lindeth waved to their adoring citizens. Chooser likewise waved to the crowd as we rode by. As we exited the carriage, the captain of the guard greeted us.

"Welcome home, your majesties," he said bowing to Firestorm and Lindeth.

That phrase hit me like a ton of bricks. Welcome home. This was after all Chooser's home. She had been born here. She at one time in the not too distant past ruled here. But it was not my home. The gravity of my situation was finally sinking in. I hadn't yet expressed my feelings about Blendell with Chooser. I looked over at her she was beaming with delight to be where she loved to be. I wondered if I could or even should ask her to leave this place.

We ate an elegant meal with all of Chooser's relatives and Anthgolia's highest-ranking dignitaries. After which we retired to our quarters, just down the hall from Firestorm and Lindeth. I once again marveled at Chooser's beauty as she prepared for bed. She caught me staring at her, smiled, came, and put her arms around my neck, then kissed me passionately. We shared a peaceful night in each other's arms.

I awoke earlier than usual. I got out of bed, trying my best not to disturb Chooser. Having successfully accomplished that, I went out onto the terrace that overlooked Blendell. The city sprawled out in front of me. Looking up I strained to see the billion stars above me. All of the major constellations were out this time of year. The light of the torches that illuminated the city hid them.

Looking back at the beauty still sleeping, I never felt more out of place. I couldn't see myself ever growing accustomed to such surroundings. At the same time, I couldn't deny my wife and as yet unborn child these things. Chooser had been raised with such trappings; how could I take them away from her now?

"You can't," Soulbinder said.

'I'm beginning to think I've made a huge mistake,' I sent. 'How could I have let myself get caught up in all of this? I'm a powerful wizard, at least by my race's standards. How could I let my emotions outweigh my logic?' To which Soulbinder giggled.

"Love is said to conquer all. And by most standards you are really quite powerful. The plane you are on is what binds you to your current level of power. On my plane you would be able to exceed even my father in power and he was a truly gifted man," she assured me.

I wasn't sure if this was flattery or honest assessing. I decided to let it go.

"Am I doing the right thing?'" I asked. More giggling.

"I assume that you mean are you doing the right thing by marrying the woman carrying your baby, in which case I can only say that you two are as in love as any beings I have interacted with. Which in turn makes it right. If you're asking if you are doing the right thing by procreating, well it's a little late to be concerned about that. The damage, as it were having already been done. It's quite natural for species with dual sexes to procreate in order to propagate the species. Had either your parents or mine opted not to follow this instinct, we wouldn't be having this conversation. Only time will tell if you were right to do so. And even then, it will be up to future generations that must interact with your offspring to determine if his or her life was of value and thus your procreating being the right thing to do," she replied.

'Sorry I asked.' More giggling.

I looked off to the southwest, toward the Plains of Dread. Somewhere out there were my brothers in arms. Soon they would be facing an army of trolls, zombies, and other such miscreants. If I didn't join them, it would be the first major conflict they would have had in twenty-five years without me. A feeling in the pit of my stomach told me that that wasn't right. Especially since I had been the one to convince Velouth that fighting Hellfire was the right way to go.

I must have been too deep in my thoughts because I failed to hear Chooser get out of bed and come up behind me. I was momentarily startled when she put her arms around my waist and laid her head on my back. I turned, wrapped an arm around her shoulder and kissed her hair.

"The suns not up yet," she complained. "Come back to bed," she urged. I found myself unable to resist. I crawled into bed beside her and held her close. She snuggled up, using my shoulder for a pillow.

It took her a couple of hours to finally wake up and want to get out of bed. She prepared us a meal in the small kitchen that was attached to our quarters. As she put the plates on the table, she said, "I was thinking that we'll have to build our place closer to the border, near your parents' village. I'm sure that they'll want to be involved in our child's upbringing."

I stared at her blankly. It was almost as if she had been reading my mind.

"You didn't want to stay here did you," she asked bringing me back to reality. I burst out laughing.

Shaking my head, I told her, "I was worried that you wouldn't want to leave. After all, this has been your home your whole life. I couldn't see bringing myself to ask you to leave it all behind."

"I won't be leaving it all behind. In a way, this will always be my home. But my life is with you now. I know that this type of lavishness isn't what you're accustomed to. And I don't want to do anything to make you uncomfortable," she assured me. "Of course, that's not to say that the home we build will be as small as the one you grew up in. We will need space to raise the kids away from our laboratory."

"I suppose a little opulence won't kill me," I admitted. After a few seconds I asked, "kids?" Laughter is all I got in response.

Firestorm and his generals began planning for the upcoming war. Every day the troops were put through rigorous training exercises to prepare them for the arduous task that lay before them. Velouth kept in constant contact so the two armies would be better able to function as one. Asmeria's once maligned army had become a real fighting force thanks largely to the training Braveer and the company had given them.

Chooser and I were going over the plans for our future home when Gambit, a member of the company, arrived at Blendell. Braveer wanted me to know that the situation was not looking good. Every night there were larger and larger groups of Hellfire's minions testing the perimeter of the company's camp. Thirty brethren had been lost or severely wounded during these incursions. I thanked Gambit and summarily dismissed him. Chooser was appalled at my handling of the situation.

"How can you be so callous? These are the men you spent the last twenty-five years of your life with," she berated me.

"I don't see where I have much choice. My heart goes out to them, but I can't abandon you especially with our child growing nearer to delivery with each passing day. It tears me up knowing that so many of my friends have met an ill fate in my absence, but what can I do about it," I implored her.

"You can do what's right and rejoin them. I won't have the blood of your comrades on my consciousness, or yours. The staff here at the palace is more than capable of helping me deliver our child when the time comes. In fact, I think I would prefer it if you weren't here when the time comes," she retorted. I sensed she was lying about the last but didn't express it.

I stood there staring at her, trying to gage whether or not her words were true or that which she wanted me to hear. I took a minute to collect my thoughts before I spoke again.

"There is nothing on this world or the next that could keep me from your side when our child is being born. But since it is your wish that I come to the aid those that I have spent the better part of my life with, I shall. However, I am going to make a teleportation bracelet that will bring me back here so that I can be here for the arrival of our child. You may object to this, but I'm still going to do it so learn to like it," I put forth boldly.

"You don't know how to make a teleportation bracelet," Soulbinder sent.

'No, but you do. You can teach me, or is that against the rules,' I asked. She hesitated then agreed that she could and would.

I found a desk at which I could write down the procedure for creating the bracelet. First, I had to get a list of materials needed for such a venture. Most were readily available in any marketplace. The one crucial item not to be so readily found was a gemstone fifteen carat in weight and of perfect clarity. After writing out the full procedure, I stared at the list, in particular the gemstone. Chooser came up behind me and put her hands on my shoulders, leaned over, kissed me then read what I had written. She laughed out loud slightly, noticeably trying hard to contain herself.

"I don't suppose you can tell me where you plan on finding a fifteen-carat gemstone of perfect clarity," she giggled as if amused. Almost instantly an image flashed into my mind. The image was that of Dragore's lair. I had been so enthralled with the sheer enormity of the beast that I hadn't really paid attention to the rest of the lair. The image that flashed in my mind showed me that the floor was literally littered with gemstones. It was obvious to me that Soulbinder had sent me the image. I smiled at the thought.

"Simple," I replied. "I'll just have to pay another visit to Dragore. I'm sure that with all the stones she has laying around her lair one of them will be suitable for the task."

Her complexion visibly paled at the mention of going to visit the beast. She looked truly worried that something might happen to me. I was touched, and slightly amused.

"Don't worry sweetheart, I'll be on my best behavior. I'll ask her if such a stone is within her possession and if so, what I might need do to acquire it. I promise I won't take any foolish chances," I assured her. "You need to relax. I'll get your assistant to fix you a hot bath. That should help."

"You're staying out of Dragore's lair would help," she snapped, annoyed at my pandering.

"It's either that or I stay here. I'm not leaving without some way of returning here quickly. Becoming my namesake and flying it's still a journey of three days from the plains, that's far too long. I can be to Dragore's lair in just over twelve hours flying at breakneck speed. I'd be back before dawn. You'd hardly know I was gone. But the choice is yours," I said leaving the final decision up to her. She bowed her head in apparent sorrow, or defeat, collected herself for a moment then looked me in the eyes.

"Go," she said firmly. "But if anything happens to you there will be hell to pay." I smiled and took her in my arms.

"Do you know that I love you with every fiber of my being," I asked as I looked down into those sparkling green eyes. She smiled, we kissed then I was off.

I'm sure I created quite a commotion as I left Blendell. It isn't every day that a flaming bird goes streaking across the sky. The cattle in the fields, just outside the city walls, scattered as I flew by. I suppressed the urge to buzz them and made a mad dash for Dragore's lair. True to my word, it had taken me just shy of twelve hours to reach my destination. The sun was just setting as I landed.

"You may enter, Phoenix," boomed inside my head as I neared the opening.

"I apologize for this unexpected and uninvited visit," I told her as I entered the lair.

"Who said it was unexpected. You will find the stone you seek in the pile to your right," she said nonchalantly.

"You knew I'd be here for this," I asked incredulously as I picked up a stone that seemed to fit my needs. She laughed and the mountain seemed to shake.

"Forgive me. But you must understand, from my perspective this has already happened at least a dozen times before. Someday you will come to understand what I am telling you. For now, take the stone with my blessing. But don't dally. If you wait too long the balance will be irrevocable thrown off. Now go," she commanded. I literally flew the coop, having no idea what the majority of the conversation was about.

I landed on the balcony to our quarters. I tried to be as quiet as I could so as not to disturb my hopefully still sleeping wife. As I entered, I spotted a figure standing over Chooser with a drawn blade, preparing to strike. Instinctively I drew Soulbinder and leaped at the intruder, slicing downward as I neared this would be assassin. There was a loud baleful scream as the blade passed through him before he could strike. The visage vanished without a trace. Chooser sat bolt upright clutching the covers. I frantically searched for any signs of the intruder or any accomplices that he might have.

After several minutes, Firestorm and several guards burst into our chambers. Chooser, gaining her composure and her senses cast a light spell, illuminating the area that we might see what it was we were after. One of the guards found a blade on the floor near the bed where I had struck at the assailant.

"Look sire," he said bending to pick up the blade. He grabbed the hilt before I could warn against doing so. There was a burst of power of a type none of us were familiar with, the guard was reduced to ashes. The blade itself was of a design and origin unbeknownst to any of us.

"Whomever or whatever it was that wielded that blade is gone. I doubt they'll be quick to return," I said sheathing Soulbinder. "I need to get some rest. I've had a long day. If you'll excuse us," I added ushering the others out of our quarters.

"Of course," Firestorm said as he helped usher out the guards. "I want the palace guards doubled and put on increased alert…" he was saying as I closed the doors.

I turned to find Chooser examining the weapon. She seemed enthralled with it. I put an arm around her shoulder and reached for the weapon. The danger I had sensed before the guard had grabbed it was gone. I cautiously grasped its hilt. Only while holding its hilt could I discern the runes floating on its blade, this weapon had been made by a wizard of at least the ninth circle. Such weapons were extremely rare, as they required an enormous amount of time and energy to make. Few wizards had the desire to give up such precious commodities to make such weapons. Those weapons that are made fetch a high price at market.

I didn't recognize the signature of the crafter. I wondered if he could be the same wizard who had struck at us several months earlier at my parent's farm. It was something that would need to be investigated after I had time to rest. I took the blade from Chooser and placed it on the desk. I stared at it a moment, then quickly drew a pentagram on the desk, complete with all the symbols for entrapping, then placed the blade inside the pentagram. I simply wasn't going to take any chances.

Before turning in, I set up glyphs of protection on the balcony. I was almost certain that the intruder had had to of come in through the same doors I had. Anyone else trying to repeat the effort would be in for a rude awakening. Feeling only slightly at ease, I led Chooser to our bed. We held each other tightly until I fell asleep.

It was midmorning when I awoke. Evidently Chooser had been up for some time. She had managed to decipher all of the runes etched into the blade. They tended to serve two purposes. The first was the ability of the wielder to move stealthily amongst even the lightest sleeper without arousing the sleeper. The second was to keep the wielder loyal to the creator.

The latter was a vital clue. Such spells had a limited life span. That is to say that the spells would only last as long as the creator of the spell lived. Upon the casters demise the blade would turn to dust. This told us that the caster we sought not only lived but had commanded the wielder to assassinate Chooser. This made finding him all the more urgent.

I gathered the blade and my supplies for making the bracelet and headed towards the palace laboratory. I would first create the bracelet I had originally planned on making then I would divine the blade and see what the wizard I sought looked like. I intended on making losing the blade a fatal error for him. If he was the wizard that had attacked us before, then he had had too many chances already. If not, then the one chance he took was one too many. Either way, he or she had to die.

Creating the bracelet had taken more out of me than I had anticipated it would. Soulbinder laughed at my gullibility. I simply stared at the blade that I wished to divine, hoping against hope that the answer would leap out at me. It didn't. I would need to nourish myself, and then rest. This meant that I would lose valuable time. I begrudgingly gave in to the inevitable. I drew a pentagram of binding on the floor of the lab and placed the blade inside it. I then placed glyphs around the room to keep out any who would disturb the blade. I placed more glyphs on the door to the lab after closing it. Only Chooser, Firestorm, I, or another initiate of the ninth circle would be able to enter without fear.

I made my way to our quarters trying not to look as weak as I felt. Inside, Chooser ushered me to a bench laden with pillows. "You look as if you've been drained by a succubus," she told me.

"That's a relief. I thought I'd look like death warmed over me," I quipped in retort. She then went into our kitchen and surprisingly quickly returned with a meal. "Using magic to fix meals now," I asked somewhat surprised at the implications.

"Don't be foolish. This is the meal I made for our dinner that I already ate, and you missed. I kept it ready just in case you might be hungry," she defended herself and berated me.

I apologized and thanked her for the meal, which I dug into ravenously. After eating, I lie back onto the pillows and fell asleep almost instantly. I awoke in the middle of the night. I was slightly disoriented, and it took several moments for me to gain my bearing. I found my way to our bed.

The moon Crothos was full and bathed the bed in its light. I stood there awestruck by the beauty lying there. "What did I do to deserve you," I asked in a whisper not wishing to disturb her.

"You found me on an altar," Soulbinder sent. I couldn't help chuckling. I glanced sideways at the scabbard next to what had become decidedly my side of the bed. "Levity makes the world a better place. At least I think so," she sent.

"Goodnight," I whispered as I climbed in beside Chooser.

"Goodnight," Chooser said as she rolled over towards me putting her arm across my chest. At this I smiled.

I awoke at dawn and skipped breakfast making a beeline for the lab. A quick glance assured me that my glyphs were still intact and undisturbed. A quick gesture and they were dispelled. I opened the door and stood there dumbfounded. All the protections were active. The pentagram radiated the power I had imbued it with, yet the blade was nowhere to be seen. I thought for a moment then began muttering the words of a finding spell. The power coalesced around me and spread to every corner of the room. It continued outward until it encompassed the entire city of Blendell. This was the limit of my ability to search. The blade was not to be found.

I stood there contemplating what to do next. It didn't make sense. The blade, for all intent and purposes, had simply vanished into thin air. The pentagram was supposed to prevent anyone from magically whisking it away. I double-checked and triple checked the spells on the pentagram. They were correct and fully intact. This meant that the blade had had to be physically removed from the pentagram, which meant that somehow, someone had entered the lab and took it.

I quickly made my way upstairs. Chooser wasn't in our quarters. I searched and finally found her in her brother's quarters. They were eating breakfast together along with Lindeth, Mildeth and Rockner. I burst into the room unexpectedly and it was evident that my countenance showed my concern. "I don't know how, but it's gone," I blurted.

"What's gone," Chooser asked confused but concerned.

"The blade from the other night. I left it in the lab under protection of spells and it's gone. I can't explain it. Somehow, someone got past my spells and removed it without being detected," I explained.

They stopped eating and got up from the table. We made our way back to the lab as quickly as was possible. We entered cautiously. I watched as each of them examined the scene of the crime. Mildeth and Rockner stayed outside, feeling the power radiating from the still intact spells that I had put in place to protect the now missing blade.

Firestorm, Lindeth and Chooser looked up at me and shook their heads as dumbfounded as I had been. They had each double-checked my work. The spells I had put in place should have insured that the blade wouldn't be disturbed in my absence, yet they hadn't. Chooser set about casting a finding spell, just as I had when I first discovered the blade was missing. Like me she allowed the power to encompass the entire city. Like me, she found nothing. Once out of the trance of the spell, she looked at me and shook her head signifying her failure to locate the blade.

"Let's look at this logically," Firestorm suggested. "We know that the blade is missing. We also know that it couldn't have been taken by magic alone. Someone had to remove it from that pentagram, which means that they had to have been inside this room. To get into this room they had to get past the spells that barred them from entry, which means they either had to have used spells of greater power or they had to be on another plane, at least partially." It was like being hit by a sledgehammer. I looked again at the spells I had set in place and realized that I had overlooked that one small tidbit. Plane shifting.

I shook a finger at Firestorm as I began muttering in the ancient language of magic. Had anyone entered the room via another plane of existence, their movement from that plane to this could easily be traced. A second circle initiate could easily cast a spell of deflection allowing the intrusion of one plane to another. In mere moments we had the riddle of how the intruder had gotten into the lab. The plane shift was quite evident. The real surprise was that there had only been one shift. This could only mean that the blade had existed on both this plane and the other plane it had been taken to. If it hadn't, the intruder would have had to enter this plane to lift the blade out of the pentagram.

I stared at each of them intently. It was now clear that our adversary was truly gifted. Magical weapons that existed on multiple plains were the rarest magical items to exist. Whereas normal magical weapons took months, sometimes years to create, those on multiple plains could take decades.

"Look at it this way, we're younger and more vibrant than our unknown opponent," I said trying to inject some humor into a humorless situation. No one laughed. Our enemy had us on multiple accounts. He knew who we were, was probably older and thus more experienced than us, and he knew where to find us.

"You'd best be going. Your friends need you," Chooser told me breaking the silence.

"Do you really think that I'll be able to leave knowing all that we have learned in the past two days," I asked showing my concern.

"Maybe your staying is what he or she or it wants. Maybe they want to be able to cripple the company making it that much harder for us to win. In any case, your place is with those men who stood by you all those years. I'll be fine. Firestorm and I can handle this coward should he strike again. Besides, you now have the bracelet to bring you back here should the need arise," she said fondling the new piece of jewelry adorning my wrist. I looked into her eyes and she kissed me, breaking my resolve. Yeah, I'm a real powerful wizard. She could make me do whatever she wished, and she knew it. So, did I and I was still helpless to prevent it.

I looked Firestorm in the eyes and told him, "Don't let anything happen to her in my absence."

"Count on it," he assured me. With that I made my way to the nearest exit. Once outside I performed my transformation magic and flew off toward the Plains of Dread.

Chapter 10

Rejoining the Company

AS I NEARED the plains, I spotted a small village. I swooped down and assumed my natural form. It seemed that all of the citizens of the village had witnessed my approach and while staring at me intently, they provided me with a wide berth to pass through.

I was about to enter the stable to inquire about purchasing a horse for the final leg of my journey and ran into Gambit coming out. "Slasher…I mean Phoenix," he gasped smiling broadly. The stable master heard him and stumbled back in awe. Someday I would have to find out how my reputation had come to frighten people so readily. As a mercenary I had killed far more people than I had as a wizard. In fact, with a limited exception, all those I had slain as a wizard had been nonhuman creatures whose diets tended to consist of humans.

"What are you doing here? I thought you were staying with Chooser until the baby was born. Did she have the baby? What is it," he asked without taking a breath.

The stable master's jaw dropped. News of Chooser's and my union hadn't yet become common knowledge.

"No, she hasn't given birth yet. She insisted I come. She couldn't bear the thought of you guys dying while I stood by and did nothing. She said she would've blamed herself if I didn't come and you guys were wiped out to a man. I tried to assure her that you guys could handle it without me, but you know how women are," I explained not taking my eyes off of the stable master. He looked vaguely familiar. I shook it off as fatigue from nearly three days of flying as a phoenix.

"You are heading back to camp now," I asked.

"Uh… yeah. I was just checking on my horse. It sort of came up lame as I got here. He says it's gonna have to be put down," he replied indicating the stable master.

"Oh Really? Let me see it. You never know, sometimes a wizard can fix things that seem unfixable," I suggested realizing where I had seen the stable master before.

"He's right in here," Gambit said showing me into the stables.

"There's really nothing anyone can do," the stable master assured me backing into the stalls while feebly attempting to bar my path though trying to appear not to so as to not offend.

"You know, when I first arrived here, and Gambit called my name I thought you recognized me by my reputation. It took me a little bit to realize that you recognized me from the same place I now recognized you, in Rin north of Grendale. What's it been, fifteen years ago," I grilled him. "Yeah that sounds about right to me," I continued. "That was about three years before you joined the company," I informed Gambit.

"Cyclops, Hermit and I were on one of recon missions when my horse suddenly came up lame just outside of Rin. We were planning on only passing through, but with my horse lame, we would have to secure another form of transportation for me. The stable master here was working there at that time and informed us that my mount would have to be put down, but he had a fine horse he could sell us for only three platinum coins. Of course that was all the cash we had on us and I thought that it was fortuitous that we had just enough cash to purchase the steed," I continued while steadily making my way towards the stall where Gambit's mount was.

"I...I...I have a really fine animal for sale for only fifteen gold pieces," the stable master stammered as I let my story lag.

"Imagine, if you can, my surprise when two days later the steed I had purchased transformed magically back into the steed I had been riding to begin with," I finished as we reached the stall with Gambit's mount. I smiled because I could feel the magic radiating from the beast within.

The stable master held his ground. He still hadn't recognized me from my reputation. Fifteen years ago, I had been a mere mercenary, having sworn not to utilize magic. I was an easy mark back then. While Cyclops and Hermit were free to utilize whatever magics they wished, they hadn't had reason to suspect a scam.

I allowed a ball of power to form in my hand. The stable master paled. I grinned. His turning white told me that this act, while effortless for those above the sixth circle, was beyond him. I allowed the ball to float over toward the horse in question. It interacted with the power surrounding the horse and as a result both were nullified.

Gambit, although a bit slow, finally realized what I was telling him, drew his sword and put it under the stable master's chin. I walked over and pushed the blade down.

"That won't be necessary," I said. "He knows that the table has turned on him, and that he's outclassed. He won't give us any trouble. Will you," I asked rhetorically. The stable master stumbled back shaking his head. "In fact, I suspect that he's probably gonna want to make amends for scamming me fifteen years ago by supplying me with a horse at no charge, hmm?" He nodded in agreement.

I looked around the stable and found a suitable mount. "I'll take this one," I informed him.

"And I'd suggest getting out of Asmeria. If I run into you again, I might not be as cordial," I warned him. "Perhaps you'd enjoy going to the coast," I suggested, the nearest of which was three thousand miles away. He started to stammer pleading his innocence, thought better of it, and fled.

We saddled our mounts and prepared to head to the company's camp. I tied the reigns of my steed on his saddle horn. I hadn't rested in far too long and had long ago learned how to sleep in the saddle. I fully intended to utilize this skill once again, knowing that Gambit would wake me should the need arise.

"Phoenix, wake up," Soulbinder told me. I awoke to see the company's camp stretched out before us. The sun was just setting as we rode in. My once fearful brethren clambered around expressing their gratitude at my coming. Braveer beamed from ear to ear as I rode up to the command tent.

"It's really good to see you," he said wrapping his arms around me in a bear hug. "But to be honest, I didn't think you'd actually come, what with the baby being due any day now."

"To be truthful, I turned you down at first. Chooser insisted that I would regret it if anything happened and I wasn't here to help. I knew she was right, but damn I hated leaving her," I replied.

"Can't say that I blame ya there," he admitted.

"So, tell me about these raids that have left so many dead or injured," I said as we entered the command tent. He went on to fill me in about each of the raids and how they had tried to prepare for each successive attack only to be taken by surprise every time. As I listened, I got the distinct feeling that magic played a bigger part in the attacks than I had first given it credit for.

Hermit and Cyclops entered the command tent as Braveer was finishing recanting the events of the last two weeks. I smiled in acknowledgement of their arrival but continued to pay attention to the commander.

"After last night's raid, Cyclops found something he said you would be able to determine the origin of. Cyclops show him the blade you found," Braveer ordered. Cyclops proceeded to pull a blade out of his pouch of holding, a magically enhanced bag that enabled its wielder to carry large objects within it without being encumbered by the large object. I was thoroughly shocked to see the blade that the, would-be assassin had attempted to kill Chooser with. If it wasn't the same blade, it was its twin.

"Where did you get this," I asked anxiously.

"An assassin attempted to kill the commander the other night. I happened to be coming over to ask about a furlough, which I still didn't get and stopped him," he explained and complained. I smiled at the grimace on Braveer's face at Cyclops' explanation of why he had been there to save the grizzled old commander.

"Let me guess, when you slew the assassin, he vanished leaving only this blade behind," I asked.

"That's right. How did you know," Cyclops asked?

"A similar event happened the other night in my own quarters. I interrupted an assassin attempting to kill Chooser with this same blade. I had it in the castle's lab under spell until I could divine its origin, but it vanished before I had the chance," I explained.

"Are you sure it's the same blade," Hermit asked shocked.

"No. I can't be absolutely positive that it's the same blade. But I find it highly unlikely that the wizard who made it would have the time or inclination to make two blades that straddled multiple planes of existence," I replied. At that revelation they looked totally dumbfounded.

"Unfortunately for the owner of this weapon, I managed to rest on my journey here and I will be divining this thing tonight," I stated boldly.

I felt it almost too late. "Look out," I screamed pushing Braveer to the ground as a bolt of power tore through the tent smashing into the ground where we had been standing. I drew Soulbinder from her scabbard with my right arm, as was my custom. Almost instantly pain shot up my left arm starting from the blade that I was holding in that hand. A tentacle of power shot out of Soulbinder's blade and encapsulated the blade in my left hand. Instantly the pain subsided. With the pain gone, I searched the area for the source of the attack but had been forced to wait too long. The trail was gone.

"Did either of you see where that bolt came from," I asked my two cohorts. They shook their heads. The bolt had stunned them. My powers had shielded me from the stunning affect. They weren't powerful enough to have such protection.

'What is this thing? I mean where is it from,' I asked Soulbinder.

"Think of it as a wraith blade," she explained. "It was created by a wizard from both your plane and mine. Only, my plane hasn't existed since the game began."

'Are you telling me that someone is straddling two planes, but one of those planes no longer exists?'

"No. I'm saying that that blade is straddling two planes, one of which no longer exists," she replied.

'How is that possible,' I had to ask.

"The masters of the game are allowing it. That's the only way possible," she stated flatly.

'And this doesn't break protocol? There's no rules against it in the game,' I asked more than slightly perturbed.

"Apparently not," she replied.

I looked up to see Braveer, Hermit and Cyclops looking at me oddly. A host of company men had gathered round to see what had transpired and were marveling at my seemingly lack of higher functioning. I sheathed Soulbinder. Her tentacle of power dissipated instantly and was no longer needed. It seemed the pain was a direct result of having both blades drawn at once.

I looked at Cyclops and Hermit. "Are you two up to guarding me while I divine this thing," I inquired rhetorically.

"Lead on," Cyclops said feigning a courtesy.

"We'll need some horses. If this goes wrong, it's gonna make quite a mess of things," I informed them.

"Things being us," Hermit put in. He wasn't wrong.

We rode out back toward Asmeria. After an hour or so of riding, I figured we were far enough from the company to be able to divine the blade without risk of wiping out the company with us should things go wrong. I set about preparing to cast the spell that would unravel the spells that made the blade while my cohorts set out putting up glyphs to help keep any would be intruders away.

"Give me to one of them to hold," Soulbinder ordered.

'Excuse me,' I retorted.

"I would be of greater service to this endeavor in the hands of someone capable of wielding me should an assault occur while you're busy divining that weapon. Don't worry, they won't be able to keep me," she said making it sound like I was only concerned with possessing her. I chuckled at the thought. I looked over at my two friends trying to gage which would be better able to wield Soulbinder should the need arise. I instantly thought how stupid that thought was and proceeded to give the blade to Cyclops. Hermit was the stronger of the two and would better compliment Cyclops with his own power.

"Cyclops, this is Soulbinder. The power encased within makes me look weak. It would be best if someone were able to wield her in case we're attacked. I'll be too involved with the task at hand, so I am letting you hold it in my stead. But don't get the wrong idea. She will be coming back to me once I've finished the casting and have regained my strength," I informed him handing him my sword still in its case. He went to unsheathe her and received a nasty jolt for his efforts. "I said only in case of an emergency," I scolded. I could hear Soulbinder laughing in my head, literally.

Just as with Soulbinder, the divining of this blade was a tricky and tedious procedure. The spells that wrapped themselves around this steel were a delicate mix of two opposing forms of magic. It seemed to take forever, but finally I was through to the first spell cast upon the blade. I felt myself once again being sucked back in time to the forging of the blade itself. This was even stranger than the forging of Soulbinder's blade, for this took place on two planes simultaneously. Two wizards each took turns striking the metal while chanting to each other and the blade before them. I didn't recognize the larger of the two men, the smaller had been in the palace with Destroyer's general, and I recognized the forge as being the one where Firewind, Destroyer and myself were taught the craft in our youth. I forced myself back to myself.

Back in the here and now, I stood up took three steps and collapsed. I should have known that I had spent a great deal of energy, more so than it felt like I had. My sidekicks picked me up and hauled me to my bedroll. "Put that back in your bag," I told Cyclops. The blade had been safe there before I figured it would be so again. I then fell into a deep sleep.

"Show me what you saw," Soulbinder demanded. I looked into her eyes. A storm of power flashed within them.

"Not even a hello, how are you? 'Show me what you saw' is how you invade my dreams," I asked feigning indignity.

"I already checked you out, you're fine. In need of some rest but perfectly healthy. Now then, show me," she demanded. I let my mind go back to the forge and the two men working the same blade on differing planes. "Drendar," she muttered.

"You know him," I asked. She nodded in the affirmative.

"I don't understand. He wasn't made a part of the game. Why is he making a blade with a wizard of this realm? And to what end," she asked just as confused as I felt.

"I couldn't tell you. But I know who can," I suggested pointing to the other wizard in the picture.

"Yes, but we still don't know who he is or where to find him," she retorted sounding more than a little dismayed.

"Maybe not. But I know where he's been. I'd recognize that forge anywhere. I learned the art of imbedding magic on steel there when I was seven. I'm betting that once there we should be able to use the blade to help us trace his movements and finally pinpoint his current location," I suggested.

Her countenance visibly improved. "If you weren't a married man and I wasn't trapped in this sword I still wouldn't kiss you, but I'd think about it," she quipped.

"First things first, we have to secure the company's position to help prevent any further incursions. I'm just hoping that no one was killed in our absence," I demanded.

"That sounds like a reasonable request. However, if we find the wizard responsible for the attacks, we can stop them completely and therefore wouldn't need to secure the camp," she countered.

"True, but we don't know how long finding said wizard is going to take. There's no telling how many attacks he can muster between now and then. Therefore, protecting the camp comes first," I countered back.

"Okay. We'll let you do it your way," she relented. I waited for the next argument that never came and drifted off into a real dream.

We arrived back at the company's camp just after daybreak. All the sentries and all the men wandering the camp looked sullen. Few, if any, looked us in the eyes. I got the feeling that there had been another attack and more of our brethren had perished. I soon found out that my feelings were once again right, damn them.

"We really could have used you guys around here last night," Braveer told us solemnly.

"I gathered as much from the mood of the men. Who bought it," I asked for all of us.

"Shameer, along with a dozen others," came the reply. It hit us like a ton of bricks. I suddenly felt the weight of the world upon my shoulders. Of all the brethren I had expected to hear of being killed, his was second to last on my list of those I expected would. Braveer of course is the last person in the company I expect to die. Not that he's immortal or any other rational explanation like that, he's just too damn ornery.

This new situation changed things. I had a new priority. Those who killed Shameer had gotten away with it. That is, they had gotten out of camp alive, or undead, whichever the case may be. I wasn't about to let one of my close friend's death go unavenged.

"Take me to where he fell," I commanded in a tone that spoke volumes of my hurt and anger. I looked Braveer in the eyes. He had been ready to question my motives, my countenance made him do otherwise. They led me to where Shameer had been slain.

There was a trace of blood on the ground, which told me that a weapon of some sort had been used to kill him.

I scooped up the dirt with the blood and began to chant an old hunter's spell. Not too many people hunted for food these days with all the farming that was being done. These spells were all but forgotten. I had hunted with Firewind in our early teens. I tend not to forget spells once I've mastered them.

The power emanated from the blood and sought out other sources of the same blood. The most powerful emanations went straight to where Shameer's body now lay. The second trail, very faint, led off into the plains. This trial was the one I wanted. It would lead me to the weapon that had been used to slay Shameer.

"Cyclops! Gather a dozen horses and men to ride them. I'm going to follow this trail the best way I can think of, as a phoenix. In that form I will be better able to see the path and move quicker. You should be able to follow my heat trail," I instructed. "Of course, if you take too long, I'll just have to kill them all myself."

"This is not what we discussed," Soulbinder objected.

"No, but it's what we're doing," I sent back.

I transformed myself quickly into the bird of prey I was named after and set off following the magical trail following Shameer's blood on the weapon that slew him. In my human form the trail was faint, barely visible. But to the eyes of a phoenix, it glowed brightly, beckoning me forth. Who or whatever was behind these attacks on the company's camp may have thought themselves cleaver in not being caught and inflicting more damage than they had so far received, but they were now in for a rude awakening. I found that I could still see the trail even at great heights. This allowed two things to happen. One, I could see which direction I would be heading in for a greater distance, and two, Cyclops and those riding with him could see me from a greater distance, making it easier to follow me.

I was somewhat surprised to see that my destination wasn't really that far at all. A small keep lay two horizons from the company campsite. It was there that the trail ended. I landed at its doorway transforming myself back to myself as I did so. I could sense the power guarding the door from would be intruders. It was of a great enough magnitude to bar even me from entering through said doorway. I scanned the entire building as only a wizard could and smiled. All of the entrances were similarly protected, but not the walls themselves.

I stepped away from the building and began to chant in the ancient language that channeled my powers into their potent form. This was a spell I had learned in a dream, while being ensnared in a trap at a great library. As the power began to emanate from me and coalesce around the building, the ground itself began to tremble.

For that was the nature of this spell. It weakened the ground, the very foundation upon which this building harboring my enemies was built upon. The trembling grew into violent shaking until the building started crumbling. Little pieces began to fall away, followed by bigger pieces until the whole of the building collapsed, except the magically protected entrances, which stood unscathed.

Cyclops and the others rode up as the dust was beginning to settle. Some of the bricks began to move as those trapped beneath them, and still able to do so, began to claw their way out from under the rubble. As the survivors clawed their way out of the rubble, the company men attacked them ferociously. Their anger and fear of the past few weeks turned them into violent killing machines. I let them vent their anger.

Suddenly a large area of stones flung themselves into the air as though being flung by a great power. A great plume of dust arose from this area keeping us from ascertaining what had been the cause or results. A figure strode from the dust, a sword in one hand, power balled in the other. I drew Soulbinder and prepared my own ball of power to combat this as yet unknown enemy.

We released our power at each other nearly simultaneously. The two powers met in the middle and canceled each other out. It appeared that we were of equal strength, though his magic was of a darker nature. I recognized the power he was emitting, from when he had attacked me anonymously. I stood my ground allowing him to close the gap between us. I recognized him as the wizard I had seen creating the blade in Cyclops' pouch with the wizard from Soulbinder's plane. The sword in his hand was obviously one of her other siblings. I unleashed another bolt of power, as did he, and then our blades took charge.

We seemed to be locked in an unending struggle. Each move was countered. Each spell was canceled. I was beginning to wonder which of us would succumb to fatigue first. Then inexplicably, my bolt slammed into his face. It was at this point that Soulbinder's power overtook her sibling. With its wielder incapacitated, it could no longer protect itself from her wrath and mine. Great beams of multicolored light shot from her to her sibling. It climaxed in a blinding flash, followed by a loud explosion whose shockwave knocked all but me off of their feet. When our sight returned, we could see that she had completely decimated her rival sibling.

Out of the battle, my body no longer generated the adrenalin that had sustained me. I staggered backward and fell to one knee. I leaned on Soulbinder's blade to steady myself. I looked up at the charred body of the wizard and half chuckled at the sight of what had given me the advantage I needed to end the combat. It was the very blade he had helped create. Cyclops had returned it to him by sticking it into his back.

I looked around at the gaping faces of my comrades. They were all in shock at the display of power Soulbinder had put on in eliminating her sibling. I was surprised to see Braveer and an additional thirty men had arrived at some point while I was busy doing combat. I looked Cyclops in the eyes and mouthed the word thanks.

"We tried to help, but our weapons kept bouncing away," I heard Spinner ramble. "You have to believe me Slasher, I mean Phoenix. We really tried to help." I smiled, put a hand on his shoulder, and pulled myself back to my feet.

"We generate a shield that only a powerful weapon can penetrate," Soulbinder sent.

"I believe you," I assured Spinner.

I walked over to the fallen wizard and retrieved the blade from his back. 'The wizard from your plane apparently is still living,' I sent to Soulbinder.

"That one at least," she replied sadly. I had forgotten that she had just slain one of her siblings, it must have been another brother. "My oldest brother, Lexstar," she explained. "He was probably the strongest of us," she lamented.

"We'd best be heading back to camp," Braveer ordered. I nodded in agreement. I had just swung up into the saddle when the bracelet I had made just prior to heading here began to glow. I felt the tingle of magic being activated and before I could say anything to anyone, I was teleported back to Blendell.

I found myself standing at the foot of our bed. Chooser lay upon the bed sweating and breathing heavily. Lindeth and two other women, midwives, were standing at her side. She was in labor.

"I'm here my love," I said as I started walking around the bed. That was the last thing I remembered until I awoke laying on the bed beside Chooser and our son. I had weakened myself more than I had imagined. Both Soulbinder and Chooser explained this to me as soon as the cobwebs cleared from my head.

Firestorm and Lindeth came in, each carrying trays of food one for Chooser and one for me. It's not every man that can claim to have been served by a king. I of course would never tell anyone out of respect for my brother-in-law.

"You need to eat, to regain your strength," they said simultaneously. They then looked at each other and smiled at the happenstance. It was obvious that they were as much in love as Chooser and I were.

"Shouldn't you be taking it easy," I suggested to Lindeth. "After all, you'll be giving birth here before too long," I explained.

"You're not very observant," Soulbinder sent as Lindeth giggled.

"She had her baby three days ago," Chooser explained. I felt my cheeks flush a little.

"Okay, so I'm not fully awake," I defended myself. "I did manage to kill the wizard who had sent the assassin that had made the attempt on your life," I told Chooser.

"More good news," Firestorm responded.

Taking that first bite made me realize how hungry I really was. I ate ravenously.

The baby started crying and Lindeth led Firestorm from the room so that Chooser could feed our son. I couldn't help but smile at the sight of the woman I loved feeding our son.

"We'll have to think of a name for him," she said looking up at me briefly. She kissed his head as he suckled her breast.

"Granger comes to mind," I suggested.

"Granger? Why Granger," she asked.

"It was Shameer's given name," I replied.

"Was," she half asked.

"We lost him the night that I spent with Hermit and Cyclops divining that blade the would-be assassin had tried to use against you," I explained.

"It wasn't your fault he died," she told me as though reading more into my statement than I had said.

"Maybe. But if I had let Cyclops and Hermit stay at the camp, they might have been able to protect him," I suggested.

"And just maybe you'd be mourning one of their deaths with or instead of his," she suggested.

"How did someone so young get to be so wise," I asked kissing her on her forehead.

"Good lineage," she replied. "And little Granger has inherited two good lines."

I got up and took our trays over to the table in the middle of our chambers. I then went back and lay back beside my wife and child. Before I knew it, I was again in a deep sleep. I slipped into a peaceful dream.

I dreamt I was back in my youth. I was following Firewind and Christina up a hill. It was a warm spring day. Firewind had heard of a small run-down castle that was once owned by a wizard who loved to transform himself into various beings and forms. Our powers were just starting to take on their full potency. Every powerful wizard before us, including our master, Cyclone, didn't develop their full potential until well into their thirties or forties. Our master often held us in awe for our youthful exuberance and skill at wielding the powers we possessed, for we were only thirteen at the time.

We found the castle in ruins. Only one room seemed to be still standing. I could see the powers that encased it from a distance. Still, it didn't intimidate me. There was no one about to wield the power therefore it was locked into its present form. I knew there had to be runes binding it to these walls. It would simply be a matter of deactivating the spells by reversing the runes in the proper order. For two young skilled wizards like us, it should be a snap.

Finding the runes proved to be problematic. It turned out that they were on the inside of the room, keeping everyone else out. The room had no windows, and only one visible door. The door had no handle or any markings on it whatsoever. Even the hinges were on the inside. Firewind decided to try to burn open the door with a spell. Christina and I stayed back out of harm's way. He took several moments to gather his strength and then unleashed a powerful fireball at the door. A big cloud of soot and ash flew back at him, covering him from head to toe. The door was unscathed. Christina laughed out loud. I had to bite my tongue to keep from doing likewise.

I spotted a tree nearby that looked easy to climb, so I did. I climbed until I was overlooking the walls of the room. I had to smile, for the room had no ceiling, no roof for that matter either. It looked to be completely empty, except for the power emanating from every crevice to protect it. I thought this was odd and leaped down into the room. I never made it. An invisible shield that carried an electrical shock sent me flying back over the wall. I was miraculously unharmed, except for my ego. Again, Christina laughed out loud, when she saw that I was unharmed and what I looked like after my encounter with the shield.

I gathered myself up and brushed myself off, unaware that my hair was sticking out in all directions. I risked leaning back against one of the walls to support my stance and fell backwards into the room. I looked around in great awe at the magnificent library that surrounded me. I wandered around the room, unaware that neither Christina nor Firewind were able to duplicate my actions. An open spell book on a pedestal caught my attention. The spell on the page gave instructions for turning into a great fiery bird of prey.

Next, I found myself standing on a hillside overlooking a great battlefield. Chooser and our son were there beside me. Below us were tens of thousands of men and other creatures engaged in an epic battle.

Swords clashed, arrows flew, and spells did too. Some of the spells were cancelled out by opposing wizards. Others wreaked havoc on unsuspecting and unprepared warriors. Fire and ice and lighting and numerous bolts of power flew back and forth from one side of the battlefield to the other.

Then I was in the middle of the field wielding Soulbinder, fighting Hellfire and casting spells. Suddenly Destroyer joined the fray and it became a three-way free for all.

Each of us knew that the only way to win was for the other two to die. No one could press an advantage for fear of being struck down by the unencumbered third party. I next saw Chooser weeping sorrowfully. I awoke in a cold sweat.

"Soulbinder, was that merely a dream or was that a vision of an upcoming battle?" I asked.

"I couldn't tell you. I don't invade your dreams. It may very well have been a vision, with dreams there really is no way of knowing," she replied.

"What do you mean you don't invade my dreams? You've invaded them at least ten times that I can remember," I reminded her.

"That's different. I had something to tell you, so those times don't count," she defended herself with typical female logic.

'Okay, then I'll fill you in,' I said as I proceeded to relay the contents of the dream I had just had.

Chooser shook my arm bringing me back to reality. "Sorry, I was discussing a dream I had with Soulbinder," I explained. I then had to tell her about the dream.

"I don't think it's necessarily a vision of things to come, but you can never eliminate a dream as a warning of things that might come to pass," Chooser remarked after my narration.

The preparations for war had gone on and were nearing completion. My son was now seven months old. I couldn't believe how alert he was. Everyone kept telling me not to expect too much from him at this young of an age, but I could sense the power surrounding and flowing through him. My son was bound for greatness. Providing I would be able to secure the present for him, he would have a bright future. His power would eclipse mine, his mother's and every other wizard born of this realm. Of that I had no doubts.

I joined Firestorm on the balcony overlooking the training field. Below us, twenty thousand troops, of an army of one hundred thousand, were busy practicing their trade. Archers were honing their skills with the bow, while swordsmen were being taught how to better wield the blades that were their craft. Calvary men practiced hitting targets with their lances and then quickly drawing the swords they carried incase their lances were broken or lost. Everyone seemed to be filled with optimism about the upcoming battles. I was dreading them. Not from fear for myself, but those I loved.

I looked off in the opposite direction, to the other side of the city at those practicing the crafts that would truly be the deciding factor in the upcoming war, magic. It had the capability to protect or destroy hundreds in an instant. These warriors were kept separate from the mundane soldiers. Simply seeing the devastating effect of some of the spells these wizards wielded could quickly demoralize an army.

I noticed that the wizards had separated into two groups. One group was casting spells of destruction, while the other was busy trying to neutralize the effects of the first. Occasionally a spell would get past the neutralizers and threaten to do real damage. At these times one of the wizard generals would step in and cancel out the spell himself. These were seventh and eighth circle initiates while the rest were sixth or lower.

"It would be nice if it really worked this way," I commented to Firestorm as I sampled a glass of tea he offered.

"What makes you think it won't," he asked. I looked him in the eye and realized he was serious.

"Ever been in a real battle before," I asked, knowing full well he hadn't. I sent a massive thunderstorm into the midst of the wizards. It wasn't my most powerful weather spell, but it took them some time to neutralize the effects. "Because in battle, nothing hardly ever goes as you plan it," I replied heading back into the castle.

"So, you're saying we shouldn't practice and plan," he asked sounding slighted.

"Not at all. I'm simply stating fact. Plan all you wish, just be prepared to be flexible with your plans in case the enemy doesn't do what you expect him to do, for they seldom do," I explained.

I went back to my quarters. Chooser was busy playing with Granger. Lindeth and Dahlia were there as well. Mothers it seemed love having other mothers around to share in the little moments that they always seem to believe are really big moments. The children were making all sorts of noises that someday would be words. I just hoped that they would have a world to grow up in that wasn't hell bent on its own destruction.

Chooser came over to me and began telling me about all the little things that I had missed in my absence. She then handed me a set of plans.

"What's this," I asked.

"Plans for our future home. I wanted you to see them before I gave the go ahead to start construction," she told me.

I couldn't help grinning. "Baby, if it makes you happy, and it's what you want, then it's what I want. As long as I have a place to lay my head, I'm happy and if you're by my side, then I'm satisfied," I said kissing her. She gave me that look women get when they can't figure out why a man can't think the way they do. I shrugged in response.

Chapter 11

Growing Evil

HELLFIRE AWOKE in the king's chamber of the palace of Dragonsvale. He looked at the decaying palace that was nearly as old as he was. Dragonsvale was an ancient city long since abandoned by the humans, dwarves and elves that had constructed it long ago. It had once been known as Dragon's end before it became a major metropolis. The ancient wizard Crelloth had slain a dragon on the spot.

Local residents began coming to the area to examine the remains, until an enterprising man built a barricade around them and charged admission fees. He became quite wealthy, giving others the idea to capitalize on the situation. First came an inn with a diner and tavern then other merchants began setting up shop as were their nature to do so. Before long, a wealthy city emerged until one day a palace was built around the remains and the metropolis of Dragonsvale was born.

Hellfire was a teenager as the palace took shape. He was enthralled with magic, dark magic to be precise. As Dragonsvale's population grew, more members of the arcane arts gathered, enabling Hellfire to gain in power. His power increased with each passing year. As his power increased, his body became ever frailer. He turned to ever darker magic to stave off death that visits everyone eventually.

Dragonsvale was at its peak of power at the same time Graveer was at its height. Hellfire had heard of the Library of magus that had been built there and fully intended to visit it once he had learned all he could in Dragonsvale. Unfortunately for him the great Dragore would unleash her wrath on humanity before he was ready to do so and all who knew of its location were slain, along with all of its inhabitants.

Walking down the great hallway that led to the throne room, he gazed at the tatters of once magnificent tapestries. When new, they depicted the destruction the dragon had wrought upon the countryside and the epic battle between the dragon and Crelloth. Others contained scenes from Dragonsvale's glory days as a mighty kingdom with a large mixed army of humans, elves, and dwarves. The kingdom lasted thousands of years until the mighty Dragore reduced it to the rubble of its current state. Hellfire had joined the wizards of the council to help defeat the beast, though many of the wizards objected to his presence there and he had fled before the final battle. He was himself thousands of years old by this time, relying on dark forces to keep him alive. Dark forces most feared to acknowledge existed, as though that would make them not real. He was living proof they did.

He entered the throne room, now his personal laboratory for conducting his dark magic. His apprentices were awaiting his arrival, several rushing to his side as he entered. Today was a special day. Today the twin counter rotating moons of the planet Asmodora, Crathos and Prothos, would simultaneously eclipse its sun an event that occurs only once every ten thousand years. Today he gathered his apprentices to perform a ritual that would restore his youth and vitality. He alone knew how to perform the ceremony that had prolonged his life for thousands of years.

The most powerful of his apprentices was neither human, nor goblin, nor orc though his mother was human his father was from a dark realm. Defiler's father was a being whose strength and age made Hellfire's appear to be an uninitiated infant. It was he who gave Hellfire the secret to prolonging his life. He had instructed Hellfire on finding him a suitable mate, and how to bring him forth so he could do so. Defiler, the offspring of that union, was to be Hellfire's apprentice, though without the ritualized oath of binding Hellfire had with his other apprentices. This ritual ensured none of his apprentices would ever attempt to overthrow him by binding their life force with his, should he die, they would also. Hellfire was allowed to encapsulate Defiler in a dampening field that would limit the amount of power he could wield while Hellfire lived, thus limiting him as a threat. Hellfire agreed to these terms having no real choice due to Defiler's father's immense strength.

A four-foot diameter pentagram adorned the center of the room, directly under the remnants of the glass dome that once constituted its ceiling. Arranged around the pentagram were thirteen adolescence, seven boys and six girls. Each child was laid down, hands above their heads, feet away from the pentagram. Each had been given a potion that paralyzed all but heart and lung functions.

Hellfire struggled to the center of the pentagram, looked up through the ceiling and waited anxiously. This was a ritual he had performed numerous times before, though this being the first with a simultaneous eclipse. Most often he would perform the ritual when the larger moon, Prothos, eclipsed the sun, which happens every twenty-seven years. The power of the ceremony returns him to a state similar to a man in his sixties, he was eager to see what would happen during a dual eclipse, when the dark forces would be at their peak.

As the moons reached the edge of the sun, it was time to make the final preparations. A silver coin was placed over each of the children's eyes. A bottle containing pungent oil was opened and a drop applied to their foreheads. As the suns light was blocked, Hellfire began reciting the words of the forbidden ritual. Dark forces began to envelope the young humans, swirling around them, becoming darker and swirling faster as Hellfire continued chanting the rites of the dark ritual. As the two moons completed eclipsing the sun, the life force energies of the children were pulled from their bodies and into the pentagram, then into Hellfire. Those present watched as his skin began to tighten and take on a youthful texture.

As abruptly as it began, the eclipse ended. As sunlight bathed the throne room again, a reinvigorated, youthful Hellfire stood in the pentagram. He gazed down at his body extremely pleased with the results. He was now ready to meet and either enslave or kill the young northern upstart Destroyer. He beckoned an apprentice who stood nearby holding a sword in a scabbard. He pulled the sword from the scabbard, pointed at one of the few remaining statues that once adorned the throne room and released a powerful bolt shattering it to pieces.

Hellfire assembled his forces, emptying out Dragonsvale of all of its current inhabitants. All save one. Defiler would have to be left behind due to the nature of his binding spell. The upcoming battle had the potential to sufficiently weaken Hellfire enough, even if only momentarily, to allow Defiler to overcome him and free himself from his servitude. Hellfire hadn't lived this long by taking such unnecessary risks.

Defiler watched as his master led his forces away to the north to find and defeat a young human wizard who dare try and stake his claim as the dominate one. Hellfire had been so kind as to grant Destroyer the right to remain ruler of his current domain, all he would have had to do was take a loyalty oath under ritual. Destroyer infected the messenger Hellfire had sent to him with the changeling disease. The messenger completed the transformation in front of Hellfire and nearly managed to injure him. Defiler had had to intercept the creature before it could reach him. The beast bit him, so Defiler returned the favor by ripping out its throat with his teeth. He was immune from the diseases of this world due to who his sire was.

With his master gone, Defiler had plenty of time to explore the place he called home. From the day he was born, he had never been left alone. Most of his time was spent perfecting his use of magic or honing his skills with various weapons. He knew that there were the remnants of a dragon in the dungeons of the lower levels of the palace and it was time he went to go see them.

The room in which the remains were housed was quite enormous. It had been built around the remains, first to create a tourist attraction, then as a laboratory for the manufacturing of potions and ointments from the various parts of the fallen beast. Little remained of the dragon except for the skull, which still lay where the dragon had fallen.

Entering the room, Defiler could feel immense power coming from the skull. This struck him as odd since the creature was quite dead and stripped of all but the bone itself. He began to circle the skull, trying to determine where the power was emanating from. After a few laps, he determined it wasn't actually emanating from the skull, but rather from below it. The skull weighed several tons, was impervious to everything that those who first encapsulated it had tried to use to move it. Defiler leaned against the skull, planted his feet, and gave a mighty shove. The skull moved barely an inch, but it had moved. He reset his feet, grabbed the bottom of the upper jaw where the long since missing teeth had once been, and attempted to flip it over. He entered a trancelike stage, gathering the dark from his father's realm, energy only he could summon, and in one swift seemingly effortless motion flipped the skull over. It rolled several times before coming to a rest upside down against the far wall.

He looked down to where the skull had once lay, trying to determine the source of the power he could sense. He brushed the dirt with his foot and discovered boards covering a hole that descended deep into the ground. He peered down the hole, then at the skull. The hole was unnatural, having been carved into the ground before the dragon fell, by who there was no way of knowing. Defiler was very large, standing over seven and a half feet tall. The hole was large enough for him to fit into, with a ladder that descended into its depths.

He descended the ladder until he came upon a tunnel from which the power, he had been trying to find emanated. He descended the tunnel until he encountered a set of large metallic doors with no handles or hinges in sight. The doors were adorned with runes from top to bottom. The runes weren't of a type used in this realm of existence. Defiler instinctively traced his fingers through the runes in a pattern that had flashed into his mind the moment he approached the doors. The doors split apart and slid into the walls on either side, revealing a large chamber with a glow emanating from a sword hovering over an altar in the center.

He entered the chamber cautiously, peering around, making sure there were no traps he might accidentally trip. Finding none he proceeded towards the altar. Raptor was carved into the altar. The power he could feel emanating from the blade dwarfed his own by many times over. He was mesmerized by it, and without the hesitation of thinking, he grabbed the hilt. Holding it in his hand he could sense an intelligent presence. He had had the same sensation once before, the one time he had dared touch his master's own sword.

Gazing at the blade, he could clearly see runes floating on its surface, though he couldn't discern their meaning. Whoever had created the blade was both skilled and powerful. He wondered how it had come to lie here in this long-hidden chamber and how long it had actually been there. Glancing around the room, he spied an intricately decorated scabbard that was obviously meant to sheath the sword. Placing the sword on the altar, he strapped the scabbard around his waist, picked up the sword and slid it into the scabbard.

He left the tunnel and made his way quickly to the library. It was quite an impressive library, eclipsed it was said, only by the library of magus in Graveer by the number of tomes and scrolls it contained. His master's personal journals from his thousands of years of existence were among the tomes contained within it. It was these tomes he had come here for, his master's sword was made by those who had made the one that now adorned his side, of this he was certain, and he hoped to find out more about it. Hellfire had told Defiler about finding the blade on an altar, just as he had now done. He doubted his master would have found such a powerful blade and not done some research and cast some spells on it to learn all he could about it. Just as he suspected, he found just what he had hoped to find, his master's attempts to communicate with the source of the intelligence he was sensing from within the sword. He was disappointed to see that all of his efforts had failed.

In the center of the library, on a pedestal covered in runes of power of elf, dwarf, and human origin, lay an amulet from which radiated immense magical energy. Defiler cautiously picked up the amulet of knowledge that heretofore only Hellfire had been allowed to touch. As he clasped the necklace holding the amulet around his neck, he was stunned to realize that the actual amulet and necklace still lay on the pedestal. He could instantly feel the amulet opening his understanding of the magic that enabled him to wear the amulet without actually wearing the amulet. As its name implied it imparted knowledge unto whoever wore it, though few beings possessed the strength and ability to do so. And there was currently no one around with the knowledge to remove the spells that kept the true amulet upon the pedestal it has rested upon for thousands of years.

He gazed around the library at the numerous tomes, knowing which he had already studied and which he hadn't noticed. The number he had were only a small fraction of those he hadn't. He glanced down at the sword and determined he would read them all if that were what it took to find a way to reach the intelligence in his sword. He started in an area that appeared not to have been disturbed since the library was built. He wondered if he could actually read them all before his master's return, being certain of his master's ultimate victory.

He came upon a tome titled forbidden dark magic. He thought it odd that they would retain a tome on forbidden magic, if it were forbidden why not destroy it? He attempted to open the tome and found it magically sealed. Gazing at the cover, he began to see runes swirling on the cover seemingly changing at random. He smiled as he recognized the same runes that had adorned the doors that had sealed the chamber where he had found the sword. Tracing them with his finger unlocked the tome allowing him to read its contents. He absorbed the spells eagerly. As he read on his power increased. He was feeling stronger than he ever had by the time he finished reading. The tome had contained many dark spells, most not from this realm.

It also contained knowledge of numerous creatures that dwelled in the bowels of the world. Some were neutral by nature, others dark. Among the neutral creatures, was a simple beast called a fireworm. These dwellers of the deep earth spent their time tunneling through the ground eating the minerals contained within it. The worms were exceptionally large and spewed fire from their orifices, anus while healthy and living, maw in their death throws while dying. These creatures could easily be controlled with little effort according to the tome.

Chapter 12

Off to War

I WAS CHECKING OUT the market early the next morning when I spotted the rider approaching the castle. I recognized his uniform as that of an Asmerian royal messenger. I followed him back to the castle. I caught up with him as he was finishing his delivery. He was escorted to a small chamber to await a reply. Firestorm spotted me and summoned me into his chambers behind the throne room. Several generals followed as well, while a servant was sent to summon Chooser and Lindeth. Firestorm studied a large map, similar to the one in Velouth's throne room while we waited for the others to arrive.

"Now that everyone's here, I can begin. Velouth has sent a message that Hellfire is on the move. Your company has been constructing defensive positions just beyond Asmeria's borders," he said addressing me. "It seems that Hellfire has gathered an extremely large fighting force. Initial estimates place it at over a quarter million strong. Destroyer is sending his men towards the plains even as we speak, his ships are sailing south on Lake Arness. It seems that it has finally begun. Whether our preparations are done or not, we must march tomorrow. Velouth has increased his strength to forty thousand. Our hundred thousand should join with them here," he continued pointing to an area on the map about forty miles off the plains of dread. I couldn't help but notice the area was quite hilly.

"It could still be just a coincidence," Soulbinder sent.

"Maybe," I replied. I looked at Chooser. She too noticed the hills displayed on the map. I gave a weak smile trying to ease the concern I could see welling up in her.

"While we're gone, we're going to need to train replacements to protect Anthgolia should we fail. Chooser, you have ample experience leading an army, so I leave it to you to gather reinforcements in my stead," he ordered. She shook her head no.

"I won't be able to help you there. You'll have to let Lindeth take care of that for you, I'll be with my husband," she informed him.

"And what of our child," I asked. She cocked an eyebrow in mock surprise.

"He'll be with us, of course," she responded.

I stared at her intently, trying to gage whether or not I could actually win this argument and get her to remain behind.

"No, you can't. That argument was lost the moment you told her about your dream," Soulbinder sent.

'Then why didn't you stop me from telling her,' I asked not expecting a reply. I was surprised when one wasn't forthcoming.

"My family will be safe with me," I assured Firestorm. He looked at me gauging whether or not he could convince me otherwise, and soon realized he couldn't. He turned to Lindeth and instructed her briefly on how to raise an army. He would be leaving her a half a dozen lesser officers to aid her in the task at hand. She too refused to comply.

"I'm just as strong as you are and would be of more use with you there than here. Dahlia will remain, for I can't see bringing her to a battlefield," she retorted taking a veiled swipe at Chooser. He stared at her intently, realized he couldn't win the argument, and finally selected a senior general to look after creating a force to defend Anthgolia in our absence.

We were dismissed as Firestorm picked up a quill and began penning a reply to send to Velouth. I took Chooser's arm and led her quickly up to our quarters.

"You know damn well that I don't want you anywhere near that battlefield," I told her as soon as we were in private.

"You know damn well that I'm not about to let you go off to battle and get yourself killed without being there to prevent it if I can," she retorted.

"And what of Granger? How do you plan on watching him and keeping him safe?" I asked?

"By keeping him near me, and," she said, grabbing the teleportation bracelet off my wrist, "sending him back here if it gets too dangerous there." I shook my head and grinned. I knew I was beat and there was no getting around it. I reached out and held her close.

"I'd never forgive myself if anything happened to either of you out there," I said kissing the top of her head. She pulled back and looked up at me.

"Now you know how I feel," she stated simply. A few seconds later, Lindeth and Firestorm knocked on our door.

"How can you let her go into a battle where we'll be outnumbered nearly four to one," Firestorm demanded as they entered. Chooser grabbed his arm and spun him toward her.

"He isn't letting me do anything! I decide where I go and when I go where I go! I can't believe that you have the gall to come into my chambers and try to belittle me in front of my husband and child! Just where do you get off trying to tell me what I can and can't do," she berated him. "I'll have you know that I've been on battle fields since I was a preteen! And I wasn't just on the field I was leading my army, which of course is now your army. You have no idea what I am capable of! So, don't you dare come in here and start that 'how can you let her' shit! Remember, brother, you may be king but I'm still the more powerful wizard," she yelled really tearing into him.

"Next time give me a little heads up before you go off and insult a ninth circle wizard. I'll be sure to put all the breakables out of harm's way," I chided him.

"Are saying you agree with her decision," he asked me incredulously.

"I can't beat her arguments; therefore, I see no alternative but to concede to her point," I replied.

"You're not really taking Granger with you, are you," Lindeth asked concern showing on her face.

"Don't worry, we've got that covered," I assured her, though not really feeling it. "In fact, I have to get to the lab to make a couple of modifications before we leave," I said grabbing the bracelet from Chooser. "I'll leave you three to hash out all of your anxieties. Now if you'll excuse me, I have work to do," I said before leaving the room.

Modifying the bracelet was a remarkably easy task. In fact, it went far quicker than I would have suspected. Soulbinder assured me that the changes were correct and since she was the one who had given me the knowledge to begin with, I had to trust her judgment on the matter. I looked around the lab to see if there was anything that I might want to give me an advantage should my dream turn out to be a vision. I spotted a small blade, not much different from the one that had been used in the assassination attempts. It radiated a power that was somehow familiar. I picked it up and put it in the pouch that hangs at my side. I would have to ask Chooser about it, surely, she would know about any weapons found in the lab.

When I got back to our chambers, the argument was still going strong. I held up the bracelet for Chooser.

"That was quick," she remarked as she retrieved the bracelet and placed in around Granger's wrist.

"I thought so too," I replied. "By the way, I found this blade in the lab," I added as I pulled the weapon from the pouch, I had put it in. "Any idea what its properties are? I know I know the power that it's giving off, I just can't quite place it." Chooser took the weapon from my hand.

"I know what you mean, I too feel as though I recognize the power it's emitting, but I have no idea why. I mean I know I've never seen that blade before in my life," she responded leaving me totally baffled. I turned to the other two wizards in the room.

"Okay, it's up to you two. Which one of you can tell me about this blade," I asked sure that one of them would know something. They each shook their head and looked bewildered. "Okay then, who else uses the lab," I asked trying to determine how the blade could have gotten there in the first place. All three of them began spouting off the names of every wizard and apprentice in their command. In other words, I got nowhere. I put the blade back into the pouch.

"Well, I'm taking it with us. You never know when a magical weapon could come in handy," I remarked. "Firestorm, Chooser, we really have to be going," I urged them, effectively putting an end to the argument about whether Chooser and Granger went or not.

"Not without me," Lindeth chimed in.

We left Blendell around noon. We had many reservations about the final outcome of the upcoming war. If all went according to plan, Destroyer's forces and ours would eliminate Hellfire as a threat. In the process, Destroyer's forces would be sufficiently weakened as to nullify any threat that they posed. I wasn't counting on any of it. I fully expected to have to join the fray and tackle both Destroyer and Hellfire. I was just hoping that

I would be up for the task and wouldn't get myself killed in the effort.

The first three weeks of the journey were uneventful as we travelled south towards the Asmerian border. Most predatory creatures tended to flee in the face of an advancing army. On the first day of the fourth week, we happened upon a herd of ogres. Big ugly brutish things that didn't have the common sense to realize that they were doomed should they attack such a force. To their credit, they managed to kill fifteen soldiers before they were finally subdued. I suggested to Firestorm that he spread his wizards out so as to better protect his forces in the future. The remainder of the journey to the Asmerian border was peaceful although tedious.

I was surprised when Braveer and the company met us at the border. He grinned in that way he had that told me he was damn glad to see me. We took the rest of that day to rest and reorganize. Granger smiled broadly at Braveer every time Braveer would do his googoo gaa gaa routine. He fully understood where I had gotten the name Granger from. Shameer and I were never the best of friends, but we had a deep respect for each other from years of working with each other toward common goals. Cyclops and Hermit acted like a couple of kids in front of Granger. Just before we called it a night, Firestorm came to me.

"Are you sure these men can be trusted? They certainly don't act very professionally," he inquired voicing his concerns. I could understand where someone who hadn't been around these guys for years on end could come to such a conclusion.

I grinned, slapped him on the back and said, "I trust them with not only my life, but that of my family as well. We couldn't be in better hands; of that I have no doubts."

The trip to the future battleground took on an interesting twist having my brothers in arms surrounding me. They each had to show off for my son. As far as any of us could recall, I was the first member of the company to start a family. Sure, some of the men had left pregnant women behind after some of our previous campaigns, but I was the first to stay with the woman I got pregnant and raised the child as a father. I spotted a couple of the men looking at my son with a hint of regret in their eyes. I was as amazed as anyone at how the presence of a child made grown men act like children. On the bright side, it made the journey go by quicker.

We topped a final hill and overlooked the battlefield I had seen in my dream. A chill ran down my spine as I looked down at the armies already amassing in their individual groups. On the far side of the valley, roughly five miles away, was a massive array of miscreants. Only a handful of which were actually human. Off to the northwest, was another group of mostly nonhumans. These were Destroyer's forces. Chooser came up beside me, Granger in her arms. In front of us were roughly a hundred and forty thousand warriors. I felt rather uneasy. We humans were outnumbered somewhere around six or seven to one. I grabbed Soulbinder's hilt for comfort. I didn't find much comfort there.

Velouth's troops had fortified the defensive structures the company had built months before. There were pike lined trenches, some filled with flammable liquids. Earthen walls behind these were set up as well. There were obvious pathways between these defenses to allow for troop advancement, though these were quite narrow to limit those attempting to skirt the major defenses.

It was getting close to sunset. Firestorm had his troops join forces with Velouth's and together they continued to set up a perimeter of defenses working throughout the night. Massive fires were lit to illuminate the area and help ward off some potential threats. There would still be some skirmishes during the night. Hellfire had a large number of night thriving creatures among his ranks. These would be sent to probe for weaknesses and inflict as much damage as possible in advance of the main assault. Firestorm sent a messenger to Destroyer's camp asking for a parlay. My cousin was no fool, he had to know that our alliance was tenuous at best and that upon Hellfire's demise our attentions would turn to him as he would turn his on us. I rode with Firestorm to a point just about halfway between our respective camps. We kept our distance as they talked.

"I've noticed that you have a number of night thrivers in your ranks. Hellfire has a number of night thrivers as well. Undoubtedly, he will use these tonight to probe our defenses. It would make our position less tenuous if you would have your night thrivers intercept his," Firestorm suggested.

Destroyer thought about this for a moment, then looked up grinning and asked, "and what would I gain from this? Hellfire surely knows I have as many night thrivers as he does. If I have mine protect your camp who will protect mine?"

"If our forces are decimated in the night, then who will aid you in battle on the morrow," Firestorm asked in reply.

Destroyer glared at me for a few minutes. I never broke eye contact with him during this time. He seemed a little intimidated by this, which was my intent.

"Okay. I'll send a quarter of my night thrivers to protect you, for tonight," he agreed, making me suspect he had other things in mind.

There was more to the story than I could figure out. Something he saw while looking into my eyes had made him decide to help us. What he could have possibly seen is beyond me. I would sleep very lightly tonight, if at all. We rode back to our camp in silence.

I had just settled beside Chooser when a booming voice filled my head.

"I need to see you," it said. I sat upright instantly. I scanned the area trying to determine the origin of the mystery voice. "Come here, over the hill," it called again. I got up as quietly as I could. Surprisingly, Chooser was undisturbed and sound asleep. I did as I was commanded to do. The last time I heard a voice that filled my head, it belonged to Dragore. This wasn't her voice, but it was just as commanding.

As I crested the hill, I was shocked by what I saw. Under the boughs of an extremely large, glowing elderberry tree that had not been there when I had passed this way earlier, lay a white dragon approximately twelve feet long. And though it was a fraction of Dragore's size, I could sense a power even greater than hers emanating from it. Its left front leg was severed below the elbow. My hand went instinctively to Soulbinder's hilt.

"You have nothing to fear from me," I was told as the scene shimmered. I felt a little dizziness and when it passed, we were no longer where we had been. In fact, we were no longer on the same planet or plane where we had been. It was now daylight, and the skies above were green, while the leaves on the trees were now blue. It was at this point I realized I was no longer wearing Soulbinder. I hadn't felt more helpless in my life then I did at that moment.

The dragon was gone. In its place was a burly man with a left arm severed below the elbow. He was familiar to me, having seen him before. His power was beyond compare. He was the same man I had witnessed forging a sword in which a young woman was encased by magical powers I couldn't imagine being able to wield.

"You're my wild card in the game," he informed me, though I had no idea what exactly a wild card was. "There has been a breach of protocol, not totally unexpected, but disturbing none the less," he continued. "As a wild card, you have given me a perfect opportunity to correct the breach and restore the balance to the game. Yes," he continued eyeing me up and down. "You have given me the perfect solution, By the way," he added, "did you know that only you and Soulsta can speak? No?"

The scene shimmered again, and I was back where I belonged, hand still on Soulbinder's hilt. 'I don't suppose you know what that was all about,' I asked her.

"What was what all about," she asked as though genuinely unaware of what had just transpired. I attempted to bring the memories of the events that had recently occurred, to come to the front of my mind, so she could see what I had witnessed. She cut me off. "I don't want to know," she replied sternly. No further discussion of the subject would be forth coming.

I returned to our tent and stealthily slid into the bed I shared with Chooser, hoping not to disturb her. She was actually awake and awaiting my return. After we made love, I fell asleep, much to my surprise, rather quickly. Once again, I dreamt of the forthcoming battle. Again, I awoke with a start as I heard Chooser crying mournfully, though this time I had heard her calling to our son, Granger. I got out of bed and covered the short distance to where my son lay sleeping. I was relieved to see him peacefully sleeping, unaware to the vision I had had. The implications of the dream were disturbing.

It was still about an hour before dawn, and the troops were already roused and ready for action. I looked back to where Chooser lay, to find her now sitting upright. Granger started fussing, so I reached down and picked him up. I gazed at him adoringly, imagining my own father would have done the same when I was his age. I carried him over to Chooser, who cooed and shushed him as she enveloped him in her arms.

"I'm just going to come right out and say it," I said not knowing how to broach the subject of what I had dreamt, "I think you need to leave and take Granger with you." She stared back at me dumbfounded by my seemingly sudden change of heart about them being here. I started to explain further but recognized the absent look on her face that she gets when her and my sword are talking. Conversations I'm not privy to. My sword... my wife... both women of power treating me like the enemy.

'Child,' Soulbinder sent correcting me. Not helpful.

We quickly dressed for the days coming activities, then headed towards the command quarters. Firestorm was giving final instructions to his generals, Lindeth stood beside him. Chooser, Granger in her arms, headed straight to Lindeth. I handed Lindeth the blade I had found in the laboratory. She gave me a puzzled look, as Chooser started to explain what she had learned from Soulbinder. Reluctantly she agreed to leave the area post haste with an honor guard of about a dozen men.

"And Chooser," I added. Chooser was about to argue, but the look on my face must have convinced her that it would be useless to do so and reluctantly agreed to go with them. I watched them ride off, yet still couldn't shake the feeling that something bad was going to happen. The sight of Chooser weeping on the battlefield for Granger again flashed in my mind. I tried to shake it off and chalked it up to lack of sufficient sleep.

I was brought back to the present by the first major assault of the battle. Firestorm had joined his wizards and was busy casting spells to ward off the approaching force. To the north, Destroyers wizards launched an offensive of their own, aimed directly at Hellfire's wizards. I watched and waited. Hellfire was perhaps the strongest wizard on the field, but even with his apprentices, he didn't out power both Firestorm's and Destroyer's combined power. He would weaken as the battle continued, then I would attack.

I looked out upon the now, well lighted battleground and saw the carnage that had occurred the night before. Destroyer had lost at least a dozen changelings who had fought with a half dozen trolls. The changelings had been torn into two pieces, while the trolls had had their spines shredded. The remains of about a dozen humans were impaled upon the sharpened timber the company had installed as a defensive barrier. From appearances, I suspected they had tried to attack a troll and got backhanded for their effort, which sent them flying onto the spikes. They should have stayed behind the barricade.

Chooser rode along with her sister-in-law until she was certain her husband couldn't see them. She called a halt. She looked Lindeth in the eyes. Far behind them they could hear the sounds of the battle that was taking place.

"Take Granger and the guards and go back to Blendell," she instructed.

"And just exactly what are you going to do," Lindeth asked in return.

"Why, save our husbands of course, what else is there to do," she quipped. Chooser ordered one of the guards off his mount, got on the horse and turned it around and she rode back toward the already raging battle. She dismounted as she neared the crest of the hill upon whose other side the battle was raging.

The battle had been raging for about two hours in earnest. I could sense the diminishing power in the spells being cast back and forth. It was time to join the fray. I sprung into the air, transforming into a flaming bird of prey, arcing up and over Hellfire's position. Hellfire could ill afford to take his concentration off of his current adversaries. Diving on his position, I sent a massive bolt of power at him. It slammed into his shields and obliterated them killing several of his apprentices in doing so.

I landed, transforming back into my human form, about twenty feet from him, drawing Soulbinder as I did so. I concentrated and used her to direct a bolt in a wide arc, cutting down those apprentices not killed in my first attack, yet bouncing off of Hellfire with no effect. It was now down to the two of us.

Firestorm witnessed his brother in law, Phoenix, attack and penetrate Hellfire's defenses. Hellfire's apprentices fell immediately. He immediately ceased his attack on the magical component of Hellfire's forces and turned his attention to the physical army advancing on his men. Velouth's wizards had managed to keep the physical contact between the two forces to a minimum. With Firestorm's help, they should be able to completely destroy, if not repel the foul beasts that made up Hellfire's army.

Destroyer watched, taken by surprise, as his cousin became his namesake and assaulted Hellfire's position. He had mistakenly not paid attention to his cousin since he watched him send Chooser and their brat away. It still stung him to have to surrender Chooser. He had been unprepared for his cousin's interference then too. Phoenix's bolt was as strong or stronger than any he had ever cast. Hellfire's apprentices were weakened or killed by its effects. Another quick blast and it was down to him and Hellfire. He looked over towards Firestorm's position and saw him preparing to attack Hellfire's army. This he couldn't allow if he were going to add their numbers to his. He prepared to hit Firestorm with a spell.

A stench of sulfur and burnt flesh struck Chooser as she crested the final hill above the battlefield. It was followed by the foul stench of death that already permeated the air. She gazed in awe and admiration as her husband leapt into the air becoming a phoenix as he did so. She watched his assault on Hellfire's position. As he landed, she scanned the unfolding events below her. Spying Destroyer preparing to attack her brother, she unleashed a lightning bolt from a bracelet her mother had given her when she was two. It struck Destroyer in the face. It wasn't powerful enough to do any real damage, but it managed to break his concentration and dissipate the spell he had been formulating.

A flash of light to his right caught Firestorm's attention as soon as he unleashed his spell upon Hellfire's forces. His spell had killed a large swath of the foul creatures, giving the soldiers at the front a space to breath in. He turned towards Destroyer's position and could see his face smoldering. A fireball went flying in from the hillside above him. He turned and saw Chooser, his sister standing there. Knowing she wouldn't have attacked him unprovoked; he too turned his attention towards Destroyer.

Hellfire drew the sword he carried on his side and felt it take control of his limbs again. It had only done so once before, shortly after he had found it, and he hadn't felt compelled to draw it since. Until now that is. He gazed across at the powerful young wizard squaring off with him. He knew from the form he had taken who he was. He had been under the belief that he was dead, if so, he's obviously risen from the ashes, though he didn't have the feel of death about him. Hellfire had lived for thousands of years, outliving even some elves he had known in his youth. Dark magic enabled him to do so. He had thousands of years of experience dealing with young powers, though he sensed something different about this one. Something that made him more cautious then would be his norm to do.

He unleashed a powerful spell intended to disable its target leaving its victim paralyzed. It had no effect on the nimble young wizard before him. He quickly deflected the similar spell his opponent sent back at him. This battle would prove to be time consuming, fortunately he was still feeling the vigorous energy he had recently stolen from the thirteen adolescents he had reared for just such a fate.

While I could contribute some of it to my having not wielded my powers for numerous years, I had to admit Hellfire was stronger than I had anticipated. My mentor had told me tales, told to him by his mentor, of how Hellfire had been an apprentice when the doomed cities of Dragonsvale and Graveer were in their infancy. If the tales were true, that would make him thousands of years older than the thirty something year old appearing man I was now engaged in battle with. We continued to tax each other's strength, neither gaining an advantage. Magically, it seemed we were evenly matched. I wondered how he was at wielding a sword while performing magic.

I closed the gap between Hellfire and myself as quickly as I could. As I swung Soulbinder towards him, I sent a lightning bolt into her. As the blades clashed together my bolt sent Hellfire stumbling backwards. In anger at the thought that my son might have perished here due to this evil excuse for a being, I unleashed all my remaining power into a massive bolt that slammed into his chest. He wasn't prepared for it, having been stunned by my lightning bolt. From there it was all Soulbinder's show, and she put on a good one.

Swirling brilliantly colored bands of power swirled around, first her, then both of us. The emerging visage coalesced into a fierce dragon. Flames spewed from the dragon's mouth slamming into Hellfire and the sword in his hand. The intensity of the light being emitted grew blindly bright. All combat had ceased, as everyone attempted to shield their eyes from the painfully blinding light that filled every crevice of the valley eliminating all shadows in the process. Finally, the power was too much to withstand and Soulbinder's sibling succumbed to the inevitable. The shockwave from the results of her final spell knocked all but me off of their feet. I turned back towards the battlefield.

Destroyer had had to turn away from the brilliant light emanating from across the battlefield. Just as he was beginning to think it would kill him, it gave off one last even more brilliant flash. The shockwave that followed knocked him off of his feet, along with everyone else. Well almost everyone else.

When he looked across the battlefield to where the blast had come from, he could see his cousin, Phoenix, still standing. He felt the unusual sensation of fear creep up inside him. It was a sensation he wasn't used to. He quickly reassessed the situation at hand. He came to the realization that things had not gone quite as he had hoped they would. Steeling himself as best he could in an attempt to hide his growing fear, Destroyer ordered a withdrawal from the battlefield. His minions, still hurting from Soulbinder's performance, did so willingly and hastily.

Chapter 13

The Price of War

LINDETH AND ENTOURAGE continued their hasty exit from the battle zone. The captain of the guard kept the pace until after the sun was well into the sky. They stopped to feed young Granger in a clearing from which they could see anyone approaching long before they truly posed a threat. As they finished their meal, a brilliant light emanated from back towards where the battle was taking place. The brilliance of the light was so intense that it began to hurt, then, with a flash, it was gone. Everyone looked around at each other starting to question whether everyone was okay when a shockwave of enormous strength, knocked everyone to the ground.

As they tried to regain their footing, the ground beneath them exploded upward. The maw of a gigantic fireworm burst through swallowing Lindeth, Granger and all but three of the guards. These remaining guards hesitated only momentarily, then quickly drew their weapons and attacked. Their blows bounced off uselessly against the creature's thick hide. It began to thrash about violently, crushing two of the remaining guards, leaving only one. He assessed the situation, and wisely retreated. The beast spewed fire from its massive maw as it continued to thrash about, searing the guard's left side, severely injuring him. He managed to call his mount to him, get aboard, and head back towards the battlefield.

His steed seemed to know right where to go and trotted there as quickly as he could. It took everything he had to stay in the saddle, but he had to make it back to inform the king of his wife's demise. He took a long drink of water from the skin attached to the saddle. Poured some on his wound and put the skin back. He hoped to make it back before sunset.

Chooser watched as Destroyer quickly withdrew his forces from the field. She was suddenly struck by a feeling of despair; it was a feeling she had never known before. She fell to her knees and began to weep uncontrollably.

Seeing Chooser weeping on the field, a field she was supposed to have vacated, sent fear and trepidation into my soul. I transformed into a phoenix again and quickly crossed the field. I landed as near as I could, transforming back into my human form and was quickly kneeling by her side. She hugged me burying her face into my shoulder weeping. I looked about frantically searching for our son.

"Where's Granger," I asked fearing the answer. She continued weeping, seemingly not hearing me, or too wrecked with grief to answer. I turned her body so I could look into her face. "Where's Granger? Where's our son," I asked again.

"With Lindeth," she finally managed through her tears. My initial fear subsided though I couldn't get any more out of her and she continued to weep mournfully. I looked around the battlefield trying to figure out whose loss could cause the reaction I was witnessing. My initial fear was for my son, but he wasn't here. I began to suspect magical sources causing her grief, but a quick spell eliminated that as a possibility. I scooped her up in my arms and carried her to our tent. I left her sobbing on our bed and went back outside to assess the situation.

The remnants of Hellfire's forces had scattered or were being systematically dispatched. Destroyer's forces had retreated back towards his domain. I guess my defeating Hellfire along with Soulbinder's show afterwards made him reassess his position. I can't say I was sorry to see him go. Yes, he would have to be dealt with, after all he was wielding one of Soulbinder's siblings and there can only be one winner, or so I'm told.

With the battle winding down, I headed towards Firestorm and company. Among those gathered were Velouth and his leading general. Braveer and several lesser important individuals were there as well.

"What's wrong with Chooser," Firestorm asked the concern showing on his countenance.

"I honestly don't know. She's apparently grieving over something though I can't say what. I asked about Granger, and she said he's with Lindeth, so he should be fine. I even checked to see if she was suffering from a spell or other magical reason, but nothing presented itself," I explained.

"I guess we'll have to wait until she gets over whatever it is," he responded. "By the way, hell of a show you put on, almost too big," he added. I didn't bother telling him it wasn't really my show.

I cast a few spells to hasten the demise of the remnants of Hellfire's forces. It had actually been a very fortuitous day. Less than three thousand humans were killed or seriously injured, while Hellfire, all of his apprentices and most of his forces were now dead on the field of battle. Destroyer had suffered significant loses and fled the field.

I found the mess tent and joined Hermit and Cyclops in eating the food that had been prepared. It wasn't the grand food I have been becoming used to since joining Chooser, but it would sate a hungry appetite.

After eating I headed back to my tent. It was now nearing sunset, and I was hoping Chooser would have recovered from whatever had grieved her so. I spotted the rider as soon as he crested the hill. He rode straight towards Firestorm. It took a moment for me to realize he had been one of those sent to guard Lindeth and Granger. I rushed over and paled seeing the scars he bore. He had been severely burnt on his entire left side. The fact that he had made it was a testament to his strength of will.

"...it came out of nowhere. It was preceded by a brilliant flash from here and a wave of force that knocked us off our feet," I heard him telling Firestorm as I got close enough to hear what he was saying. The look on Firestorm's face told me I had missed something important.

"Where's my son," I demanded of the guard. The sorrow in his eyes spoke volumes.

"Swallowed by some sort of gigantic creature that burst up out of the ground then spewed fire," he replied.

I staggered back dumbfounded for a few moments, trying to comprehend what I had just been told. It couldn't be real. I leapt into the air transforming back into a phoenix and headed off into the direction he had come from, climbing as I went so as to see further. In the distance I spotted it. I flew faster than I had ever done before, landing next to the now deceased fireworm. Lying nearby were the crushed bodies of two of the guards. I drew Soulbinder and sliced open the beast, not really knowing what I expected to find by doing so. Several bodies emerged from the gash I had made in the beast, though none were recognizable due to the fact that the beast's digestive acids had already taken its toll on the human flesh.

I staggered back away from the foul stench that assaulted my sense of smell. I stared at the mess in front of me. It took a little while, but I finally spotted the small bones of a child's hand and knew that my worst nightmare had come to fruition. The teleportation bracelet I had made adorned the wrist. My son was dead. I now knew why Chooser grieved so. The mother and child bond had been broken leaving her in despair.

I stood there numbly staring at the enormous carcass, seeing the aura of dark magic that encompassed it, wondering two things. Primarily, I wanted to know who had controlled the beast directing it to kill my son. Then, as I stared at the grotesque visage in front of me, I wondered what had caused its death. Continuing to scan the scene gave me the answer to the last question at least. Among the bones, I spotted finger bones still grasping the hilt of the dagger I had given to Lindeth. No longer wanting to look at the image I know I'll never forget; I used my powers to move enough dirt to cover the entire area. A quick-fire spell fused the dirt into rock ensuring it would remain undisturbed in the future. Afterward I fell to my knees vomiting.

I spotted the horses and carriage that had been carrying them a short distance away. I approached one of the saddled animals and mounted it, turned towards the now buried grim remains for one last look. I spurred the horse back towards the battlefield, in no great hurry to get there. As I rode, I tried to figure out what exactly I was going to say to Chooser, my tears flowing freely. What was there to say? She already knew our son was dead, and there was nothing I could do to change that fact. I grieved for my loss, but truly hurt for hers. She had carried him inside of her for nine months then nurtured him for the last eleven. A mother's grief is something no man can truly comprehend.

It had been a few months since his master had headed off to war against Destroyer. Defiler had completely mastered the spells in the forbidden tome he had found in the library. He could now see the events taking place to the north. One of the spells enabled him to take control of weak-minded beings, even those at a great distance, he just had to have met the individual he would possess. Having spent his entire life among his master's forces, most of which were such simple-minded creatures, he knew exactly the orc he wanted to possess. He would be near enough to his master to hear what he was saying.

He had timed his possession exactly right, as he witnessed the start of the battle. Before the battle began, he had a precognitive event flash in his mind. It was discombobulated and he wasn't completely sure of its meaning, but he sensed that a child of one of those he could see fleeing the area before the battle began would lead to his demise. He used another of his recently gained powers to ensure it never happened. He connected with a fireworm near enough and large enough to suit the task and sent it to consume the entire party.

Turning his attention to the battle, he watched as two forces clashed with his master's forces. One was Destroyer's and made up of mostly nonhuman creatures of the type usually loyal to his master. The second was a large army of humans. Defiler realized his master was in trouble, and he was doing all he could to help him. He cast a fear spell on Destroyer. If Destroyer were truly a great force of darkness, he wouldn't succumb to its effects.

After the battle had been raging for several hours, and his master was greatly weakened, a powerful human wizard joined the fray. He had taken the form of a fiery bird of prey and smashed into his master's defenses, shattering them. His master fought hard but proved to be no match for this new wizard who wielded a sword the same as his.

The display that followed his master's demise told how incredibly powerful the weapons were, when the explosive end result knocked everyone to the ground and Defiler back into his own mind. His head ached with pain as though his brain itself had received the blow. Through his pain he was able to witness the fireworm he had sent complete its mission, swallowing all but three members of the group he had sent it after. He smiled knowing his fireworm had completed its task, despite the pain he was in.

Chapter 14

Heading Home

I FINALLY ARRIVED BACK at camp close to midnight, my tears subsiding as I crested the last peak. Chooser was sleeping when I got there. Knowing the grief, she was feeling, I let her sleep and made my way towards the still bustling mess tent. Everyone in the tent stopped speaking as I entered. The mood in the tent was sullen. The knowledge of the loss of Lindeth and my son Granger was by now common knowledge. I grabbed a helping of food and found a mostly empty table to occupy and ate. I was numb taking the first bite. I didn't realize how hungry I was, though I had expended a lot of energy.

After eating, I found an area to relieve myself before heading to my tent to turn in. I slipped in beside Chooser, trying not to disturb her. She wiggled herself right up against me, so I wrapped my arm around her and proceeded to doze off. I awoke in the morning, refreshed, but still grieving. Someone or something had commanded the fireworm to kill my son and Lindeth. That same someone or something had attempted to kill me the same way a while ago, only my ability to become a phoenix had saved me. My child and Lindeth didn't have that ability, and so had perished.

The mood in camp was mixed. Most were elated at not only having survived, but they had witnessed the demise of one of the greatest evils to plaque this world. Then there were those like me who were grieving what we had lost, none more so than Chooser, my wife.

I arrived at the command tent to find Firestorm in a heated discussion with Velouth and their generals about what exactly should be done next. Most were for chasing down Destroyer and thus finishing what it was we had said we wanted to do. Firestorm, grieving the loss of his wife and nephew, my son, wasn't having it. He wanted nothing more to do with this war that had already cost him so dearly. There would come a day when he would want to find and kill Destroyer, everyone knew he had ample reason for wanting to do so, but that day wasn't today. Rather than pursue Destroyer, we would be heading home.

The journey home was sullen and depressing, for me at least. Chooser remained in a state of despair, blaming herself for the death of our child. Three months into the journey, when we were almost at our destination, she began to suffer bouts of vomiting. Upon arrival in Blendell, she finally allowed the healers to examine her, and we were informed that she was once again with child. We stared at each other in disbelief since we hadn't been intimate since before the battle. Reunited with his daughter Dahlia, Firestorm began to show signs of overcoming his grief. Hopefully as the pregnancy advances, Chooser will get over her grief enough to get back to living instead of mourning.

Dahlia was becoming quite a handful and brightened the spirits of all who came into contact with her. She reminded me of her mother in that manner. We had been back in Blendell for three months and Chooser was starting to show. Dahlia's constant giggles and other innocent responses had finally removed the anguish Chooser had been suffering since the day her son Granger had perished. Chooser had become a surrogate mother to her since our return. Dahlia hadn't been able to grieve the loss of her mother, being too young to understand what death was. She was beginning to talk though complete sentences were still a little beyond her.

Firestorm, finally getting back to the business of governing ordered his wizards to find out where Destroyer was with his army. His grief had turned into a desire for revenge, especially after spending time with his young cousins who wanted revenge as soon as they had been cured of the changeling disease inflicted upon them by Destroyer when he had killed their uncle, Firestorm and Chooser's father, king of Anthgolia and almost all of their other relatives. The wizards began casting spells to allow them to see things occurring in the distant lands beyond their own border. Spies were sent into Destroyer's domain.

Chapter 15

Rebuilding the Forces

DESTROYER HAD LEFT the battlefield in defeat. He had been overcome by an unnatural sense of fear he had never experienced before. His forces were pretty well intact, Hellfire's forces having suffered the greatest losses. He wondered what had come over him and began to suspect a magical explanation. He was well out of sight of the battlefield and finally called a halt to his retreat.

Had his cousin's remarkable display while slaying Hellfire been the cause of his fear? If so, what did that mean about any possible confrontation in the future? As he began to think about it, he realized he had witnessed just such a display of power before and hadn't been overcome with fear then. At that time, it was the sword that he carried that had put on such a display when it destroyed a sword of like origin. He determined he would camp where he was for the night and consider his options.

He slept in the next morning, arousing from his slumber shortly before midday. It was a crisp, cool day mostly cloudy with a light mist about the higher regions of the hill they were on. He emerged from the tent feeling refreshed and kicking himself for having fled in fear. He still didn't know what had come over him, but he wasn't going to dwell on it either.

First they would head back to the battlefield to see if he could determine a magical source for the fear he had felt then they would travel south to Dragonsvale to try and bring whatever was left of Hellfire's forces into his fold. He figured they would retreat the way they had come in the face of the power they were up against and do so as rapidly as they could.

Upon arriving back at the field where the battle had raged the day before, Destroyer began casting spells to enhance his memory of the events of the day before. These same spells would actually allow him to examine every inch of the battlefield as though it were frozen in time and he himself standing at any point he chose to see from. The fear he felt started immediately after his cousin's swords display, and he could sense a magically created sense of fear emanating from that direction. He attributed the fear to the shock wave from the destruction of the sword Hellfire had wielded, for it had been completely obliterated. The same thing had happened when the sword he carried had destroyed another in the line, and like his cousin he had been immune from the effects of the shockwave that had occurred during that incidence. He would never give it another thought.

He headed towards Dragonsvale picking up those creatures that lagged behind the fastest of the remnants of Hellfire's forces. The journey to Dragonsvale would take several months. He expected to pick up vast numbers by then. The fear was gone, a distant memory as though it had never happened, replaced by a sense of confidence that Hellfire's former servants would gladly obey as more and more joined his ranks. Some of the larger, intelligent, harder to control types began eyeing his lesser apprentices as a possible food source so he decided to send them back to his domain and await further instructions. He would need them when he turned his forces on the human kingdoms.

Destroyer rode into Dragonsvale with the air of a conquering hero. Hellfire and his apprentices had all been killed. Though he could sense power emanating from within its walls, Destroyer didn't think the source would be a living creature. The power he sensed was greater than that which Hellfire would have been able to create, so he expected to find an artifact of some sort on a par with his sword, which he drew from its scabbard. It couldn't be another sword of the same line he thought, for every time two of the blades had come into close contact with each other one would end up destroyed. He had a sense that there could only be one sword remaining, though the purpose for making such blades escaped him.

He couldn't pinpoint the power's source, as it appeared to move every time, he thought he was closing in on it. He had those apprentices he had brought with him spread out so they could triangulate and pinpoint the source. As their spells began to home in on the source, it appeared, standing right behind Destroyer. As Destroyer turned around, Defiler lunged his hand deep into Destroyer's abdomen and up into his chest. Defiler's fingers tipped with sharp talon like claws grasped Destroyer's heart yanking it out while still beating. He raised it over his head and squeezed the blood within into his mouth before taking a bite of the organ savoring the taste.

Destroyer's apprentices stood there momentarily stunned at what they had just witnessed and been unable to prevent. Several attempted revenge for their master and were struck down immediately for their efforts. The changelings under Destroyers control began attacking everything and one in sight. Two were near Defiler and attempted to assault him. He snapped the nearer one's head off with his left hand while snatching the second one out of the air by its throat. He squeezed this one's throat until its head burst, let out a howl that knocked everyone off their balance causing most to fall to the ground. He unleashed a lightning bolt that jumped from changeling to changeling, killing the remainder of them. The remaining apprentices either scattered like rodents or pleaded with the dark being before them to allow them to serve him. He eyed these up and down and determined they may yet be useful at a later date, for fresh food if nothing else.

He pulled Raptor from its sheath to cut off one of Destroyer's legs to eat. Removing the blade from its scabbard allowed it to take control of the situation. Defiler was unaware that such a thing was possible as he felt himself become a puppet to an unseen force. Massive amounts of energy swirled around the sword in his hand and then him, just as he had witnessed happen when Hellfire fell. When it was over there wasn't much left of Destroyer's corpse that he would consider eating.

He headed towards the hall, down which were the king's chambers, swung Raptor in an arc slicing off the leg of an apprentice still flailing on the floor from the effects of the burst of energy. Another apprentice who was more powerful than the one on the floor cast a fire spell to cauterize the wound and staunch the flow of blood. A troll nearby grabbed the still in shock apprentice and bit off his head. The second apprentice scorched the troll enveloping the room in a horrid stench that left everyone's eyes burning. Defiler laughed at the display.

The strongest of Destroyer's former apprentices asked Defiler "master what is your will?"

"Multiply the forces," was the response he got.

Chapter 16

A New Joy and Sorrow

CELESTE ENTERED THE WORLD in the hours just before dawn, having kept her mother and I up all night. I didn't know what I expected to feel as she was placed in my arms for the first time, umbilical cord still attached. I cradled her in my arms as she wiggled about crying loudly exercising her lungs for the first time. I gingerly handed this precious bundle to her exhausted mother, beaming a broad smile as I did so. I could sense a power emanating from her, stronger than I had felt from her now deceased brother when he was born.

After seemingly endless sleepless nights, Celeste was finally sleeping through the night. She was six months old and accomplished something I had never heard of in one so young. Chooser had removed a stuffed doll from the crib, given to her by her uncle Hermit, put it on a shelf and watched with amazement as our daughter levitated it back into her crib. Not even I could wield my powers at that young of an age. My mother once bragged that I had saved my blankie at the age of one, which had been the youngest anyone had ever been heard of wielding magic.

The months passed quickly, and before I knew it Celeste's first birthday was upon us. Velouth had sent an emissary in the form of the company's upper echelon headed by Braveer. It was really good to see my old comrades again, especially on a joyous occasion such as this. We hadn't seen each other since we parted ways after the battle. They fawned over Celeste even more than they had Granger. I suspected it had more to do with her gender than anything else. Her hair was now shoulder length and the same shade of blonde her mother's was. Her eyes were the same green her mothers were as well. I suspected she would grow up to look a lot like her mother, the same as her cousin Dahlia was doing in regard to her late mother Lindeth.

Dahlia came rushing into the room to greet us, as was her custom these days. She talked up a storm telling us great tales, which we would pretend were new and astonishing to us thus encouraging her to use her imagination, a vital tool for wizards. She had an adorable little girl lisp that no human with a heart could resist.

I picked up Celeste in one swift motion tossing her into the air as she enjoyed me doing and was rewarded with a delightful giggle.

"Stwong," Dahlia said.

"What was that," I asked not quite understanding what she had said.

"Stwong," she repeated mispronouncing the r in strong.

"She doesn't weigh much," I assured her confusing her intent.

"Not you," she said stomping her foot in frustration.

"How's that," I asked.

"Celeste," she corrected me. Though she was only slightly less than two years older than her, Dahlia could already sense the power Celeste had at her disposal. Everyone in the room had had a good laugh catching my and Dahlia's exchange. The kid was as adorable as they come.

Braveer strode over to us and pulled a necklace from his pocket. "Thought you could use this," he said as he presented it to me.

I could feel it trying to sap my strength as I held it in my hand. "What would I want with this," I asked, momentarily unable to think.

"Put it on the baby," he suggested. It didn't sink in at first, but then dawn came the light and I realized it was to limit the amount of power Celeste could wield, thus preventing her from accidentally doing irreparable damage. It brought back the memory of a necklace I had worn as a child that I had all but forgotten.

"It had been Firewind's," he said solemnly. I stared him in the eyes for a moment.

"I wish he could still be here," I remarked as I slipped the necklace around her neck.

"As do I," he replied.

The party was over, and the dignitaries returned to the lands they were from. Firestorm returned his full attention to locating Destroyer and his forces. They had vanished shortly after the battle and hadn't been seen or heard of since. The ships that brought his forces across Lake Arness still sat on the Southeast shore, untouched since being grounded there. The days turned to weeks turned to months, which eventually turned to years without a sign of them.

Celeste was now six years old and quite the skilled wizard. Where she once asked her uncle Hermit and Uncle Cyclops to show her tricks, they were capable of, she was now eager to show them what she could do, all of which was beyond their powers to achieve. She made me look like an under achiever even though I had been hailed a child prodigy in my youth. After creating a sphere of energy hovering over her hand, similar to the one I had created the first time I had approached Chooser's camp many years ago, when I was in my early fifties. She just as easily dissipated it then ran off to play with her cousin Princess Dahlia.

"Is she aware of how destructive that force could be if handled incorrectly," Hermit asked the concern evident in his voice. The look I shot back made him apologize for he could see I found the remark insulting to not only me, but my wife as well, who spent nearly every waking minute of her time nurturing and tutoring our daughter and her niece Dahlia.

Firestorm, convinced Destroyer must be plotting to assault us at any moment, had dispatched an envoy to the library of magus to retrieve some of its tomes and scrolls that could prove to be more useful in Blendell then there in Graveer. I tried to remind him that the library had trap spells that could kill them if they weren't strong enough. He informed me that in Blendell was kept an artifact, a key in essence, that would neutralize those spells. It had been brought to the then small kingdom for safe keeping during the time of Dragore's wrath.

His cousins, Mildeth and Rockner, would lead the expedition remembering the way from our return trip from there after they had been cured of the changeling disease. Chooser had lectured them on being careful and alert for danger. Firestorm assured his sister that the guards accompanying them were the best at traveling through hostile territory, a fact she should be better aware of having spent many more years as their sovereign.

Wrapped up in the education of my daughter and niece, I failed to notice the passage of time and before I knew it the expedition returned from the library. During their travels, they had passed through a village, where they had heard a rumor of Destroyer's death. According to the tale, an even greater evil slew Destroyer when he attempted to claim Dragonsvale. I had a hard time believing that Destroyer could be killed by a darker evil, if there really were such a thing, for Destroyer wielded a sibling of Soulbinder.

"Could it be?" I asked her.

"Yes" was her one-word reply.

They hadn't been able to remove any of the tomes or scrolls from the library, despite having the royal artifact Firestorm had given them to take with them to unlock the library. The artifact had actually been used to seal the library from all except the most powerful since the time that the council of wizards summoned all to join the battle against Dragore. While it allowed them unimpeded entry in and out of the library, it did not allow items to be removed.

Celeste's eighth birthday had come and gone, and she no longer wore the necklace that had limited the amount of power she could expend, greatly increasing the potency of every spell she now cast. To nearly everyone's surprise, Dahlia's strength was approaching that of her cousin. The two were sparring in the courtyard, healers nearby incase an accident should occur. Chooser and I had cast a shielding spell around the compound to contain the energies they were throwing back and forth. Dahlia's slight age advantage gave her the edge in most of these bouts, though Celeste made sure they were never easy victories.

When the bout was over, and Dahlia once again declared the winner, the two combatants raced over to where Chooser was standing, wrapping their arms around her waist, and hugging her upon reaching her. I couldn't help but smile at the sight of my beautiful wife and by now equally beautiful daughter standing there with Dahlia whose own beauty can't be denied.

I felt a shove from behind and fell forward to my knees, a sharp pain in my chest. Somehow Soulbinder flew from her scabbard and landed at Celeste's feet. I looked down and saw the long blade of a spear sticking out of my chest dripping my blood. I felt a wave of power rush over my head. I looked up into the horrified face of my wife, and saw my daughter wielding my sword. My vision blurred, and when it refocused, Chooser was standing next to younger looking version of herself. Blood spewed from my mouth and my vision blurred again, this time when it refocused, I could see the big burly one-armed man sitting at a table smiling and beckoning me to him. Sitting next to him was a young woman and a small boy. I recognized them both as Lindeth and Granger.

Chooser rushed to her fallen husband's side. She had witnessed in horror as the spear blade came thrusting out of his chest. Before she could react, her daughter had eliminated the assassin and his cohorts who had suddenly appeared behind her husband. Celeste had picked up Soulbinder, her husband's sword that had somehow managed to fly to her feet and used it to focus a powerful ray that instantly turned them to dust, a power Chooser was unaware her daughter possessed.

"Granger," she heard Phoenix say as she cradled his head. It was his dying words. She cried out in anger and anguish at her current loss. Celeste came over and put her hand on her mother's shoulder to comfort her. She knew she should feel a sense of loss at the sight of her father lying there dead, but somehow, she didn't really believe he was gone for good.

Firestorm and his wizards began investigating the area of the courtyard where the creatures that had killed his brother in law had suddenly appeared. It had a very dark feel about it. The power that had been used to send them was all but imperceptible. The wielder of that power was stronger than anyone Firestorm had ever encountered, surpassing even his sister and her now deceased husband. The trace was too weak and the source too far away for him to do anything with it.

Before his body was carried away, Celeste retrieved the scabbard for Soulbinder and the medallion of a phoenix that her father always wore. Touching it made her certain she would see her father again someday. Royal guards delicately lifted the remains and carried them to be prepared for the pyre. Celeste headed to the marketplace and went straight to the merchant who sold vials and jars and asked to purchase a small vial in which to hold some of her father's ashes. News of Phoenix's death had already swept through the kingdom. Teary eyed the merchant gave her a vial refusing to accept any coin for it.

"Your father was a great man who helped this entire kingdom, we are all forever in his debt," he told her as he handed her a vial of the size she had indicated. He threw in a leather strap he had that would be suitable to the task of attaching the vial to the necklace that now adorned her neck.

Her father's body was wrapped in multiple layers of cloth, laid upon a large pile of wood, and doused in oil, which was then set on fire. Chooser wailed mournfully for her dead husband, Celeste tried to comfort her, but it didn't really do any good. She would need time to grieve and that was all there was to that. The two of them stood by and waited until the pyre turned to ash, while most left shortly after the blaze was set. Celeste removed and unstopped the vial on her necklace and scooped up some of her father's ashes. Chooser was puzzled by this but didn't question her daughter who had yet to shed a tear for her deceased father.

Braveer and company arrived three months after the funeral, which was as quickly as they could traverse the distance from where they had been stationed. They had once again been assigned to the southern region near the border of the ancient forest between Asmeria and Dragonsvale. Celeste and Chooser were advised of their approach and rushed to the gates to greet them. Celeste ran and gave Braveer a big hug overjoyed to see her uncles again. Chooser stood in the gateway solemnly.

"It's good to see you," she said as Braveer walked up to her bowing as he did so.

"How are you holding up," he asked the hurt and caring evident in his voice.

"I have good days and bad," she informed him.

"I still can't believe he's really gone," he replied.

"Neither can our daughter. She's convinced she'll see him again someday, though she can't explain why or when," she added.

Braveer told Chooser there have been rumors of an evil greater than either Hellfire or Destroyer in control of Dragonsvale now and that he was building a powerful army to destroy humanity. It was also rumored he wielded a sword of immense power. Celeste carried such a sword, and there was now only one other in existence. Soulbinder hadn't spoken to either Celeste or Chooser since Phoenix's demise, as he had been the connection between them and with him gone the link was broken.

Braveer had informed Chooser that the company had elected to sever their contract with Velouth and pledge their swords and skills to the protection of her and Celeste. Hearing the rumors and now being offered the services of a small army gave Chooser an idea of what to do about Celeste's future education. They would travel to Graveer and study in the library of magus taking advantage of the protections it offered. She would have to bid farewell to Dahlia, for she did not intend to come back until Celeste was a fully trained adult wizard, or an emergency requiring her assistance occurred.

It was difficult for Chooser to say goodbye, having raised Dahlia as her own after Lindeth had perished with

Chooser's son. She wished she could take her with her, but that would mean Dahlia would have to leave her father behind, something Chooser was loathed to do.

A number of people interested in seeing the ruins of the ancient stronghold, decided to tag along, among them were many craftsmen, carpenters and masons looking to make some gold off of the endeavor. Merchants, never ones to miss an opportunity began to organize caravans to ship goods that would be essential to reviving Graveer. What better an opportunity to do so than when an army led by a ninth circle wizard and her equally powerful, eight-year-old daughter were making the trek?

The women of a brothel that the local wives were forcing to close its doors decided to follow the army, their best customers. This pleased the members of the company beyond anything they had been through since this adventure began.

Chooser and Celeste rode at the head of the column, alongside Braveer, Cyclops and Hermit. The trio had gelled since Phoenix first revealed himself, especially after Shameer's death. There were no incidences on the journey to the library. The road that had long ago connected the two lands was once again traversable, cleared by the company and craftsman as they made their way. Once they reached Graveer, Braveer had the company prepare the area for defensive purposes, paying special attention to the pathways to the library.

With the aid of some of the civilians who had come along, large building stones were removed so as to not impede passage through the streets of the ruined city. The masons set about rebuilding the cities outer defensive wall, while carpenters set about providing suitable housing so that no one would have to sleep in tents for too long.

After setting up their temporary housing, Chooser led Celeste up and into the library of magus. A number of lesser wizards had arrived earlier and were in the process of straightening out the library. The thick layer of dust that Chooser remembered from her last visit still covered almost everything. It was easy to determine where her cousins had searched during their visit by the footprints in the dust.

"Yuck," Celeste said upon seeing the condition of the library.

"Instead of just commenting on it you could help clean it," Chooser replied. "I'll see if I can find you a broom."

The main entry area was clean in relatively short order. The dusty smell still lingered as it was quite a large library and they had only cleaned the entry. Chooser had watched her daughter work diligently and decided it was time to reward her with a break from the tedious task and show her where she would be honing the craft. She led her to the laboratory where Phoenix had crafted the spell that had cured him and her family of the changeling disease. The civilians who had tagged along and weren't strong enough to help with the defenses, set about cleaning the library for the royal wizards. With everyone's assistance and a few days' time, it was ready to get on with Celeste's education.

As she delved deeper into the library's vast treasure of knowledge, Celeste could sense her father's medallion giving her energy which seemed to aid her in reading and remembering what she had read so she could fully grasp it's meaning. Her father knew what he was doing when he had made it even though he was quite young when he had done so. She would often grasp the medallion in her left hand while holding whatever tome it was she was studying in her right hand as she paced across the floor of which ever room it was that housed the tome in question. She would spend nearly every waking minute either studying from the numerous tomes and scrolls, or exploring the vast library trying to learn it's hidden secrets.

She eagerly approached a shelf of tomes emitting enormous amounts of power she was sure would contain a powerful spell she could add to her repertoire, she grabbed one of the tomes from the shelf. It was large and quite heavy, and she struggled as she carried it to a nearby table and placed it upon the table with a thud. She was puzzled when she noticed this tome had no title. She was even more confused when she opened the tome and found the pages blank. Chooser walked up and glanced at the tome Celeste had tried to read. The runes on the page contained dangerous powers, concerning Chooser until Celeste looked at her and asked, "momma, why isn't there anything written in this book?"

"Because you're not ready to see it yet," Chooser said closing the heavy tome and pushing it aside. She had been concerned that her daughter who emitted more energy than anyone prior to her would be able to read the advanced spells written in the tome. Fortunately, merely possessing the power didn't automatically convey the ability to read the runes.

Celeste's childhood now revolved around the knowledge stored in the great library. Chooser discovered many ways to turn lessons into a game, making learning something Celeste enjoyed doing. Mixed in amongst the magical training, Chooser would include an occasional civics lesson. On numerous occasions Chooser would catch Celeste speaking to her medallion as though she were really talking to her father.

When she was twelve, Celeste discovered a tome labeled how to discover the hidden. It was a tome she had picked up shortly after she had first arrived at the library. She was certain that it had been blank the first time she had looked at it, along with a number of others. She had matured and learned a great deal in the four years since she first arrived. Studying the ruins floating on the page, Celeste formulated the spell in her mind and released the power. She watched as the energy she had sent forth swirled around the library. She felt herself drawn towards one room in particular where the energy from the spell irradiated the strongest feedback. At the back of the room, she found the energy outlining a doorway that she never would have noticed without the spell. But finding a door and opening a door were two different things. This particular door would take time to open.

As Celeste studied diligently in the great library, the city of Graveer roared back to life. The masons and carpenters had managed to reconstruct most of the buildings in the four years since their initial arrival. A stately manor that had once belonged to a long ago deceased wealthy citizen had been renovated and transformed into Braveer's headquarters. Merchants had set up shops and now supplied all the wares needed for everyday life. Braveer looked at his best fighters sparring with each other and had a thought about the girl who called him and the rest of the company uncles. While her mother was seeing to her magical studies, no one had been attending to her skills with a sword. He decided to take the subject up with Chooser. She could see the merit in his argument and conceded to allow her to train with a sword if she desired to do so.

Celeste's time became a regimen of learning to wield a sword during the morning of the first day of the week, staff during the morning of the second. On the third day of each week she learned to fight unarmed, while on the fourth it would be the bow. A lesson on wielding daggers was the day after that with axes, hammers and maces being next. After her weapons training, she would have two hours of free time before resuming her magical studies. Celeste eagerly absorbed all of the training she was offered, and it wasn't long before she was proficient in a wide array of weapons to add to her spell casting abilities.

Every couple of months Dahlia would come and study with her aunt and cousin for a couple of months. During these stays, Celeste and Dahlia were inseparable, with Dahlia just as eager as her cousin to learn all the wizened old men of the company could impart. These lessons evolved to include every type of weapon and all forms of unarmed combat as well.

Celeste would often start a sparring match whether with weapon or magic. These matches were now ending in draws as Celeste's powers continued to outpace Dahlia's. Only her slight experience difference kept Dahlia from losing outright, though some suspected Celeste held back purposefully. Braveer would watch with amused pride having watched the hardened troops of the company become patient adoring instructors to the young princesses. They in turn came to love the old men as though they were true uncles, and not just a bunch of men Celeste's father had served with.

During one of her free hours between physical and magical training, while exploring the few remaining ruins, Celeste entered a building that had yet to be renovated. Her mother had cautioned her against entering such buildings knowing they could possibly collapse should the wrong support be moved. Like most teenagers, Celeste believed her mother was being overly cautious and entered the building anyway. No one had entered the building yet and Celeste was shocked to find skeletal remains inside. There were the remains of numerous armor-clad warriors, not all of which were human.

From their stature, Celeste could easily tell that nearly a dozen of the fallen were dwarves, while she suspected some were elves. Two of these were wearing golden rings on their skeletal fingers from which she could feel emanating a great power. She eagerly plucked these rings from the remains and put them in a pouch she had taken to wearing for holding items she wished to keep or examine at a later date. The pouch was a magical one given to her by her uncle Cyclops called a bag of holding.

Back in the library, after her daily lessons, Celeste removed the rings from the pouch and began to examine them. Both were quite pretty. The first one she examined had a canary yellow diamond rectangular in shape and multifaceted. Inscribed upon the ring was a language she didn't recognize but knew that it was the reason the ring radiated power. The second ring had a cobalt blue diamond of a size and shape similar to the first and was inscribed with yet another language she didn't recognize. After admiring the jewelry for a few minutes, she returned them to the pouch and set out to find her mother.

The days and years passed quickly, and before Chooser realized it, her daughter was a grown woman. Chooser lamented about the events that unfolded those many years ago, when Celeste was merely eight years old. It felt like yesterday, instead of the decade it had actually been. The years had not diminished the grief she felt over her losses.

Celeste could no longer be called an initiate of the ninth circle, as her power greatly exceeded the amount of power one would associate with that level. She was beyond a tenth circle if one was to be honest, in fact the only being Chooser had ever met with more power resided in the sword Celeste wore on her hip. She was also a skilled swordswoman, having been trained by her uncles of the company her father had been a part of when she first met him. Unlike her father who relied on Soulsta, the powerful woman enslaved in and the source of power for the sword Soulbinder, Celeste's skills were all her own. She could swing a sword, axe, or staff against the best and come out on top. Her skill with a bow was unrivalled and her unarmed combat skills were equally impressive.

After years of searching, Celeste had found the one tome she had thought she would never find, the one for opening sealed doors. She returned to the room where she had found the secret doorway years before, this time convinced she would get it open. She placed the tome on a table in the room and began to flip through its pages examining each spell before turning the page again. Finally coming upon the spell, she felt would do the trick, she cleared her mind, and focused on the spell on the page of the tome before her. As she recited the words required by the spell, she could see the energies forming around her, then the door. It opened unlike any door she had ever opened before. Instead of sliding into or swinging open, it floated inward then the bricks became a bridge. She walked across the bridge, mesmerized by the powers she could see swirling all around her. The bridge ended in another room similar to the one she had left.

Celeste gazed upon the tomes lining the shelves of this new room. The power they shed was remarkably strong. She grabbed the first tome and time seemed to stand still as she eagerly studied each and every page. She moved on quickly to the next tome in the room. The last was the most intriguing, dealing with transformational magic. Being the daughter of the late great Phoenix, she should have an edge in this field.

Celeste told her mother Chooser she had found a new spell amongst the old tomes and headed to the basement to try it out for herself, she closed the door behind her keeping out everyone, fearing distraction could spell disaster. Her uncle Firestorm and cousin Dahlia had just arrived for a visit, but she wanted to try this spell more than she wanted to visit with her relatives. She thumbed through the ancient tome until she found the spell she was searching for. Pulling a pouch of silver dust off of her belt, she drew a circle around her for protection. Reading the spell one last time, she put the tome aside and began the chant. Energy began to swirl around her in the form of various colored light. The spell was taking effect.

Defiler had built his army for the last decade. He had believed he had directed his orcs after the correct target by going after Phoenix, but the way they were killed had convinced him he was up against a greater power than he had expected. They were slain so quickly and with such intense power, that even with his dark magic he was unable to penetrate the light emitted by the spell to see who had cast it. His forces now numbered in the hundreds of thousands, and the dark magic at his command would allow him to transport them right inside the human's defensive perimeter. His success with sending the two dozen he had sent after Phoenix showed him it could be done.

"Prepare the forces for battle," he ordered the last remaining human wizard under his command. The wizard bowed as he backed out of the throne room. He made a gesture with his hands, fingers moving quickly to weave magical forces into his desired effect. Defiler's forces became immediately aware of their master's bidding and hastily set about obeying the command they had received.

They formed ranks outside the remnants of the once great city walls. Defiler came forth amongst them and began the dark magic spell that would transport them to Blendell and the final battle of the swords. The human inhabitants of Blendell had managed to ensure he could no longer see what was taking place within its walls with the ruins they had added after his first raid, but he could sense that they lacked the ability to prevent him from transporting his army behind their walls. He chanted the words of his father's realm and continued as the dark forces surrounded his army and him turning them vaporous, then whisking them all off to Blendell.

Horns blared out the warning of the breach of their defenses. The handful of wizards training in the courtyard quickly turned their magic on the creatures that had suddenly materialized within the palace courtyard walls. An extremely large human looking creature with talon tipped fingers and dark leathery looking skin stood at the forefront. With a wave of his hand he slew the human wizards before they had done any damage to his troops. He focused his senses on trying to locate the power that had slain his assassin orcs. The wielder of the power was no longer in Blendell.

A surge of power came from the northwest it was the power he was searching for and it was far from his current location. He didn't want to lose time reorganizing his forces, so he left them there in Blendell and quickly recited the incantation again, only this time the spells energy enveloped only him and sent him straight to the source of the power he was seeking.

Celeste had just completed reciting the words of the spell she had attempted to cast and was now standing there in the form of a dragon. She was the first of her species to do so, though she was unaware of that fact.

Just as she completed the transformation, a large dark figure appeared inside the laboratory she was in. This wasn't supposed to be able to happen with the spells imbedded in the walls of the library from when it was built, and yet there he was. She sensed darkness about him, it was a darkness she had felt the day her father was slain.

Without hesitation, she exhaled spewing fire instinctively as a real dragon would. The beast backed away shielding his face with his arm. He drew the sword hanging from his side, and Celeste could sense its power immediately and knew it was the same type she wore on her side. She was instantly transformed back into her human form, holding Soulbinder in her hand. The combatants assaulted one another neither hesitating both believing they would be victorious. They unleashed their might against the other and proved to be of equal strength. Defiler was impressed, and more determined than ever to kill this human female.

Chooser, Firestorm and Dahlia were slightly startled that Celeste had locked them out of the lab. She hadn't seen her cousin and uncle in nearly a year, and here on their first day in Graveer she locked them out.

"She has been obsessing over her magic lately," Chooser informed them after a few second of staring at the now magically sealed door.

Even with the protections placed upon it to contain the spells cast within, they could sense the immense amount of power being generated inside the laboratory. It was beyond anything any of the three of them could hope to wield, even if they combined their powers. A dragon's roar from within caused them to storm the door.

Celeste and Defiler clashed their swords against one another while simultaneously casting spells at one another. Neither seemed to be weakening the other, no matter what they attempted to do. Without warning, Celeste stumbled on the tome she had used to cast the dragon transformation spell she had cast just prior to Defiler's arrival. As she fell backwards, he reached out to grab her with his left hand, snatching her deceased father's medallion and clasping it in his hand. The effort was rewarded with the stench of burning flesh as the medallion turned blazing hot and branded Defiler's palm with an image of a phoenix.

He pulled his hand back ripping the chain from Celeste's neck and flinging it across the room. A brilliant flash and a slight odor of ash filled the lab. Defiler, sensing the energy, turned to see what had caused the flash of power and came face to face with a flaming bird of prey. It opened its mouth and blasted him in the face with a burst of energy. He raised his branded left hand up to shield himself from the blast, and as he did so Soulbinder came bursting out of his chest.

I transformed back into my human form and gazed at Chooser standing there, Soulbinder in hand looking back at me. I looked around and realized I was back in the laboratory of the library of magus. I also realized I didn't really have any clothes on, but rather was wrapped in cloth of the burial type. I was about to ask who that was and how I had gotten there, when a brilliant flash of light stunned me.

When my eyes focused again, we were standing in the presence of the creators of the swords. Soulsta was also standing there with us. The burley one-armed man approached me. Patted my back and said, "wild card indeed."

I stood there dumbfounded, especially when I spotted one of Soulbinder's siblings still grasped by the dead hand of the beast that had been attacking Chooser. The shadows around the room began to coalesce and turned into the form of a dark being, with a strong resemblance to the thing grasping the sword on the floor.

"You violated the rules of the game," the female admonished it in a voice that was somehow familiar, yet I couldn't quite place it. An image of a great dragon filled my mind and I realized it was the same voice I had heard when I encountered Dragore in her cavern.

"Why whatever are you talking about," the dark being pleaded innocently.

"Don't try denying your interference, the proof of your meddling is lying right there," one of the men retorted while pointing to the body lying on the floor.

"If you are suggesting that I sired this thing of my own volition, you are mistaken," he protested. "Why you know yourself you made it so I can only enter this realm when either summoned by you or when someone here performs the correct ritual in the correct manner, and when they do so I am bound to obey their commands."

"Don't take me for a fool," the burley one-armed man shot back. The rest of the group huddled together discussing their options, finally nodding in agreement.

"You will never influence this realm again," they informed him and with the slightest gesture on their part sent him back to whatever dark realm it was that he was from.

They turned their attention to me, looked upon Soulbinder and asked me, "What would you have us do at this point?"

I didn't know how to respond at first, but after a few moments of contemplation, I finally said timidly, "Release us to live our lives as nature would allow us to."

The burley one-armed man picked up Raptor and asked, "and what of this?"

"If he has to die so that Soulsta can live free then so be it, but knowing how much she grieved over each of her siblings she was forced to kill or whose death she had felt, I would hope you could see your way to free him as well," I replied.

He smiled as he waved his hand and suddenly all of Soulsta's siblings were standing there with us. "You seem to have great wisdom," he told me, before adding, "for a mortal."

In an instant everyone except Chooser, Soulsta and myself were gone and we were left standing there. The doorway to the lab burst open and Chooser, Firestorm, Dahlia, Cyclops, and Hermit came rushing in. I was shocked to see a second Chooser standing there, almost as much as they were at seeing me. I looked over towards the first Chooser who appeared to be a younger version, and asked, "Celeste?"

"Dad, "she replied, rushing to me, and hugging my neck. Everyone rushed over to me and embraced me in a group hug, each trying to convince themselves they weren't seeing things.

"How," Chooser asked after finally breaking away from me and looking me up and down still in disbelief.

"His medallion with the thanks of his master," Soulsta informed them.

Everyone now turned their attention to the beautiful goddess standing there. My mind and memory went back to the time I had fashioned the medallion that was my namesake. I was thirteen and did almost all of the work on my own. After I had imparted all of the magic I had intended to imbed in the medallion, Cyclone came over and examined my work.

"Very good," he had said, "but there are a few runes you're currently not mature enough to handle that I really think need to be added," he continued. He then proceeded to imbed a few more runes into the medallion. "For protection. You'll understand when you've got a few more years on you," he assured me.

"When Defiler grasped your medallion, his dark energy enacted its spells bringing you forth from the ashes your daughter had carried in a vial attached to the medallion's necklace. You truly became a phoenix rising from your own ashes," Soulsta explained.

"And what will you do now," I asked her.

"My realm has been restored to where it had once been, I plan on returning there," she said with a hint of melancholy in her voice. And with that she faded leaving me with my family and friends.

We exited the library, and I was shocked to see the nearly fully restored metropolis of Graveer. Quite a bit had come to pass in my absence. My hand instinctively went to my medallion, only to discover it was gone, consumed by the energy, which had restored my life. I would have to forge another.

Epilogue:

On the island of Lillewellyn, Lord Lowendelphyn, King of the elves, strode onto the balcony of his palace and gazed in the direction of Asmodora's mainland, his ancestral home and birthplace as he did every morning. Driven out along with the dwarves during the time of Dragore's wrath, he longed to return, but a shield of magical energy lay like a dark shroud over the land preventing him from doing so. He was a mere child when those events had taken place.

On this particular morning he could feel magical energy, enormous energy, coming from somewhere on the mainland. He had felt such energies in recent years, getting stronger each time. It was beyond the abilities of mortal men, as they were limited to the ninth circle. The energy he was sensing dwarfed his own tenth circle powers.

All at once he felt a strange shift and realized that the shroud of energy that had been cast upon the land was gone. For the first time that he could remember, he could feel the power of the artifacts the elves and dwarves were forced to leave behind, giving him hope that someday soon his people might be able to retrieve them and reclaim their ancestral homelands once more.

ABOUT THE AUTHOR

Joseph Hearl is a fiction writer specializing in fantasy adventure stories. The youngest of nine children, he has served in the United States Navy as a sonar technician.

Mr. Hearl has traveled all over the world, experiencing numerous cultures and traditions encompassing the wide variety of lifestyles and customs which helped in the writing of this book.

He currently resides in Florida with his beloved dog, Lil.